THE GRAVITY
OF SHADOWS

ALSO BY DAVID RAMUS

Thief of Light

DAVID RAMUS

THE GRAVITY OF SHADOWS

A NOVEL

HarperCollins*Publishers*

HarperCollins books may be purchased for educational, business, or sales promotional use. For information please write: Special Markets Department, HarperCollins Publishers, Inc., 10 East 53rd Street, New York, NY 10022.

FIRST EDITION

Designed by Kyoko Watanabe

Library of Congress Cataloging-in-Publication Data

Ramus, David
    The Gravity of shadows : a novel / David Ramus. —1st ed.
        p.   cm.
    ISBN 0-06-018779-4
    1. Art dealers—New York (State)—New York—Fiction.   2. Art—
Collectors and collecting—Florida—Fiction.   3. Art—Forgeries—Fiction.
I. Title.
PS3568.A4745G7   1998
813'.54—dc21   98-10175
                                                                                          CIP

98 99 00 01 02 ❖/RRD 10 9 8 7 6 5 4 3 2 1

This book is dedicated to my mother,
Connie Kaufman

Acknowledgments

I want to thank Larry Ashmead and Jason Kaufman at Harper-Collins for believing in this book and remaining patient in the face of hard times; also Jason's able assistant, Jen Charat; Molly Friedrich and Paul Cirone at the Aaron Priest Agency, both of whom provided more encouragement and guidance than they probably know; Sherri Holman, whose sharp criticism and wise counsel I tried to heed; Professor John Tone at the Georgia Institute of Technology; Mr. and Mrs. R. D. Hoffman, Joel Babbit, Mark Goldman, and everyone at 360 in Atlanta; John and Patsy Smith; Dr. Fred Ruder; Jackie Williams; and most important of all, my wife and partner, Cathryn, and our crew—Jessica, Juliana, and Nikki.

Remorse—is memory—awake—

EMILY DICKINSON, POEM 744

1

WHO COULD BLAME THE Peraltas for being nervous? They weren't rich, and they weren't looking to play a rich man's game. Even so, their financial future was riding on the auctioneer's gavel this afternoon. I knew all about it. I'd negotiated the deal. And I'd promised to be with them when their painting sold.

You see, there is no such thing as auction-room etiquette. The days of tuxedoed gentlemen bidding with demure signals, spending millions of dollars and never showing the slightest emotion, have gone the way of the gold standard. Art collecting has become a blood sport. A game for the wealthy. And the rich don't like to bleed; they play to win.

Christie's is usually a short cab ride from the midtown apartment that doubled as my office, but because I was late, the drive took forever. It was gray and drizzly, cool for early October, and the Manhattan traffic was snarled. The unopened letter in the breast pocket of my suit coat whispered my name as the cab crept up Park Avenue, but I ignored it. By the time your banker resorts to return-receipt postage, it's just a formality anyway. Maybe Ev Lenoir's bad news would go down a little easier after the auction. Assuming we ever got there.

Two o'clock had come and gone by the time we pulled up in

front of the auction house. As I paid the cab fare, a tall man with blond hair, a tan to match, and a bulky briefcase jumped out of a black limo. I wasn't the only one arriving late. Together, we hurried inside. He nodded at me, but we didn't speak. And although he was vaguely familiar, I was too busy thinking about the Peraltas to pay him much attention.

Isaac and Lara Peralta had first come to see me almost four months earlier with a package wrapped as carefully as an Egyptian mummy. The two of them had teetered into my apartment late one muggy, New York summer afternoon with all of the halting grace and careful economy of motion that frail bones and stiff limbs teach the elderly. They each held tightly to opposite ends of the package. Isaac was a man somewhere between seventy and ninety, round and pink with a fringe of white hair surrounding his bald pate. Lara looked just this side of a hundred, prim and proper in a navy blue dress and heavy, sensible shoes, her fine white hair pinned tightly to her birdlike head.

They carried their burden with as much care as they had wrapped it. Isaac backed into the small living room I'd set up as an office, an inch at a time, straining to hold his end waist high, instructing Lara to be careful of her hands—not to bump them on the door frame.

She stopped short, halfway through the door. "I am not a cripple, Isaac—not yet."

I hurried over and took the package from them. It weighed four, maybe five pounds. "Please, come in. Sit down." I pointed at the pair of chairs in front of my desk.

Isaac took Lara's arm and escorted her in, but neither sat. They stood, slightly stooped, arm in arm, in front of the chairs.

I set the package down on top of my desk and held out my hand.

"I'm Wil Sumner."

Isaac took my hand and shook it. Then, instead of letting go, he covered my hand with both of his and looked me in the eye. "We are the Peraltas."

His hands were smooth and dry, his grip mild—but his eyes

were piercing. He looked up at me and smiled warmly, still holding my hand in both of his. The force of his gaze surprised me. It wasn't harsh or judgmental, but full of recognition, of amused pleasure at seeing me, as if we had known each other but hadn't met in many years and he was gauging the way I had weathered the time. It was a damned strange feeling. I found myself wanting to explain the why of my reduced circumstances to him. I wanted his approval even though I'd barely met the man.

"I am Isaac, and this is my wife, Lara." He pronounced it *eey-sock,* and spoke with a slight Spanish accent.

Lara took my hand, much the way Isaac had. Her gaze was softer, but no less direct. "We are pleased to meet you, Wil Sumner."

Then Isaac, dressed, in spite of the heat, in an old-fashioned, three-piece suit, turned to Lara. She nodded. He turned back to me and smiled again. I got the feeling I'd passed some sort of inspection. And odder still, I was glad of it. The two of them were quite a pair.

"We have brought this to you to appraise," Isaac explained. Then, with a flourish, he began peeling layer after layer of clean white linen off an unframed painting the size of an overnight suitcase. His wife watched silently.

"You see, Lara and I, we are married over fifty years." He paused, a fold of the white cloth in either hand. "Like a dream it's been. Like a long and lovely dream. Now we are getting on— each day is like a gift. But money is short. I no longer work. We would like to have you buy this painting."

Lara murmured something in Spanish.

Isaac frowned. "She doesn't like me to say such things, but to be frank, we need money, Mr. Sumner. For *what,* she will not permit me to say. But it is not by choice we sell."

"I understand." I nodded, sympathetic to their situation. You see it often enough in my business. Older people, struggling to make ends meet, having to sell that which they cared most about. More often than not, their prized possession turns out to be worth far less than they had thought. I hoped that wouldn't be the case here, but if he didn't get the thing unwrapped, we'd never know.

Isaac ever so slowly folded back the linen. I wanted to take the painting from him and pull the cloth off myself. But he was handling it with such care—such proprietary tenderness—that I couldn't bring myself to interfere.

Finally, he nodded at Lara, and the two of them sat down in the chairs facing my desk.

I looked down at their painting.

"*Esto es privado*—personal. Quite private. No one need know we are selling?" Lara asked. "This is possible, no?"

I had to tear my eyes away from the canvas. It had been worth the wait. "Your business is just that—*your* business. If I can be of help, I will. If not, no one else will ever hear about it from me."

"Good. We heard you were trustworthy," Isaac said. He looked at Lara and stroked her arm. She put her hand over his, then gazed owlishly at me.

I looked down at the painting again.

"Lovely, isn't it?" he asked, waving a pair of soft, pink hands.

"Yes, Mr. Peralta, I think it is."

"Please, call me Isaac. And I know my wife would prefer Lara. We think it to be French. And we hope it is worth your time. Mr. Abraham Mendez recommended you. He says you are having bad luck, but that you are one of the best in the business—that you know everything there is to know about such paintings." He looked around my living room office—a desk, the chairs he and his wife occupied, a couple of old wooden file cabinets, a bookcase loaded with reference books and auction catalogs—then his face broke into a kind smile. "I too am down on my luck. Maybe together we can turn our luck around. Abe says you are something of a genius."

"He lied," I said, lifting the canvas. I tilted it to let the glare from the window behind my desk slide over the surface of the paint at a raking angle.

There is a scientific theory called "naïve realism." The basic tenet of this theory is that the world does not necessarily exist the way we see it. Forty-nine percent of all our cranial nerves relate to vision. It is a highly complex series of actions and reactions that translate reflected light into recognizable images. Suffice it to say that absent injury or disease, we all do it in about the same way. But even though our optical equipment is pretty standard, most of the time we can't agree on what we see. Ask any group of witnesses to an accident or a crime. By the time light is fed through our eyes and along that river of cranial nerves, it has been filtered through our brains and enhanced with all the preconceived notions and prejudices we each carry. It's a wonder that most of us can agree that the sky is blue and the grass is green.

When an artist paints, he adds in his own mix of vision and emotion, his own aesthetic theories and styles. Some work, some don't. Scholars, experts, and critics can't come up with a universal definition of art, much less a definitive opinion of what makes it any good. Most art critics live small, frustrated lives in faux-ivory towers trying to accomplish that task. And most of their opinions aren't worth the paper they write on. A painting either speaks volumes or is silent. I have a rule—the Sumner Rule of Collecting. It's simple. Never buy a painting if, after spending time with it, it remains a mute mystery—decipherable only by some critic or expert. Buy a *Sports Illustrated* swimsuit calendar instead. Great scenery, good photography, careful lighting, and the models need little explanation. You'll get exactly what you pay for.

The painting the Peraltas had brought me needed no deciphering. Even if it wasn't exactly what Isaac and Lara thought it was.

Isaac cleared his throat. "Well, it is good, no?"

"I'm not sure *good* is the word," I answered.

I looked at the painting once more to be sure. It depicted a pretty young girl, ten or eleven years old, with a head full of dark curls. She wore a white silk dress and was blowing bubbles from a clay pipe. Her face and white dress were stark against a boldly figured red-and-blue oriental carpet, her cheeks a radiant pink, her eyes half closed as she puffed into the mouthpiece of her toy pipe. The artist had chosen an unusual perspective—the viewer looked down at the child, who practically filled the canvas. The background was obviously a study or a library, suffused with a mellow glow of daylight. But the only clearly distinguishable background feature was the colorful rug. The bubbles, as big as tangerines, shimmered, hanging wet and iridescent in the air over the girl's head. It was a quiet moment full of charm and innocent delight. The girl looked ethereal, caught in that magical time between androgynous childhood and the onset of puberty. The artist had captured both the child she was and the woman she would become. Isaac was only half right. It was better than lovely. It was beautiful. The canvas was signed C. Beaux.

"Isaac, where did you get the painting?" I asked.

"We bought it after we left Spain and came here to America," Lara answered for him.

"Left? We were driven out!" Isaac exclaimed indignantly, as though it had happened yesterday. "Anyone who sympathized with the miners were no longer welcome in Oviedo—not in all of Asturias. Especially Jews. Not after 1934. They assumed we were all communists."

"To dwell on the past does not change it," Lara said calmly.

He frowned. "You make it sound like ancient history."

Lara sighed. "Because it is, Isaac. It is a lifetime ago."

"No, my dear. It is still happening. Last winter, in Florida, you saw the graffiti. It hasn't changed. It never will." He closed his eyes, a resigned expression on his face. "We must never forget what happened. We must bear witness."

"The *painting*, Isaac. Wil wants to know where we got the painting," she reminded him.

I'd nearly forgotten the original question myself.

Isaac nodded. "Forgive me, Wil. The painting reminded Lara of her younger sister, Sasha, who was killed during the civil war. That is why we bought it."

Lara added sadly, "We were going to bring Sasha over here to live with us. But she wanted to finish school in Spain. Then the war came . . . It looks just like her when she was little . . ."

My history was pretty good, but I had no idea what they were talking about. I started to ask what had happened in Oviedo, but Isaac said, "Manuel Mendoza and his wife, Elena, knew of this resemblance. We admired the painting often in their home. When the war ended, they decided to go back to Spain and practically gave it to us before they left. We insisted to give them something, but they accepted only a token. Fine people—they were very fine." He closed his eyes again and shrugged. "We regret that we must sell. But life goes on."

I looked again at the painting, but could find no family resemblance. Too many years—too wide a gulf separated the two sisters. *Life goes on . . .* Well, Isaac and Lara were proof of that, in spite of their age and their financial troubles. It made what I was about to tell them taste even sweeter.

"I'm sorry you're forced to part with it. It's not French—it's by an American painter named Cecilia Beaux. Generally, she doesn't sell for more than twenty or thirty thousand dollars. But this painting has enormous appeal. I recommend you put it up at auction. It's bound to attract a great deal of attention. It could bring a big price."

This got Lara going. I couldn't understand a word.

Isaac touched her hand, said something in Spanish, and then looked at me.

"How much is this great price?" he asked.

"The auction house will say less, but perhaps as much as sixty to eighty thousand."

"Dollars?" Lara blurted out, the color rising in her papery cheeks.

"Yes." I nodded.

"*¡Bueno!* We'll take this money now," she said.

Isaac stood. "This is good. Yes! We are very happy to take eighty thousand."

He reached for his wife and pulled her to her feet. Then he wrapped her in his arms and squeezed her harder than I thought medically safe for so frail a woman.

Her smile convinced me otherwise.

"Wait," I said, holding up my hands. "I'm not offering eighty thousand."

It took over an hour to sort it out and explain that I wasn't in a position to buy it from them, although I would have liked to. Instead, I agreed to help them negotiate the best deal possible with an auction house. It would take longer to sell the painting, but once Isaac and Lara understood the potential upside, they decided they could afford the delay. They also decided I should take a commission above the auction house commission. Five percent.

Four months had been a long wait for people who counted each day as a gift. We were about to find out if it had been worth it.

By the time I walked into the sale room, the auction had already started. Isaac and Lara had saved me a seat in the third row. He was turned around in his chair, his face tight, his eyes wide as he scanned the sparse crowd. I caught his attention and waved, gesturing for him to meet me at the back of the room. He leaned close to Lara, then did so.

"Isaac, it's better that we stand back here. That way we can see the action."

"What do you mean?"

"If we sit up front, we can't see who's bidding. I like to know."

He shrugged. "Okay. Let me tell Lara."

As Jay Burgess, head of Christie's American paintings department and today's auctioneer, waded through a sluggish sale of a still life by a follower of Rembrandt Peale, Isaac returned to his seat. I scoped the room.

"I have twelve hundred. Twelve hundred. The bid is in the front of the room. Who will say thirteen? Can I hear thirteen?"

I tuned out Burgess's clipped cadence as he called the bids. It was a minor sale, a tune-up for the important auctions that would take place later in the month. But the Peraltas had wanted their painting sold in the first auction of like paintings. It meant a lot to them, and to me. The turnout was disappointing, even for a nuts-and-bolts auction like this one. But Christie's had displayed the Beaux prominently during the pre-sale exhibition; I'd come to think of the painting as "Sasha," and I knew at least some of the right people had seen it.

Most of the die-hard players were in place. A handful of ambitious dealers from Florida to California stood at the rear of the room, nodding and waving to each other, comparing hastily scribbled notes in the margins of their catalogs. Low-end collectors and bottom feeders were spread out across the mostly empty chairs facing the auction block, avidly watching the proceedings, waiting for any misstep, any opportunity to walk away with a bargain. Not likely, but hope springs eternal. The big players, the New York boys, weren't in attendance. But the auctioneer was only on the fifth lot. It was early. A sprinkling of civilians sat, relaxed, enjoying an afternoon's free entertainment.

Nicole Brabant waved from across the room. She owned a small gallery on Eighty-third Street, and was one of the few dealers I trusted enough to confide in. I'd shown her the Peraltas' painting and she had agreed with my opinion of its value. She smiled, her blue eyes flashing under the dark mop of her hair. "Good luck," she mouthed.

I blew her a kiss.

"The bid is at thirteen hundred. The bid is at the desk now. Thirteen against the room. Who will say fourteen?" Burgess looked bored on the block, but you couldn't tell it from his voice.

"Sasha" was lot number twenty-two. Based upon Cecilia Beaux's previous auction prices, Burgess had agreed to offer it with a reserve of thirty-five thousand dollars. It was less than the fifty thousand we'd turned down from a Boston dealer to preempt the auction. But we'd decided to gamble. It could fetch much more if a couple of bidders fell in love with it. And there was plenty to love about our "Sasha." Burgess had featured the painting full page in Christie's catalog and promised to give it plenty of play on the auction block. Unfortunately, the color reproduction had turned out dark. The painting had looked flat and lifeless on the printed page. I told myself to quit worrying, that "Sasha" was the best thing in the auction, that it hadn't gone unnoticed by the big boys. But I worried anyway. Isaac and Lara hadn't hesitated when I suggested we turn down the offer of fifty, but I knew they were nervous. I didn't want to let them down.

Isaac returned to my side and told me that Lara would prefer to sit where she was. She was excited enough without trying to guess who would bid and how much.

By the time the auctioneer finished selling lot number twenty, I was getting a lot worried. Then, out of the corner of my eye, I saw Vance Blome, a dealer who specialized in nineteenth-century American paintings, walk in, armed with a catalog and a bidding paddle. He leaned nonchalantly against the wall on the far side of the room. He was in his mid-forties, casually attired in dark green slacks and a tan cashmere pullover, a bloodless, effeminate man with lank brown hair and gold-rimmed glasses. He barely looked my way, but I didn't doubt for a moment he knew who was in the room, and where they sat or stood.

A minute later, Henry Harper and then Clay Dupre, two other big dealers, walked in and took up positions about ten feet apart, across the room from Vance. Harper and Dupre were both in their sixties. Prosperous, middle-aged; gray men in gray suits. Thick around the middle, but their quick eyes missed nothing. Dupre nodded to me. Harper avoided my eye. He could afford to avoid anyone's eye he wanted to avoid. Less than a month ago he'd outbid a consortium of Europeans, paying two million dollars for a rare, postcard-size drawing by Velázquez. One of only three drawings the master was known to have executed. A world-record price made all the more astounding by the fact that within a week he had turned around and resold the drawing to the Getty Museum for a profit of almost a million dollars.

The three of them studiously ignored each other. These were men at the top of the heap, serious players in a world of wannabes. But even to men like Harper, Blome, and Dupre, no matter how good the art, it always swelled in desirability if someone else wanted it too. Even they trusted their own taste only so far. So they moved in packs. Always sniffing each other's business like hungry dogs. Nose to ass—or wallet, in the oh-so-refined reaches of the art world.

I nudged Isaac. "They're here. If the painting doesn't sell to one of the three men who just walked in, keep my commission. I don't deserve it. If they go hard against each other, who knows? It could reach eighty thousand."

Isaac smiled, then lifted his eyes toward the ceiling. "From your lips to God's ears."

I put my hand on his shoulder and whispered, "Amen."

Burgess started "Sasha" at ten thousand. It stalled at twenty, then picked up a few bids from the audience.

The bidding slowly climbed to thirty—then thirty-one, thirty-two.

It was like pulling teeth. Isaac stood rigid beside me. I was as calm as a dinghy in a storm. You'd think *I* owned the damned thing.

At thirty-five thousand the bidding stopped. Cold. Right on the reserve. Vance Blome held the bid. Neither Harper nor Dupre had made a move.

"Thirty-five thousand. I have thirty-five. Who will say thirty-six?"

You could touch the silence.

"The bid is thirty-five. Going once. At thirty-five." Burgess eyed the room.

Not a peep.

"Shit!" I cursed under my breath.

"Why?" Isaac asked, looking confused.

"They've ringed us," I whispered. "Harper, Blome, and Dupre. Agreed not to bid against each other. Keep the price down; then they'll hold a silent knockout among themselves. They'll each write an offer on a piece of paper. High offer wins, then pays the other members of the ring the difference between his written offer and what the painting actually brought at auction. It's against the law but it happens."

"What do we do?" Isaac asked.

Lara was turned in her seat, a stricken look on her face.

"Going, then, at thirty-five thousand. Final call. Any advance?"

"Forty!" It was my voice, but I couldn't have been that stupid. I didn't have forty thousand dollars, hadn't been near that kind of money since losing my gallery. But I couldn't watch Blome walk away with "Sasha." Not for thirty-five thousand.

My bid broke Burgess's rhythm. He knew exactly what I was doing and didn't like it. But there was little he could do to stop me.

"Uhhm, right you are, sir. Forty thousand, in the rear of the room." He directed his gaze at Blome. "The bid is against you, now."

Blome smiled. "Forty-one."

Back to me.

And Burgess looked apoplectic. He glared daggers and imperceptibly shook his head. He was doing everything he could in the way of sending a nonverbal message to stop. Now. While I was ahead.

I ignored him. "Forty-five."

If for any reason I had read the situation wrong, I was up the creek. I'd be obligated to pay what the auction house calls a buy-in commission. The price you normally pay if your property doesn't reach its reserve is 1 percent. But if you consign an item, then purposefully bid above the reserve in an effort to push its price higher, they hit you with both the seller's and the buyer's commission. Something on the order of 20 percent. Twenty percent of forty-five thousand. I took a deep breath. If nobody bid against me, it was going to cost me nine grand I didn't have—for nothing. The Peraltas would get their painting, but they'd be back at square one. Isaac was squeezing my arm. He had a powerful grip for such a sweet man.

Now it was Blome's turn to stare at me. He glanced at Dupre across the room, but what transpired between the two of them I couldn't tell.

"Fifty," Blome bid.

"Fifty-five," I shot back.

Burgess was turning the color of eggplant.

Dupre and Harper huddled, deep in conversation. Probably wondering when I had gotten back into the game—where I had come up with new financing. Judging from the look on Blome's face, it was a discussion he would very much like to be a part of.

Most of the audience was oblivious to our drama. But I don't think Isaac and Lara were breathing.

Harper pulled away from Dupre and shook his head. Then he held up his own paddle. "Sixty," he called out.

Dupre shrugged at Blome, who frowned at Harper.

But the damage was done. In spite of the auctioneer's strange demeanor, neither of them could be a hundred percent sure of my interest. Both Blome and Harper wanted the painting, but didn't trust each other. The ring was broken.

"Sixty-five," Blome bid.

Now the bidding was between two players who could actually pay if they won.

When the price topped eighty thousand, Burgess's face faded from purple to a more becoming shade of red.

Isaac and Lara started breathing again. And I rubbed life back into the arm he had nearly squeezed to death.

Harper finally bested Blome at a hundred and twenty-five thousand dollars.

When Burgess cracked the gavel finalizing the sale, Isaac grabbed me and gave me a hug. The smile on his face was bright enough to light an airport runway. At that point, Harper and Blome must have read the situation, but it was too late. My 5 percent wasn't going to make me rich. But that didn't matter. I felt as though I'd sold the *Mona Lisa*.

Christie's would write me a strong letter. Hell, they'd probably threaten to bar me from future sales. But they wouldn't. I'd brought "Sasha" to them in the first place.

2

THE PERALTAS LEFT THE auction shortly after their painting sold, but I decided to sit down at the back of the room and enjoy my self-congratulatory buzz. Nicole, still standing against the wall, clasped both hands together and shook them. "Bravo!" she stage-whispered, loud enough to be heard above the chant of the auctioneer.

Smiling, I closed my eyes, leaned back in the chair, stretched out my legs, and listened to the sale drone on. A smug and satisfied man, at the peak of his game, able to compete with the best of them. I'd been four times around the Central Park reservoir that morning and I was feeling cocky that six miles no longer felt like a marathon. Hell, I felt almost good enough to face Ev Lenoir's letter. Taking a deep breath, I pulled it out of my pocket and tore it open before I changed my mind.

It was even colder than I'd imagined:

> Mr. Sumner,
>   Our records show that you are now over ninety days past due on interest and principle payments totaling $38,465.32. According to the provisions of your note and loan agreement, you are now in

default. This letter shall serve as notice that the bank hereby demands payment in full, and that foreclosure proceedings to collect this arrearage will begin in forty-five days if this matter is not successfully resolved within . . .

I crumpled the letter and closed my eyes.

Thirty-eight thousand . . . I'd owed them a hundred times that amount and never missed a payment. Bankers will fall all over themselves to lend you an umbrella on a sunny day, but they want it back quickly if anything resembling a cloud appears on the horizon. Hell, I couldn't blame Lenoir. I wasn't suffering a cloudy day—more like a goddamn typhoon. But the timing . . .

I wracked my brain trying to think of a way to come up with enough money to keep him happy. I could picture him sitting in his corner office, looking out over the East River. A pudgy man with pudgy hands and a quick smile. A smile that never touched his eyes. He'd take no pleasure in forcing me out of business, but I didn't doubt he'd do it. Even with the Peraltas' commission, I couldn't dent the debt. Not in forty-five days.

At first, I paid no attention when someone sat down next to me and cleared his throat. But when he did it again, I cracked my eyes and found myself looking at the blond man who had followed me into the building. I shook Ev Lenoir out of my head.

The blond man nodded, and this time offered a card.

I didn't take it.

"You followed me in here." It was a statement, not a question. But if he took offense, he didn't show it.

"Yes and no," he said. "I tried to catch you at your office—but you left in a hurry. My time in the city is limited so I had my driver follow you here. Once I realized this was your destination, it seemed like a good idea to watch you in action. Your bidding war was damned interesting. Impressive as hell—although, to be honest, I have to admit the nuance escaped me. Go ahead, take it. Please." He thrust his card at me.

I did.

In elegantly engraved letters the card identified him as Broward Gaines Jr., partner in the law firm of Gaines and Gaines. There was a Palm Beach address and telephone number. I sat up and looked him over. Now I knew why, walking into the building, he'd seemed vaguely familiar.

He'd grown up since I'd seen him last. Even seated, you could tell that Broward Gaines was better than six feet. About my height, but slighter of build. He was younger than me—late twenties, thirty at the most. He wore a gray flannel suit that looked soft enough to sleep in, and black Gucci loafers, polished to a bright luster. His heavily lashed eyes were brown, his blond hair thick and wavy. He was handsome in a kind of pampered way—his country-club upbringing showed in the look of well-fed contempt hiding behind the smile in his eyes. After handing me the card, he sat back and met my gaze.

"What can I do for you?" I asked, wondering what he was doing following me around the streets of Manhattan.

"You are Wil Sumner, aren't you?"

I nodded. Did he really need to ask?

He accepted the confirmation of my identity without blinking. If he recognized me, he gave no sign of it. Opening his bulging briefcase, he pulled out a single sheet of stationery. "I represent a man named Stevenson—Andrew Stevenson," he began, pausing to study my reaction, but I kept my thoughts to myself. After a moment, he continued. "Mr. Stevenson has asked me to engage the services of a competent art appraiser to value his collection of drawings. The art is located in Palm Beach—we're prepared to pay your normal fee as well as expenses if you'll come down to Florida and provide a fair-market appraisal. My client wishes to sell the collection intact, but first he wants to establish its value. The collection comprises a group of Impressionist and modern master drawings—Picasso, Renoir, Monet, and the like. They're currently insured for well into seven figures . . ."

He tossed out the names casually, as though everyone owned drawings by the likes of Monet and Picasso. In the art world, the term "drawing" is a generic one, encompassing any work on paper. Gaines made it clear that Stevenson's collection included watercolors and pastels, as well as black-and-white images. But the lawyer sounded rehearsed, and as he spoke, his eyes rarely held on any one place for more than a few seconds. He rolled the piece of paper he'd pulled from his briefcase back and forth between the thumb and forefinger of his right hand, worrying the stationery the way a child worries a security blanket. He was a product of wealth and privilege. Ivy League. And even though it looked as if he were handing me the break I'd been praying for, there was something else working under that blond hair and golden tan. I couldn't put my finger on it, but Broward Gaines Jr. seemed wound a little too tight.

"Why me?" I asked when he finished.

The question surprised him. After a slight hesitation, he said, "If you're not interested—"

"I'm interested, all right. Just a little curious."

Gaines stood and looked toward the door. "Is there someplace we can get a drink, assuming you're finished here? I've been instructed to give you Mr. Stevenson's phone number. If you decide to take the job, the two of you can work out the fee and the details." He held out the paper he'd been caressing. It was Stevenson's Palm Beach address and phone number.

"How soon does he need this appraisal?" I asked.

"Yesterday," Gaines admitted.

I raised my eyebrows. What he was offering might be the chance of a lifetime, but I knew enough not to let my excitement show. So I put on my poker face and lied. "I'll have to check my calendar. I may have a conflict—I usually go to Italy this time of year. It's the height of the auction season there."

He was smiling at me, but his porcelain grin lacked any semblance of warmth. "Italy will be there next season—Palm Beach won't. Not this collection. Be on a plane tomorrow. I have a feeling you'll thank me."

As I stood up and shook his hand, a warning bell was ringing somewhere in the back of my brain. It was telling me to find out more before I jumped at the deal. But I didn't listen. I thought about palm trees swaying in a gentle breeze, the muted murmur of waves licking a white sand beach. But *that* was some advertising genius's idea of Palm Beach. Not mine. I knew the real place. After all, I'd grown up there.

3

ANDREW AND AMANDA STEVENSON lived on the north end of the island in the old Eckes estate, a sprawling, two-story, stucco and stone Tuscan villa sitting on three acres of Palm Beach oceanfront property. The house was surrounded by coconut palms and hidden from the street by thick hedges of oleander and ficus. I pulled through a pair of tall wrought iron gates and up the pea-gravel driveway, which ran along the north side of the house, a little before three o'clock on a humid, sun-washed Friday. The place drowsed in the heat, looking deserted. Not the slightest breeze stirred the thick air; even the palm fronds drooped, limp and exhausted. Cicadas buzzed angrily at the growl of a lawnmower revving on a neighboring property. My brown Ford Escort was the only vehicle in sight. In front of that house, it looked like a cockroach that had fallen into the caviar.

Stepping out of the car, I approached the portico facing the drive. According to the radio in the car, South Florida was experiencing the worst autumn heat wave in decades. Aside from an occasional shower, it hadn't rained in weeks, and the thermometer had topped a hundred degrees sixteen days in a row. Apparently the Everglades were about to dry up and blow away. If they didn't burn first. I could smell the distant swamp fires, but as far as I could tell, nothing was burning in Palm Beach. I hadn't seen a brown lawn or shrub since I'd crossed the bridge spanning the half mile of water and the million light-years of circumstance separating the island of Palm Beach from the rest of the world. The truly rich weren't about to be inconvenienced by anything as pesky as a drought. The locals seemed far more concerned with next month's elections. Every other car I'd passed seemed to have a bumper sticker touting Roberto Salgo for governor. The name tweaked some vague memory. But I couldn't track it, and it was too hot to pursue the thought.

My telephone conversation with Andrew Stevenson had been brief—confined to the logistics of travel and the size of my fee. In my haste to get down here, I hadn't bothered to ask about the weather. I was a native. I thought I knew what to expect. But this was ridiculous. I reached for an iron knocker the size of a small cannon ball, and banged as politely as you can with that amount of metal on a pair of carved walnut doors that looked as though they'd once hung in a Spanish monastery.

No response.

I knocked again, this time a little louder. Again to no response.

After waiting a moment or two, I tried a third time, beginning to think no one was home. Maybe there had been some kind of mix-up, although I thought I'd been clear about my arrival time. Stepping away from the doors, I considered my options. I wiped the sweat off my forehead with the back of my hand, peeled off my suit coat, and decided to have a look around.

To the east of the portico a flight of six coral-paved steps led up a low hill from the drive to an elevated lawn facing the Atlantic. A ten-foot drop separated the thick, emerald carpet of grass from the beach, the elevation buttressed by an imposing concrete seawall into which steps had been cut. A fancy iron-work gate denied strangers and uninvited guests access to the house from the beach. I stood on top of the seawall for a moment, admiring the view, hoping for a breeze. Turning, I took in the oceanfront facade of the house. It was one hell of a house—two stories of creamy stucco arches and balconies, trimmed with quarried-coral masonry and topped by a terra-cotta barrel-tile roof. A home is a man's castle. This one had the Atlantic for a moat.

In the art world, it's considered something of a natural law that collectors sell their collections for one of three reasons. The three D's. Debt, divorce, or death. It didn't look like debt was motivating Stevenson. Then again, looks can be deceptive. I wondered about the collection. Gaines had said it was made up of Impressionist and modern master works on paper—insured for millions. Stevenson had confirmed that he owned some serious art. But if his collection matched his house, why hadn't I ever heard of it?

I scanned the lawn and gardens, then, shielding my eyes against the tropical glare, I studied the house again. On a second-floor balcony above a coral-decked sitting area, an empty wicker chair sat in front of an open pair of French doors but not a soul stirred.

Wondering where the hell everyone was, I turned and found myself face-to-face with a frowning black man.

"I'm Maj," the man said in a voice heavily accented by the islands. "Be short for Major." He was the color of licorice, short, with a slim waist. His hands were huge and his arms bunched with ropy muscle. "You got bidness here?"

I stuck out my hand. "Wil Sumner. I knocked, but no one answered. Thought Mr. Stevenson was expecting me."

Maj nodded as we shook. He looked about fifty, but it was hard to tell. His catcher's mitt of a hand was rough and callused.

"Sorry 'bout that. He knew to be expectin' you now?"

"I thought so."

"Mon been sick—plenty on his mind." He shook his head. "Charteen—the maid—she say he good one day, not so good the next. Cancer. Come, I take you to her."

Maj took off around the far side of the house. I lingered for a second looking up at the empty chair on the balcony. Gaines hadn't bothered to tell me Stevenson was sick. So much for debt or divorce. What else had the young lawyer neglected to let me know?

As I rounded the corner of the house, the pool came into

view, a long, Olympic-size affair, lined in smooth dark stone. I
stopped to take it in. At the deep end, a man-made waterfall
tumbled over rough-hewn coral boulders. At the shallow end, a
Jacuzzi built into the pool bubbled and frothed. If it had been
less well designed, it would have looked tacky—something
more at home in Las Vegas. But whoever had put it together had
done it right. The effect was of some ancient grotto, straight out
of a Greek myth. On the far side of the pool, lying on the cushions of a cast-iron chaise, was a young woman—mid-twenties,
maybe a little older. Barely clad in a minuscule black bikini, she
had shoulder-length blonde hair and a healthy tan. Her eyes
were closed, and her skin shone with a mixture of suntan oil
and perspiration. Sitting on a table next to the chaise was a tall,
sweating glass of something clear with a wedge of lime. All that
was missing were the white-jacketed waiters and a towel boy or
two.

I hadn't realized I was staring until Maj tapped me on the
shoulder.

"That be M.K.—the Stevensons' daughter," he whispered, as
though he didn't want to disturb her.

"M. K. Stevenson . . . ," I repeated, remembering a long-
legged, skinny blonde kid in pigtails—a bossy little girl who'd
acted like she owned the Bath and Tennis Club. "Filling out"
didn't begin to describe her transformation. "She lives here?"

"Yeah, mon. The cabana house be hers." He pointed to the
one-story stucco bungalow just past the foot of the pool. It was
separated from the main house, but built in the same style. "Got
it fixed up very, very nice, you know."

I didn't doubt it. M.K. hadn't stirred. If she knew she had
company, she gave no sign of it.

"She's something," I said, feeling suddenly thirsty.

"Come now, I take you to Charteen. Plenty a time for lookin'
at M.K.—later."

I followed him through a shaded courtyard complete with a
gurgling marble fountain. Water music and bougainvillea.
Drinks by the pool. Suntan oil. Bikinis. The stomp and growl of
New York a rapidly fading memory. As we stepped around to

the rear of the house, I wondered why Gaines had chosen me for this job. Then I decided not to think about it.

Maj, standing by the back door, gestured for me to hurry up.

We stepped out of the sun and into the cool bowels of the house. I didn't like using the servants' entrance. I wasn't one of the help, not anymore, and I didn't want to be treated like one. But if Stevenson was really planning on selling his drawings, he'd need someone to represent his interests. And if I wanted the job, I had to get into the house.

"Charteen," Maj called as we stepped inside. "Got you a visitor. Where you be?"

"Stop your yellin', Maj." Charteen appeared in the back hall, folding a large pink towel. "You ain't in no Jamaican cane field." She looked about sixty, with skin halfway between the color of paprika and cinnamon. A sprinkling of chocolate freckles dotted her cheeks. Her hair was hidden under a flowered scarf, her face dominated by a wide nose and a generous mouth.

The air-conditioned interior of the house was a relief after the afternoon heat. She glanced first at me, then at Maj. "Well?"

"Well—you ain't in no Georgia hill town either. Is you, Charteen?" He pointed at me. "Mon knocked at the door, but say no one answered. Must be getting too old to hear the doorbell, girl." He flashed a grin at her. "Maybe it's time you done took my offer."

Charteen snorted. "Maj, I ain't near old enough to want to lay up with a goat like you. Now, out my house. I just mopped this hall."

He shrugged. "Maybe you change your mind. Got work to do, you know." Turning, he winked at me and walked out.

Charteen stood blocking the hall, arms crossed over the towel she'd been folding. Whatever Georgia hill town she was from still shaded her voice. She eyed me with suspicion. "Well, don't stand there listenin' to that old fool. What you need?"

I smiled at her. "Sounds to me like that 'old fool' likes you."

"Don't believe I caught your name, Mister," she grumbled. "You sellin' something?"

"No. I'm Wil Sumner. Thought I was expected."

Without budging an inch, she asked, "S'pected by who?"

"By Mr. Stevenson." When that gained me nothing, I added, "I just flew in from New York."

At the mention of New York, she stiffened. "Jesus Lord. You the art man?"

I nodded.

"I'm so sorry. Should'a come in through the front. Maj know better than to bring you 'round back. Thought you was another of those fellas sellin' pest control. Don't pay no mind to me and Maj. We just talks too much." She shook her head, and led me toward the front of the house, dropping the towel on one of the counters as we passed through a spotless kitchen, roughly three times the size of my current apartment.

She looked over her shoulder at me and said, "S'pected an older man—to be truthful. Someone . . . Well, you no older than my grandson—same size too. An' he used to be a ballplayer."

"What kind of ball did he play?" But I was talking to her back and she was having none of it.

I hurried to keep up with her. We passed through a formal dining room. Centered on a fine old green-and-gold Oushak carpet was a Hepplewhite table surrounded by two dozen heavily carved mahogany chairs. A rock-crystal chandelier almost the size of a Volkswagen Bug hung over the table. I wanted to stop and take a closer look, but Charteen was already halfway down a wide, barrel-vaulted hall that led from the dining room into the marble entrance vestibule.

Just inside the front doors, she turned and faced me, as if we could start over. "I'm Charteen. Been with the Stevensons almost twenty years." She offered a small, damp hand. I took it. As she looked into my eyes, I had the feeling I had grossly underestimated her age. "Couldn't hear you knockin' from the laundry room. Should'a come in this way."

"No problem." I smiled and tried to put her at ease. "I'm glad to be here."

I looked around the vestibule. It opened on one side to a high-ceilinged living room, and on the other side to a mahogany-paneled formal library. A Regency rosewood table occupied the center of the space. On it sat a Chinese export bowl filled with a lush arrangement of large white roses that were a good three days past their prime. A wide, elegantly curving staircase led to the second floor. The scale of the house was impressive. But so far I hadn't seen anything worth millions on the walls.

Something happens to a household when one of its members becomes seriously ill. As an appraiser, I'd seen it often enough to know the symptoms. It begins with a cessation of time. The days blur and turn soft around the edges. Things that were once important no longer seem to matter. A sense of impotent waiting takes over, a brooding atmosphere I now recognized in this house. Almost as though the rooms themselves, and all the furnishings and art, were slumbering—waiting for some event, some burst of energy that would return everything to the way it once had been.

I turned back to Charteen. She was studying me the way I was studying the house. It was a little unsettling.

"What time were the Stevensons expecting me?" I asked.

She shrugged. "Mister Andrew's resting and Miz Amanda won't be back till four or so. Your bags still in the car?"

"Yes."

"You need any help, or you want me to show you to your room?"

"Nah. I'll handle my bags," I answered. When we had negotiated my fee on the telephone—five hundred a day, plus expenses—Stevenson had offered to put me up while I appraised the collection. From what I'd seen of the house, the guest room ought to make the best suite at the Ritz look shabby. "You're busy enough without having to look after me. Why don't you show me my room, Charteen? Then I'll find something to do until Mrs. Stevenson gets home."

"Suit me just fine," she said, neither smiling nor frowning. "Since M.K. moved back, got enough laundry to finish. . . . That girl use in a day what'd last most folks a week." She shook her head, then led me up the sweeping staircase and toward the back of the house.

We entered a small room overlooking the pool. It wasn't the

lavish guest suite of my imagination. Furnished simply, the room contained a single bed next to a country-pine nightstand. A lamp made out of a clear glass vase filled with seashells sat on the nightstand. A naïve seascape hung crookedly on the wall behind the bed. To the left of the bed stood a pine dresser with a plain mirror hanging over it. No television, no telephone. It wasn't the Ritz. Hell, it wasn't the Hilton either. What it was was the old servants' quarters. But it was clean, the price was right, and there was a nice chintz spread on the bed and curtains to match.

I straightened the seascape. Then, edging around the bed, I stepped to the window and looked down at the pool. M.K. was on her stomach now, her rear end aimed directly at me. A lot of work keeping an even tan.

"Already put fresh soap and towels in the bathroom."

I tore myself away from the window.

Charteen was pointing to a door facing the foot of the narrow bed. "Call if you need anythin' else," she said, then left me alone.

4

I WAS LEANING INTO THE trunk of the Escort to retrieve my bags when a cream-colored Rolls-Royce coupe, the convertible model, roared into the drive and skidded to a halt in a spray of gravel uncomfortably close to where I stood.

A tall woman, dressed casually in khakis and a white linen shirt, jumped out of the car, glanced at me, and began shouting for Maj.

"Maj! Come here! Quickly! I need you!"

If this was Amanda Stevenson, she wasn't what I had expected.

Leaning back into the car, she blew the horn. Two loud blasts. Then she shouted again, "Maj! Where are you?"

At first, her panic didn't register on me. I thought she was in a hurry, that she wanted Maj's help with some packages, or maybe the groceries. But when I stepped toward her, I saw that it was more than that. She was in her late fifties with thick, blonde hair, cut short and swept behind her ears. Her skin was tanned, her face attractive but clouded now with anxiety.

Glancing back down the driveway, she shouted once more for Maj, then started for the house.

"Can I help?" I called.

Before she could answer, Maj came running around the side of the house clutching a pair of garden shears. "What happen? What wrong, Miz Amanda?"

It was Amanda Stevenson. She pointed toward the end of the drive. "There! He's there again. I saw him—just by the bushes at the foot of the drive."

"He come on the property this time, ma'am?" Maj asked.

She shook her head. "No . . . But he was standing there—looking up the driveway like he intended to do something."

Maj frowned. "Go on inside, Miz Amanda. I'll deal wit him—if he still be out there."

Without another word, Maj took off down the driveway.

She stood there for a moment, watching him. Then, suddenly, she turned to me. "Who are you?" she demanded.

"I'm Wil Sumner." I stepped over to her and offered my hand. "From New York . . ."

She repeated my name. "Wil . . . Wil Sumner?" Her blank expression clarified as we shook. "Oh God. You must think I'm awful." She hesitated. "I'm Amanda Stevenson. Please forgive me—I should have been here to greet you. It slipped my mind. Things are a bit crazy. I'm sorry."

She glanced past me at Maj, who was walking back up the driveway, a disgusted look on his face.

"Is there anything I can do?" I asked.

She studied me for a moment, then shook her head. "We seem to have attracted an unwanted admirer. That's all. Excuse me."

Turning to Maj, she asked, "Did you see him? Was he still there?"

"No, Miz Amanda. Found this, though. Sittin' on top a the mailbox." He held out a small package wrapped in brown paper. It was addressed to Andrew Stevenson, but there was no postage or return address.

She took the package and tore it open. Inside was a slender, old, sterling-silver lighter. The initials AFS were engraved on one dented and tarnished side.

She held it up, a curious expression on her face. "Did *he* leave it?"

Maj shrugged.

"Was there anything else? A note? An envelope?"

"Didn't see nothin' else," Maj said.

She thought about it for a moment, then said, "I'll show it to Mr. Stevenson—but I want you to look around again, make sure there wasn't a note or a card."

Maj threw an indecipherable look at me, then headed back down the driveway.

Amanda started toward the front doors, then seemed to remember I was there. She stopped and frowned. "I really am sorry to greet you this way. Do you need Maj to help you with your things?"

I shook my head. "Just a couple of bags. Charteen already showed me my room."

"Good." She glanced at her watch, calmer now. "I want to check on my husband, then I have some calls to make. Meet me at five-thirty in the library. I'll see to drinks—we can talk about the appraisal then."

I watched her walk into the house. She wasn't the high-society woman I'd expected. Aside from her Rolls-Royce and a pair of diamond-stud earrings, each the size of a small grape, splashing fire in the late afternoon sun, she looked like any other handsome, middle-aged woman who happened to have great bones, kind eyes, and the weight of the world on her shoulders.

I glanced at my own watch. It was just past four. I could be there and back within an hour.

Why not?

There was nothing I could do here, not until I met with the Stevensons.

Then again, there was nothing for me there either. Not now.

Maj was coming up the driveway, empty-handed. Whoever had delivered the lighter was gone now.

I closed the trunk and climbed behind the wheel of the Escort. I don't know what I expected to find, but I wanted to go back to the neighborhood I'd left behind. If for no other reason, just to mark the distance I'd traveled in the fifteen years I'd been gone.

5

PALM BEACH SITS ON A long and narrow spit of land comprising four square miles of some of the most expensive real estate east of Bel Air—bounded on one side by the Atlantic, on the other by the intracoastal waterway—tethered to the mainland by three narrow bridges. I cruised along in the Escort, taking in the manicured lawns and stately homes, smiling like a tourist.

The island hadn't changed much. Places like Palm Beach never do. Money, enough of it, can buy a sort of status quo. And unlike most places, money was no rare commodity here. There are no bad neighborhoods on the island—they just get better and better. And the best rival anything in the world. The great estates, barely visible behind their impenetrable hedges and wrought-iron gates, looked exactly as I remembered them. Impressive—private. Secure and serene. Peace of mind at a price. But one hell of a price. As a kid, I used to ride my bike across the middle bridge and along these streets, wondering who lived in the mansions behind the hedges. I still wondered. But these days, I didn't wonder who—I wondered how much.

Now I drove across the bridge going the opposite way, thinking about the difference the narrow channel of water separating Palm Beach from West Palm Beach can make to the way you grow up. The two worlds might as well have been on different planets. Oh, I could point out the lawns on the island that I'd cut as a kid, the Bath and Tennis Club where I'd worked winters as a cabana boy. I'd been a busboy for an exclusive Palm Beach catering service, probably knew the geography of the island as well as anyone. But those credentials didn't make me a Palm Beacher.

A mile inland, everything changed. Suddenly, the stores and strip centers looked sunbaked and tacky. An endless commercial district, broken up by subdivisions and tract houses. Some nice, most, not so nice.

I drove south on Dixie, then west on Southern Boulevard, past the airport and the gleaming rows of private jets and helicopters, past the Mermaid Club and its neon sign advertising girls, girls, girls, past Bill's House of Television and Repair. Old man Picknell's hardware store was gone, replaced by a restaurant, Cantinas Criollas. I wondered if the old man was still alive—and what he would think of the new restaurant serving tacos and empanadas where he had once sold cane poles and saw blades.

I slowed at the entrance to Flamingo Lakes and asked myself what I was doing here. But I didn't know the answer. Wasn't even sure I understood the question.

Flamingo Lakes. Where the name had come from in the first place had always been a mystery to me. There were no lakes, and the closest thing to a flamingo I ever saw as a kid was the Bussey's parrot, a rotten-tempered bird with moldy-looking yellow feathers and a sharp black beak. Back then, this neighborhood had seemed as if it was in the middle of nowhere. But civilization had moved west, farther and farther inland as the population of South Florida swelled. Unfortunately, civilization had hopped right over the Flamingo Lakes subdivision, leaving a little pocket of poverty smack in the middle of all the new car lots and middle-class residential developments. Once a decent, working-class neighborhood, it was now an eyesore.

The streets looked narrower than I remembered them, the houses meaner, several abandoned and derelict. Everything needed paint. Everything except the graffiti and the burglar bars, which looked shiny and as solid as hell. Garden hoses snaked across a few of the yards, sprinklers working overtime against the glaring sun. But it was a losing battle, and even the few patches of dusty, green grass mired in the sea of brown seemed to know it.

Two kids in baggy shorts practiced jumping their skateboards over the curb onto the cracked sidewalk. When I slowed to watch, one of them flipped me the finger.

The boxy little house I had grown up in seemed to be listing slightly to one side, the paint peeling, the roof tiles curling. Engine parts were scattered across the yard. A redwood picnic table in front of the house held a plastic ice chest; someone had lit a rusty charcoal grill near the tree that shaded what had once been my bedroom. I stopped the car, started to pull in behind the pickup truck in the drive, then thought better of it. My parents had died the year I'd left town—almost exactly fifteen years ago. I didn't know the new owners of the house, didn't want to know them. I sat there anyway, engine idling, staring at the front door, trying to imagine a gangly kid pedaling home from the beach on his bicycle. His bathing suit still wet from the sea, his skin sunburned and matted with salt, his head full of big, expensive dreams.

Some of those dreams had come true. I'd worked my way through school, then sold for other art dealers, struggling and saving, doing without until I had enough put away to open my first gallery. Along the way, I met Peter Jacobs—a smoother salesman had never been born. Together, we learned to wheel and deal, leveraging each sale into better and better inventory, until we were buying and selling paintings by Matisse and Renoir. Works of art worth millions of dollars passed through our hands every week. We formed a great team—at least until Peter, without bothering to ask my opinion, took money out of a client's trust account, money that didn't belong to us, and used it to buy a folio of Albrecht Dürer watercolors. The greedy bastard thought we'd make a killing. Instead, the watercolors turned out to be fakes; we lost everything. In the blink of an eye, my high-flying career, over a decade of work and effort, had come crashing down out of that thin air. I'd fallen fast and hard. Peter disappeared—Costa Rica, I heard later—leaving me holding the bag. I sold everything I owned at half of what it was worth and barely managed to pay off the debt. These days I worked alone, out of my apartment, perpetually one sale, one appraisal fee, one deal shy of total insolvency. And on those nights when sleep came late and I dreamed of how high I'd risen, I could hear myself screaming bloody murder all the way down. I wanted it back. I was prepared to work for it. And Andrew Stevenson just might be the opportunity I'd been waiting for.

The click of a pebble hitting the windshield snapped me out of my daydream. Three Hispanic-looking kids sporting blue gang colors, arms full of tattoos, stared at me from across the street, their young faces set with open hostility.

Shaking my head, I pointed the car east and stomped on the gas. Whatever I'd hoped to find here had faded and peeled away like the layers of old paint on the house that had once been my home.

6

Amanda Stevenson had her back to me when I walked into the library. She'd changed into a green-and-white-striped beach cover-up, and stood holding a cordless telephone to her ear.

"No," she said into the phone, "I won't intercede, Broward." She listened for a moment, then said, "If it's that important, I'll ask him to call you. But I don't want you hounding him, do you understand me?" She listened for another second, then lowered the phone from her ear and pushed the disconnect button.

I cleared my throat.

She turned, looking exhausted. "I didn't hear you come in," she said, placing the telephone down on the Chippendale desk that dominated the room. Late afternoon light filtered in through the floor to ceiling windows at her back, but the leather-bound volumes lining the walls seemed to absorb the bluish light rather than reflect it, giving the hushed room a submerged quality.

"I hope I didn't keep you waiting," I said.

She shook her head. A second ago on the telephone she had sounded tough, in control. Now she stood there, looking shaken, on the verge of tears. "No. You didn't keep me waiting," she said, visibly struggling to regain her composure.

I waited, not sure how I could help, or if I should try.

Stepping around the desk, she took a deep breath and pasted a brave smile on her tired face. "Come on. Andrew asked me to show you the collection."

"Will I meet him tonight?" I asked as we walked out of the library.

"I doubt it. He has good days and bad. This hasn't been a good one. But he wants to get this done—now."

She led me toward the kitchen, her bare feet silent on the hardwood floor. "We keep most of the art in the old silver safe—something around three hundred works." As we walked, she told me more about the collection.

Located between the kitchen and the pantry, the old silver safe, a feature not often included in modern houses, was a walk-in vault behind an old-fashioned steel door with a dial-combination lock. Amanda tugged on it and the heavy door swung silently open. The interior was large enough to accommodate two of her Rolls-Royces side by side. Standing at the threshold, I tried to imagine the vault as it would have appeared back when the house was built in the roaring twenties, back in the days when rumrunners ran their cargoes in from the Bahamas on open speedboats. When the house parties lasted for days and you could count on one hand the number of guests who weren't related either by marriage or merger. The silver safe would have been filled with stacks of heavy sterling platters, gleaming tea services, candelabra and chafing dishes, mahogany boxes of gilded flatware, service plates and goblets to match—all counted and polished, safely locked away until the next Gatsbyesque celebration.

No precious metals gleamed in the light. Whatever silver the Stevensons owned rested elsewhere. The vault now held a more subtle and far more valuable treasure. It had been turned into an art repository. According to Amanda, only a few of the three hundred drawings in the collection were framed and displayed on the walls of the mansion. True collectors don't buy to furnish the walls. Once it's in their veins, collecting is like dope—an itch that can't be scratched. But they try. So they need silver safes.

And their insurance agents drive better and better cars. I couldn't help smiling. Whoever had designed this room had known what they were doing. The walls were paneled in shiny, bleached oak, into which had been built wide drawers, each marked in numerical sequence. Thick, forest-green carpeting covered the floor. Cool fluorescent lights recessed into the ceiling illuminated the space; an elaborate dehumidifier stood in one corner, blowing a stream of pleasantly dry air toward the door. Mounted on the wall opposite the dehumidifier was a complicated-looking piece of equipment, tracing a record of the room's temperature and humidity on a drum-shaped scroll. A seventeenth-century walnut refectory table sat in the center of the room, surrounded by four pale-green leather captain's chairs.

Amanda Stevenson put her hand on my back and ushered me into the vault. Pointing to a notebook on the table, she said, "M.K., our daughter, helped Andrew put that book together when she came back from London. She'd had a rough time. Working on the book was like therapy—it helped her get over—" She stopped suddenly, as though she'd said more than she wanted to. "In any case, the drawings are listed there, alphabetically by artist, along with the corresponding number of the drawer in which each work is stored."

I nodded, wondering what had happened to M.K. in London. "Good. That will make my job easier."

She frowned. Her mouth pressed into a hard line.

I was ready to begin opening those drawers, but Amanda's bleak mood seemed amplified within the close confines of the vault. She seemed on the verge of saying something.

I waited.

She stood, arms crossed over her chest, staring past me at the wall of drawers. "You can set up shop here," she said finally. Placing her hands on the back of a chair, she continued, "Andrew sat *here*. He spent hours and hours in this chair. These drawings are his great love. I helped him when I could, but he's the one who really understands these things." She paused and met my eye. "The fact that he's suddenly decided to sell them disturbs me more than you can imagine. I don't know why he's doing this. He wants them out—sold as quickly as possible. I don't understand. It isn't like my husband to act so . . . so . . . impulsively. God knows, we don't need the money." She drew a deep breath. "Andrew is an intensely private man. Never showed off the collection publicly—it's always been his baby. I'm shocked he's parting with them. I told him—begged him—not to. But he's set on it—keeps talking about putting things in order. Maybe it's his way of letting go. But I'm not ready. Damnit, not yet." She looked away, eyes moist.

I nodded dumbly. What the hell was there to say?

The silence grew until it filled the room.

I kept my mouth shut, giving her time to work it out.

"Any questions?" she asked finally, in a hoarse voice.

"Are you going to be okay?"

She studied me

I returned her gaze.

"I'll be fine. I don't have any choice." She sounded more resigned than bitter, but that was there too. She reached up, absently fingering one of her diamond earrings. "If I seem less than thrilled at what you're here to do, forgive me. It's not your fault. I'll try my best not to take it out on you. Are you ready to start?"

The way I felt, I might never start. But I didn't voice the thought. I needed this.

"I'll take a look tonight, find out what I'm up against," I answered. "I'll start the actual appraisal in the morning."

"Fine. The notebook lists everything but the contents of *that* drawer." She pointed to the bottom drawer at the back of the vault. "Andrew loves a bargain. He buys anything that catches his eye. Calls them his mystery collection. He brings them home . . ." She stopped and touched the hollow place at her throat. "That's wrong . . ." She shook her head. "He hasn't bought anything—taken any interest in the collection—in almost a year. He *used* to spend weeks researching his mystery drawings. Always hoping for that overlooked masterpiece. But it never happened." She fell silent again.

The existence of Andrew Stevenson's mystery collection, a

collection within the collection, didn't surprise me. Some men scuba dive in far-flung locations, looking for sunken doubloons; others pan for gold dust and nuggets in mountain streams. Andy Warhol bought cookie jars. Men, who in the ordinary course of their businesses think carefully before making even a minor move, will sometimes do the damnedest things with their weekend money. I know a pediatric surgeon in Nashville who spends his Sundays at flea markets buying every old oil painting he can get his hands on for under twenty-five dollars. He carts them back to the hospital and x-rays them. He lives to discover a Rembrandt or something equally distinguished—waiting, long forgotten, hidden under layers of old oil paint. The odds against him are devastating. But golf never appealed, and at twenty-five dollars a pop, he explains, it beats the hell out of betting the ponies. One big treasure hunt for grown-ups. A game. But it's not just about money or winning. It's about looking as much as finding. The grand quest.

With this in mind, I asked, "Do you think your husband will want to look them over before I start?"

She shook her head. "I wish . . . God knows I wish he would. But Andrew's not very interested in art these days. Something's on his mind." She hesitated, her eyes fixed on something far away, something I couldn't see. "Sometimes I wonder . . . Maybe that's what cancer does to you. It's not easy to watch."

We stood in the vault, neither of us saying a word, the silence growing again.

The dehumidifier clicked off. I hadn't been aware of its humming until it stopped.

Amanda sighed. "Don't worry about the mystery drawings. I'll probably just keep them anyway. They'll remind me of happier days."

I nodded.

"That's it . . . I'm afraid I won't be much of a hostess tonight. There's food in the refrigerator—help yourself—or find Charteen if you need anything. Any questions?"

I looked at the heavy steel door. "Do I have to worry about getting locked in?"

She actually smiled. Not much of one, but enough to brighten her lined face. "Don't tell a soul, but I don't think we've ever actually locked it."

"Never?" I asked, still eyeing the door.

Her smile deepened. "Not even once. But if you do manage to get yourself locked in, don't panic. I won't forget you're here."

7

THE VAULT SEEMED LARGER after she left. I stood still for a few moments, letting her presence ebb out of the room. Then I stepped to the table.

Appraising art isn't a science, but there is a standard methodology that most good appraisers use. I'd brought with me from New York a duffel bag loaded with books and auction catalogs, a Polaroid camera, an ultraviolet light to detect restorations and over-painting, and a strong magnifying glass. I began unpacking my gear, thinking about the job in front of me. A work of art's value is based on a combination of five factors: authorship, medium, subject, period, and condition. The relative importance of each one of these factors can vary depending upon the artist. A work of great rarity, a Vermeer, for example, can be extremely valuable even if it has been heavily restored, whereas the value of a work by a more prolific artist like Degas would be drastically lower if it was in poor condition. A watercolor by Cézanne is worth less than an oil by the same artist, but more than an oil by any of a thousand lesser artists. By weighing these five factors against the history of an artist's prior sales record, you can come up with a fair idea of what an individual work is worth on the open market. There is, however, a sixth factor that must be taken into consideration: quality. This is the most subjective and difficult factor to apply. Like everyone else, artists had good and bad days. And the difference in value between a good drawing and a bad one, all other factors, such as medium, size, subject, and date being equal, is dramatic. It takes a damned good eye and a lot of confidence to decide the difference between a good Picasso and a mediocre one. In the morning, I planned to begin the painstaking process of examining each drawing in Stevenson's collection, good, bad, and indifferent. By the time I finished, I'd know them as intimately as he did.

But tonight, I just wanted to look.

Randomly selecting the drawer marked 129–140, I opened it. Inside sat a black solander box, the standard archival container used by museums and institutions to store works on paper. In the box, stacked one on top of the other, separated by sheets of glassine, were twelve pastel still lifes by Redon. I gently lifted them out of the box and spread them on the table. Twelve Redons! I looked at them for a few minutes, then shook my head in wonder. I opened the next drawer. Another solander box. This one contained four Renoir sketches of nudes, and two, slightly differing, fully finished sanguine studies of his famous painting *Lady at a Piano*. The Art Institute of Chicago owned the painting. How much would these studies be worth to them? My hands started to tingle. I wiped damp palms on the front of my shirt. The two drawers I had randomly selected contained drawings worth well over a million dollars.

Amanda's grief slipped my mind. I began opening and closing drawers like a breathless kid on Christmas morning, unable to choose which gift to play with first. There were six Cézannes— two watercolors of apples, two almost abstract still lifes, a pencil sketch of *The Bathers,* and an important study for *The Card Players.* In one drawer I found three pointillist Signac watercolors and seven brooding Seurat drawings, five Schiele nudes, powerfully erotic, stunningly graceful. In another, three completed Degas pastels and another five sketches the artist had rendered of ballerinas in motion. One drawer was full of

Matisses. I counted twenty of them. The tingling moved from my hands up my arms and down my spine. I was practically vibrating.

Works on paper can be sketchy—shallow scribbles. Some are mere notes in the margins, reminders artists wrote to themselves of observations or subjects that deserved further exploration. Stevenson's drawings had bones. So far I hadn't seen a single one that was indifferent or weak. They were full of heat and blood—powerful testaments to the creative genius that separates great artists from the rest of us mere mortals. I'd sampled fewer than half the drawers, but it was enough to know I was sitting amid a treasure unlike any I'd ever seen in private hands. It was too much to take in at one sitting, too much to describe in any way that would do the individual works justice. The overall effect was monumental. I fell into one of the captain's chairs and tried to gather my thoughts.

When a collection achieves a certain mass, a weight based on either its quality and quantity, or its owner's celebrity, its value soars beyond the sum total of its individual parts. Price becomes irrelevant. Consider the auction of Jackie O's personal property. I scanned through the notebook. No golf clubs, rocking chairs, or humidors here. It wasn't, as Gaines had suggested, worth millions. The Stevenson collection was worth tens of millions. There wasn't a dealer in the world who wouldn't gladly give his right arm, and maybe a whole lot more, to have these drawings. Besides what I'd already pulled out of the drawers, the notebook listed works by Manet, Modigliani, Monet, Morisot, Picasso, Pissarro. It was a goddamn who's who. There were eight Delacroixs. A sketchbook by Bazille. Works by Gris, Braque, Miró, and Kandinsky. The provenance of each drawing was listed in the notebook. They were impeccable. The collection was stunning. Alone, it would be enough to establish the dealer who controlled it as a major force in the art world. Stevenson had quietly amassed what might be the finest extant group of modern drawings. The collection would be a boon to any museum. I could think of a half dozen off the top of my head that would build a wing for them—and render the Stevenson name forever synonymous with collecting important works on paper. Why hadn't I heard of it? Why hadn't the collection been published? Who else knew about it? Had Gaines talked to other dealers? My head was spinning.

I paced around the table a couple of times, then sat and picked up the notebook again. Along with its provenance, each work was listed with its date of purchase as well as its vital stats: measurements, detailed notes on condition, if it was signed or inscribed and where. The dates of the purchases shed a little light on things. I began to see how the collection had been assembled without causing unwanted attention. Stevenson had inherited the nucleus, some twenty or thirty drawings, and had then added to them for over forty years. The original group of drawings had been purchased directly from the artists, either by Stevenson's mother or his father. According to the notebook, various letters and bills of sale from the artists authenticating the works were now stored in one of the drawers. The rest of the drawings had been acquired by Andrew Stevenson himself, using no one source any more often than any other source. Dealers all over the world had sold to him. They all knew him as a buyer, but none of them knew the full extent of his holdings. He'd bought smart. But why the secrecy?

I was sitting in Aladdin's cave and it was for sale. But I didn't have the money to insure it for a month, much less buy it. If Stevenson was intent on selling, there were ways to liquidate the collection properly. A quick sale was not the way to go. The collection needed to be cataloged—displayed, shared with the public—not dumped haphazardly. If money wasn't the issue, what was? Why had Stevenson suddenly, and according to Amanda, without reason, decided to sell? Obviously his approaching death was motivating him. But had his illness made him irrational? What could drive a man to part with his most prized possessions in such a hurry? Especially now, when he was so ill? All of these questions turned in a circle inside my skull—a tightening spiral that set my temples aching. They were questions only Stevenson could answer. I wanted to run upstairs and wake him. Pull him down here and find out what the hell was going on. If he was ready to sell, I could guide him—and make sure it was done properly.

I sat back and took a deep breath. To be involved with this collection would secure my reputation for life. The dehumidifier kicked on, its sudden steady hum loud in the confined space of the vault. If I understood his motivation—had a better handle on Stevenson himself—I could win his trust.

I glanced at my watch; it was after seven.

Dropping the notebook onto the table, I stood and walked out of the vault, careful to turn out the lights and pull the steel door closed without locking it.

I hesitated outside the vault, suddenly sure I should lock it. But I didn't know the combination.

My stomach rumbled. First, a hot shower, then dinner.

Great art gives a man an appetite.

Monet knew.

8

I CLIMBED THE STAIRS AND stood for a moment on the top landing, listening. The door was closed to the suite of rooms I took to be the Stevensons', but I could hear running water and the television—the evening news, turned loud—someone making a speech. A deep, heavily accented voice saying, "The Cuban American Political Foundation is proud to support one of Florida's great philanthropists, a senior statesman of the highest integrity, a man with a vision, a vision for a better and brighter future, for ourselves, and for our children. Please join me in welcoming our next governor, Roberto Salgo!" At this the crowd began chanting, "Salllgo . . . Salllgo . . . Salllgo."

So Stevenson *was* awake. The crowd was still chanting Salgo's name. I stepped to the door, trying to decide why that name seemed so familiar, started to knock, then lowered my hand. Disturbing Stevenson now wasn't likely to impress him. It wasn't going to be easy, but I had to remain patient, let him tell me what I needed to know in his own way—and in his own time.

I had turned my back on the door when Amanda's voice rang out over the sound of water splashing into the sink. "Why do you do this to yourself?"

There came a muffled reply I couldn't understand.

I moved closer.

"Andrew!" A note of exasperation had crept into her voice. "If it upsets you so much, turn the damned thing off. After what you've told me, I don't understand how you stomach looking at our next governor."

"Someone has to."

"Louder, honey. I can barely hear you."

The chanting stopped.

The anchorman's monotone replaced the chanting of the crowds. "After this afternoon's rally, Roberto Salgo and his entourage . . ."

"Turn it down, Andrew!"

The television went silent. Then, in a voice that scraped like a blade on bone, Andrew Stevenson said: "Bastard. I know. You know I know—and I'm waiting. *On my eyelids is the shadow of death.*"

Abruptly, the water cut off.

"Your room is that way—last time I looked."

I spun around and found M.K. standing at the top of the land- ing, staring at me.

"I—uhhhmmm . . ." I shook my head, fumbling for an explana- tion. "I wanted to meet your father—but the TV was on and . . ."

She smiled coolly. "It's okay. I wasn't spying on you. I came up to ask if you had any plans. If not, some people are giving a little cocktail reception at the museum—my mother asked me to include you, she thought you might enjoy it."

"That was nice of her."

M.K. crossed her arms and nodded. "So, would you like to come?"

We stood regarding each other. Her eyes were pale green. She wore a short, black-linen sheath and no jewelry. She didn't need any. The dress showed her long legs to good advantage. Her thick blonde hair was pulled back off her neck into a ponytail; her skin glowed from the sun. The skinny kid I remembered from the Bath and Tennis Club had grown into a beauty, but if she recognized me, she didn't let on.

"Do I have time to clean up and change?" I asked.

She shrugged. "Take your time. It's a fund-raiser. I don't even know what it's for, but I promised Broward I'd show up. We don't have to stay long."

"Broward Gaines?"

"I think you met him—in New York." Then she turned and started down the stairs.

Halfway down, she stopped and looked up at me. "You do want to come, don't you?"

I started to laugh.

"What's so funny?" she demanded.

"I was waiting for you to bat your eyelashes—but you forgot to. Has anyone ever turned you down?"

For a moment, she looked flustered, almost angry. Then she smiled thinly. "You wouldn't believe it if I told you."

"You're right, I wouldn't. By the way, I'm Wil Sumner."

"I've heard. My name is M.K."

"Does it stand for anything?"

"My name?"

I nodded.

"It stands for M.K." She started back down the stairs, calling over her shoulder, "I changed my mind. Hurry and do whatever it is you have to do. I want to get there sometime tonight."

9

THE NORTON MUSEUM OF ART was crowded by the time M.K. and I pulled up to the curb in her mother's Rolls-Royce. The exterior of the dun-colored building was brightly lit, maroon-jacketed valet car parkers running back and forth under the watchful eyes of a dozen sheriff's deputies.

"Why all the police?" I asked one of the valets as he shoved a ticket at me.

"Roberto Salgo's in there making a speech," he called, hustling to the next car in line.

"That's just great!" M.K. said, frowning as we walked away from her mother's car. She studied the crowd milling around the entrance to the museum. "Broward should have told me. He knows how my father feels about Salgo—damn him."

"Why? What's he have against Salgo?" I asked, thinking about what I'd overheard outside her father's bedroom.

M.K. took my arm and steered me toward the doors. "Who knows? My father doesn't always make sense."

More than a few heads turned to stare at us as we walked into the museum, but it wasn't me they were looking at. M.K. pretended not to notice the attention, accepting it as her due. I walked beside her, wondering what she'd meant about her father not making sense, hoping it had nothing to do with his decision to sell the collection.

A couple of television news crews were setting up lights just inside the doors; several still photographers stood around talking. M.K. eyed them and shook her head. "Broward should have told me—we could have skipped this."

"Obviously he didn't want you to skip it. That doesn't mean we have to stay."

She looked at me like that was the stupidest thing she'd heard in a month. "We're here—people have seen us. If we left, they would wonder why. We might as well enjoy ourselves—or at least act like we are. Let's find the bar."

I shook my head. "Complicated lives you Palm Beachers lead."

She didn't bother to answer.

We pushed through the great hall, to a central courtyard. A sculpture garden, tented for the evening, crowded with well-dressed men and women. A podium had been set up at the far end of the garden, but no one was speaking yet. The night air was hot and heavy with humidity. The crowd milled restlessly, faces shining under the floodlights, drinks glasses sweating, voices raised to be heard.

She either knew half the people there or they knew her. Waves and shouted greetings, kisses blown by men and women alike.

"What do you want to drink?" I asked as the line at the bar cleared.

Before she could answer, a chubby man in his early forties, wearing an Italian suit at least a full size too small, rushed over and grabbed her hand.

"M.K., you look beautiful," he gushed. "When this is over, we're all going to Taboo for drinks. Meet us there, okay? It's Minnie's birthday."

He tried to kiss her on the cheek, but she skillfully avoided his plummy lips and pulled her hand out of his. "Maybe, Ronny. This is Wil—"

But before she could finish the introduction, he spotted someone else he wanted to greet and was pushing his way through the crowd.

"Who was that?" I asked.

She shook her head and laughed. "That's Ronny Cavetto. No one you need to know. Did you see the way he crams those fat feet of his into those little Italian loafers?"

"I didn't notice," I said, watching the man cross the garden and make a beeline for a well-dressed heavyset older woman standing alone by the fountain.

M.K. watched too, a look of disdain on her face. "Look at him! Would you believe he's a gigolo? It's disgusting, isn't it? Who would want him? Even for free. But he manages to find them. It's all very *complicated* and *Palm Beach*—hard for an outsider to understand, I suppose."

I turned and stared at her. But before I could say anything, she lowered her eyes and batted her lashes.

We both started to laugh.

She began to say something, then seemed to think better of it. "I'm thirsty. Let's get a drink."

Just then Broward Gaines appeared out of the crowd and took her by the elbow. "M.K., you're late. Come with me, there are some people I want you to meet."

"Hello, Broward," I said.

He looked surprised, not at all pleased to see me. But he flashed that phony smile of his anyway. "I heard you'd arrived— welcome to Palm Beach. I take it you've settled in comfortably."

"Cozy as a clam. The Stevensons couldn't be more accommodating."

His smile faded a little. He glanced uncertainly at M.K., but she had turned her back and was talking to someone else.

"Well, I hope the appraisal goes well. Now, if you'll excuse us . . ." He pulled M.K. after him into the crowd.

"Get me a scotch," she called over her shoulder. "Heavy on the ice. I'll be back in a minute."

I ordered a couple of Dewar's, heavy on the ice, and was digging in my pocket for some singles to leave a tip when I heard the bartender say, "Wil? Wil Sumner?"

It took a moment, but slowly the round, doughy face in front of me resolved itself into a much thinner face I remembered from childhood. "Rick? Ricky Turk?"

"In the flesh, asshole. I should have known I'd see *you* here. When'd you get back in town? Last I heard you were rollin' in dough up there in the big apple. *Mister Art Expert.*"

He still managed to make it sound like a suspect way for a grown man to make a living. But that was the only thing about him that *hadn't* changed. His hair, once a shoulder-length thatch of thick brown curls, was thinning, his soft belly bulged over the waist of his trousers. His deep water tan had faded and his nose was swollen and red, a drinker's nose. I couldn't help smiling at him anyway.

"Question is, what the hell are you doing back there, Ricky? Last I heard, you had your own shrimp boat."

His smile faltered a bit, then reasserted itself. "Hell, you know how it is. Got divorced and one thing led to another. I'm working the party circuit for Mes Ami Catering—just till I get back on my feet. Like the old days, huh?"

"Yeah." I nodded, working hard to keep my own smile intact. "Just like the old days. Is your family all right? Your pop still fishing?"

"Same as ever. I meant to tell you how sorry I was to hear about your folks. But by the time I got around to it, you'd already split. Some tough luck, huh? Both of them in the car like that . . ." He shook his balding head and swiped at the bar with a white dish towel. "That blond you're with tonight . . . That's money, man. Class. Total fucking class. What's she doing with you?"

A couple approached the bar and Ricky excused himself. "Gotta hustle the tips—you know how it works. Look me up—anytime, bro. We'll grab a couple a brews, catch up on old times."

I promised I would.

Then, as he filled the couple's drinks order, I stuffed a ten-dollar bill in the tip cup and walked away. Ricky Turk—the last person in the world I would have expected to run into at the

Norton. He'd grown up three blocks from my house and it struck me as ironic that we would meet here, after all these years. I took a large swallow of scotch and watched the party ebb and flow around me. You don't grow up in West Palm Beach without visiting the Norton Museum of Art at least once a year on school field trips. Where else would a kid from Flamingo Lakes see great works of art? But unlike most of my friends, Ricky Turk included, I'd been captivated by the place. By the fifth grade, I'd begun riding my bike here on weekends. One of the curators, a man named Andrew Height, noticed me. I guess he didn't see too many fifth-graders arriving alone at the museum under their own power. One Saturday afternoon, he made a point of introducing himself. From then on, he had encouraged my interest, giving me books, taking the time to explain some of the whys and hows. He taught me to look with my heart, as well as with my eyes and my mind. If not for Andrew Height, dead for almost a decade now, I would never have become an art dealer. Taking another swallow of scotch, I made a silent toast to his ghost.

M.K. was nowhere to be seen, so holding both of our drinks, I wandered through the sculpture garden, happily recognizing no one else.

I was looking at a bronze statue of a satyr when an old man with a craggy, sunburned face and red-shot eyes, wearing a frayed blue blazer and stained regimental tie, attached himself to me. "CeeCee Pearson's son, right? I never forget a face. You're the polo player—put on a few pounds, haven't we?"

"I'm sorry?" I said.

"You're CeeCee's boy, aren't you? Recognized you right away. I'm Joe Schultze. I've known your mother for forty years."

I started to deny it, but he wasn't listening. "I see you're with the Stevenson girl. Sharp as a whip—looks too. Came home as soon as her father got sick—more than most would do in this day and age. You two serious? You better have a good seat with that one. I hear she's thrown more than one high goaler. Come see me at the farm in Wellington, we'll work a few of the ponies, see how good you are."

I tried to tell him he had me mixed up with someone else, but he was already waving to a couple near the bar.

The crowd suddenly quieted.

A distinguished-looking man wearing an impeccably cut navy suit stepped to the podium. He was tall and fleshy, his broad face tanned and patrician, his thinning hair combed straight back over the high dome of his head.

"My name is Roberto Salgo, and I want to thank all of you for coming here tonight . . ."

As the crowd applauded, M.K. suddenly appeared at my elbow. She took her drink out of my hand and whispered, "I hate these things. Sorry to abandon you—Broward wanted to introduce me to some clients from Miami. What were you and Mr. Schultze talking about?"

"Polo," I said. "He thinks I've gained weight."

She shot me a funny look.

The crowd quieted again and Salgo continued speaking in a rich, baritone voice almost devoid of accent. "It's not with a little pride that I tell you I've been a patron of this museum for over thirty years. I came to this great country from Spain, and now, as a collector of Spanish old masters, I am pleased to announce to you tonight that the Norton will be exhibiting my personal collection next spring. But not all of us are so fortunate. Not all of us have the wealth to collect art. There are hungry mothers and babies living in fear, afraid to venture out of their homes. Gangs have taken over our streets. Vicious kids, predators without conscience, who have declared war on the rest of us. A war we must win!"

As he spoke about the decline of our neighborhoods, the need for firm leadership in the war on crime, the dime dropped. I recognized Salgo's name not as a politician, but because he was an art collector. I'd never met the man—never sold him anything— but his reputation preceded him. He'd recently paid big money to a dealer I know on Madison Avenue for a painting by Zurbarán, and rumor had it that he was always in the market for important Spanish works. It's the kind of information you file away if you want to succeed in my business. I studied the man.

He was old to be running for office, but he looked strong and healthy and he carried himself with authority. As he began to list the ways he would fight the gangs and free the streets from the fear that gripped them, I decided I liked him. Not because of his rhetoric. All politicians speak a good game. But because there was something appealing about the man—an air of leadership. Which made me wonder again what Andrew Stevenson had against him. I didn't have a clear picture of Salgo's politics, but it was easy enough to imagine Stevenson's hard-core brand of social conservatism.

M.K. listened to the first five minutes of the speech, then whispered, "I'm starved. Let's get out of here."

10

M.K. PUSHED A STRAY WISP of hair out of her eyes and shook her head. "It's not that I don't want him to sell the collection—it just seems a little hurried. I don't understand what's motivating him. That's all."

I'd taken her to Charley's Crab, a little fish restaurant near the beach, and watched in amazement as she polished off a dozen oysters, followed by a Caesar salad, then a lobster the size of a lapdog. On the short drive from the museum to the restaurant, she'd started talking about art and her mask had slipped. At a stoplight, her eyes had held mine a second too long, and what I had seen there wasn't the spoiled little rich girl I had pegged her to be. M. K. Stevenson was so goddamn beautiful, it was easy to want to sell her short in the other departments. But away from her crowd, talking about something we both understood, she'd let her guard drop and I saw reflected in her pale green eyes the remnants of something that had hurt, and hurt badly. Something I hadn't expected to see, and the depth of it had surprised me.

Unfortunately, now that the conversation had turned to her father and his collection, she'd slipped back into character. I chewed on a dry chunk of swordfish, figuring the meal was going to cost me something like half my appraisal fee, while she managed to dip chunks of lobster meat in drawn butter and eat and talk and sip white wine and look elegantly bored while grilling me about my job. I got the impression that this was why I had been invited to tag along with her in the first place.

"Both of us, my mother and I, are worried," she said between bites of lobster.

"Have you gone to him? Told him how you feel?" I asked.

"I don't want you to get the wrong idea . . . If he wants to sell the drawings, fine. I just want to know why."

I speared another piece of swordfish and started chewing. There were things I wanted to know too, and I wasn't going to learn them by talking. If I waited, I had a feeling she'd speak her mind.

She played with the empty lobster shell on her plate, then lifted her wineglass.

The silence had a weight of its own.

I squeezed lemon on my fish, but it didn't help.

Finally she spoke. "This entire business of selling the collection, I just don't know . . . It seems so unlike him. To be honest, I can't believe he's doing it. Neither can anyone else. Those drawings represent years of work. He's not thinking straight. I'm afraid he might do something in haste that he'll regret later."

I lifted my own glass and nodded, wondering if she meant to say he might do something *she* would regret. But that didn't seem fair. There was a fortune at stake. Who could blame her for being concerned?

"On the phone, he sounded like he'd made up his mind. What's he said to you?"

She frowned. "Not much. He's not himself. At times he seems so impulsive—almost irrational. I want him to be careful. But he's in a big hurry to put things right—too big a hurry if you ask me."

"He hasn't said anything about how he plans to go about selling the collection?"

"No. All he's said is that he wants to put things right. Everything. Before it's too late."

I hesitated, then asked, "Is it because he's sick?"

M.K. swallowed some wine and set down her glass. "He's not

dying, if that's what you mean. Not yet. Something else is driving him. I don't understand what it is." She paused and looked at me. "But I want you to know, neither of us will let him be taken advantage of."

"And you're afraid I might be trying to take advantage of him?"

My question hung in the air.

She shrugged. "If you are, you're wasting your time."

I met her gaze and held it. For a moment, neither of us said a word. Then she looked away.

The waiter appeared and began clearing the table. "Dessert?" he asked a little too cheerfully. "We have the best key lime pie in Florida."

M.K., still avoiding my eye, shook her head.

I ordered coffee.

When the waiter left, I said, "Go to him—tell him you're worried. See what he has to say before you decide I'm the enemy."

She brushed some crumbs off the edge of the table. When she spoke, her voice was hard and flat. "This isn't what you think. It's not some contest. It's not about money—my goddamned inheritance." She looked at me, her eyes fierce. "I could care less about the money."

I stared at her, almost believing her. "Your father's collection is amazing—anyone would be thrilled to be involved with it. But I didn't ask for the job. Talk to Gaines. He ought to know what's going on. He hired me."

"I have talked to him. Broward hired you because my father told him to. But my father keeps his own counsel. Lately, he refuses to listen to anyone. Even his doctors. That's why I'm so worried."

"What else does Gaines do for your father?" I asked, surprised to learn that Stevenson himself had instructed Gaines to hire me.

"Why?" she said, narrowing her eyes.

I shrugged and lowered my voice, trying to lessen the tension between us. "Just curious. He seems young to be representing a man like your father."

She took a deep breath. "He is. Broward Senior used to handle

things. But when Little Ward—that's what they used to call
Broward Junior—God, he hates that nickname—when he
became a partner in the firm, my father gave *him* the work.
He's always taken an interest in Broward's career, his educa-
tion." She lifted her glass and changed the subject. "I don't want
you to misunderstand me. My father is sick, very sick. It *hasn't*
been easy on my mother, on any of us. He shouldn't be making
important decisions. Not now."

I raised my eyebrows. "That sounds pretty strong. Maybe
your father has his own idea of how things should be handled. It
is his collection."

"Of course it's his collection," she snapped. "He should do
whatever he wants with it. But whatever he does, he should do
it as carefully as he collected those drawings. It took him
decades to assemble the collection—I don't want him to piss it
away."

We fell silent. M.K. *was* more than just another pretty blond.
Unfortunately, my future depended upon her father doing the
very thing that she didn't want him to do. And that was a wall
between us. I wanted to tell her that I wouldn't let the collection
get pissed away—that if I were involved, the drawings would be
handled with every bit as much care and effort as her father had
put into assembling them. But now wasn't the time for a sales
pitch, so I played with my coffee cup.

After a minute or two, she looked across the table at me. Her
expression softened. "I'm sorry. This isn't about you. I know
you didn't create this situation. It's just so damned frustrating."

"You have every right to be concerned. I would be too."

Those eyes locked on mine, then broke away again.

"I'd like to ask you a favor, Wil . . ."

I saw it coming, but nodded anyway.

"Keep me informed. Tell me what my father says—what he
decides to do."

I finished the lukewarm coffee thinking she was right, that
being rich wasn't as easy as it looked.

Then I flagged down the waiter and asked for a check.

11

THE SUN HUNG JUST OVER the eastern rim of the world, its light fractured into a million molten-white shards on the surface of the sea. I'd slept fitfully. The bed too small, M.K. too large in my dreams. She'd wrestled the collection to a draw for space in my unconscious brain, but two miles on wet sand had driven both the drawings and M.K. out of the fevered slums of my imagination.

Chest heaving, slick with sweat, I waded waist deep into the tepid Atlantic, waiting for my breath to slow. I'd played football as a kid, soccer and wrestling in college. Nothing spectacular, but I'd always handled myself well. Now, running was work, keeping fit a matter of disciplined effort. I fell back into the sea and floated on my back. Face full of sky. Weightless. Pulse throbbing in my ears. When my heart stopped trying to pound its way out of my chest, I checked my watch. Not yet seven-thirty and the sky burned pale blue. Later it would glower, ash colored, unrelenting.

I stepped out of the water and walked back toward the house, thinking about breakfast. A lot of breakfast. Thirty dollars' worth of overcooked swordfish hadn't dented my appetite. Amanda Stevenson had said, "Help yourself," and that was exactly what I planned to do.

A brown pelican floated effortlessly through the air, inches above the water. Circling gulls swooped low over unsuspecting bait fish swimming in the shallows. A crab darted to its hole and clung on the edge, half concealed, eyeing me suspiciously. It was good to be back on the beach. Something familiar, an age-old sense of recognition stirred inside me. The tension in my shoulders faded, dissolved. Perhaps the sea rhythm is hard-wired into our genetic code—awakened by the salt tang in the air—a simpler cycle of life forever dictated by the tides. I thought about New York, the Peraltas. Then I let it go. New York was in another solar system.

Brushing a fleck of seaweed from my thigh, I noticed some-one standing at the far end of the Stevensons' seawall. I jogged back to take a closer look.

It was a kid, spray-painting graffiti on the seawall.

"Hey!" I shouted. "What the hell are you doing?"

The kid, dark and swarthy, broad shouldered, not more than eighteen or nineteen, looked at me, then took off down the beach.

I chased him for a hundred yards or so, then realized I had no idea what I'd do if I actually caught him. So I stopped and went back to see what he'd done.

The kid had spray-painted the concave face of the seawall with a curvy blue horizontal line pierced by five vertical lines. I'd seen the design before, on a deserted house in Flamingo Lakes. But it meant nothing to me.

I wondered briefly if it might have been the same kid Amanda had seen hanging around the driveway. If so, why was he harassing the Stevensons?

After a shower, I set to work in the well-equipped kitchen and soon had a pot of coffee brewing. There were steaks and eggs and mushrooms in the refrigerator, potatoes and onions in the pantry.

I started the onions and potatoes sizzling in two big iron skil-lets as the broiler warmed up. That's the trick. Fry the onions and the potatoes separately in a mixture of butter and oil.

Then, when they're nicely browned, combine them. I cracked whole black peppercorns over the steaks, sprinkled on some Worcestershire sauce, and let them sit while I sliced the mushrooms. The smell of frying onions filled the air. I scrambled half a dozen eggs and poked at the mushrooms as they turned golden brown in a pan with a little butter. My mouth was watering by the time I got the steaks under the broiler.

"Christ. I haven't smelled anything that good in months— maybe years." His voice was creaky, hoarse.

I turned from the stove, surprised to find Andrew Stevenson leaning against the kitchen counter opposite where I stood. These Stevensons had a bad habit of sneaking up on people. He was tall, and even thinner than I'd expected. His white hair rumpled, his noble face unshaven. A silvery stubble looked scratchy on his sunken cheeks and frail neck. From across the kitchen, he regarded me with something of a curious expression.

I introduced myself. "Mr. Stevenson, I'm Wil Sumner. I didn't hear you come in, but there's plenty for both of us."

The old man grinned, and my fears about his irrational and impulsive behavior evaporated. He wore a striped robe and a pair of pale blue pajamas that hung on his skeletal frame. His hands trembled, his bare ankles, protruding knoblike from maroon velvet slippers, were mottled with blue, broken veins and purplish spots. A lion of an old man, ravaged by his illness, bowed but not yet broken.

He looked me up and down too, his bloodshot gaze finally settling on my face. "Hmmph. Look as bad as that, do I? Well, don't stand there staring at me. I'll take a cup of coffee—and a little of whatever you're cooking. Amanda won't approve. But, God love her, she's sleeping. Come on, Wil. Get a move on. Before she wakes up and starts in on me about my bad habits."

How many bad habits did he have left in him? Not many, I thought, pouring a cup of steaming black coffee and handing it over. He grinned, raised it in a silent toast, then held it to his lips.

He took a small, shaky sip, lowered the cup, then shuffled to the kitchen table and sank into a chair. "Been a long time since I've had a good cup of coffee. Too long. Goddamn doctors tell me caffeine is no good."

"We've got steak and eggs and mushrooms and potatoes. I'll fix you a plate."

He nodded. "Real food. None of that wheat grass or herbal free-radical crap my wife seems to think I need." He paused, and for a moment the look on his face made me think of a much younger man. "Don't get me wrong, Amanda is as fine a partner as a man could ever wish for. But the woman thinks a little red meat might hasten my final journey." He shook his head.

"She showed you the collection, eh?" he asked as I dished out the food.

I set a plate in front of him. Then, grabbing my own and another cup of coffee, I sat across the kitchen table from him and nodded. "I've seen it."

He poked with a fork at his steak, then looked up at me. "Well? You've nothing to say?"

I shook my head. "There aren't words."

His red-rimmed eyes lit up. "No. There aren't."

We didn't say much as we ate. As hungry as I was, I tried not to inhale my steak and eggs. Stevenson ate a little, then for the most part pushed his food around on his plate. He didn't mention the collection again. I waited for him to bring it up, willed him to ask about the appraisal. But he didn't. I had a thousand questions, but bombarding the man while he ate wasn't likely to get me far. Patience, I reminded myself, spearing a forkful of mushrooms.

My first helping didn't come out even. Plenty of steak, not enough potatoes. I got up to get more, and a coffee refill.

As I stood, Stevenson shook his head in what I took to be admiration. "You eat like the condemned. I'd rather clothe you than feed you. You always put away this much breakfast?"

"Only when I'm hungry," I said, sitting back down and taking a swallow of coffee. "Aren't you going to eat anything else?"

"I don't think I can afford for both of us to eat."

I looked at him and he smiled. Andrew Stevenson, I discovered, had the kind of smile actors and politicians practice in the mirror and rarely get right. But his was warm and genuine, and when he let it shine, it made you feel lucky to be orbiting his sun.

Then, he grew serious. "I've checked you out, you know. That trouble with your ex-partner—Peter Jacobs, wasn't it?—cost you your gallery, eh? They say you've struggled since then. Have you put it right yet?"

He caught me off guard.

Knife and fork poised, I nodded. "As well as I could. Some people hold a grudge. Paying what I owed wasn't enough."

He nodded. "Money is God to some people. They talk about the principle of a thing—but principles are best judged by a man's actions, not his words. Not his intent. To forgive a mistake . . ." He paused and mashed down on his eggs with his fork. His hand trembled. "I know about mistakes. Everyone makes mistakes. A man who can't forgive another generally has something in his own heart he can't forgive himself."

My mouth was wrapped around a good-sized chunk of rib eye, so I nodded again to show that I agreed.

"How much is it worth?"

"Mmmphh. The collection? I haven't—"

He waved me off. His entire demeanor changed. "No! Not the collection. Honor. How much is honor worth to you? It has a price, you know. Some men hold it dear—others give it away without a backward glance. It was important in my day. Nobody talks much about honor anymore."

I set down my fork, not at all sure where he was going with this. "The price isn't always calculated in money. There are other ways to pay."

He nodded. Then, placing his hands on either side of his plate, he slowly pushed himself up from the table. "Let's go in the vault."

Once inside, I stood across the refectory table from him. He looked around and a smile settled on his thin face. "How old are you, Wil? Thirty-four? Thirty-five? Consider yourself knowledgeable though, don't you?"

"Thirty-four. 'Knowledgeable'? I know what I'm doing, if that's what you mean."

"So you say." Stevenson pursed his lips. "What do you know about Jean-Frédéric Bazille?"

A pop quiz. I shook my head and smiled. If this was what the old man wanted, I'd give him a run. "Died too young—Bazille joined the French army—got himself killed in battle around 1870. If he'd lived, he might have become as important as Monet."

"And Monet? What do you think of Monet?"

"'Monet took color from a tube of paint and made us believe it was light.'"

Stevenson grunted. "Hefflenberg wrote that. Tough old son of a bitch—dead now. One of the few I could never do business with. Thought he knew more than everyone else put together." He closed his eyes. "Who knows? Maybe he did."

Stepping slowly to the back of the vault, he pulled open one of the drawers, then looked inside the solander box it contained. "Matisse," he said, as if nothing further needed to be said.

Using both hands, he picked up a drawing. Then he turned, and with his hip, struggled to bump the drawer shut. "What do you think of this?" Favoring his left side, he slowly stepped back to the table, holding the finest Matisse ink drawing I had ever seen.

It depicted an elegant, long-necked woman sitting at a round table in front of an open window, looking out over the coast of the French Riviera. A large bowl of lemons sat on the table, along with a stemmed glass and a cut-crystal decanter. Looking at the Matisse, I could almost hear the sea, smell the lemons, the woman's perfume. I wanted to take the drawing from the old man, hold it in my own hands. Instead, I looked at Stevenson and said, "'Finally, there is only Matisse.'"

Stevenson smiled. "Picasso's words. After hearing Matisse died."

Suddenly his expression changed. Still holding the drawing, he lowered himself into one of the chairs, an ineffable sadness etched in the lines of his face. I took the chair opposite his.

"They're old friends, these drawings. Over the years they've almost seemed alive to me, more than any painting ever could. They're spontaneous. It's as if you could peer into the artist's head and see his mind at work—ideas firing other ideas, thoughts colliding. What painting lets you do that?" he asked, holding the Matisse above the table in trembling hands. "Bits of paper. That's all they are. But they're marked by the shadow of genius. They all are. Nothing but shadows—but they have gravity."

He let the drawing drop from his fingers and I watched the Matisse fall, angling back and forth through the air, finally coming to rest on the table in front of me.

"I want you to put a value on them, Wil. Tell me what they're worth in dollars and cents."

"Why now?"

He looked curiously at me, his eyes intense under tangled white eyebrows. "That's a goddamn funny question for *you* to ask."

"Maybe. But—"

He cut me off before I could phrase the question. "They mark a life that no longer exists. If I had taken a fraction of the time I spent on the collection and . . ." He hesitated. "The time for collecting art is over. It's time to make amends—time to right a wrong," he said cryptically. "I want them sold—quickly—all of them. They have come to symbolize a part of myself that I do not admire. I want them gone—and I can't do it till I know what they're worth."

I opened my mouth but didn't speak. I didn't know where to start.

The dehumidifier clicked on.

Stevenson stared as the drum-shaped scroll began to turn. But he was distracted now, focused on something far away. He tapped absently on the scarred walnut of the table. Then he reached into the pocket of his robe and pulled out the silver lighter Maj had found on top of the mailbox. He turned it over and over again in his skeletal fingers.

"There is a line," he said. "Every man knows when he is confronted by that line. It's different for each of us." He stopped playing with the lighter and stared at me. "Some of us falter— don't do the hard thing. It might cost us something we deem precious—a reputation, a career, our freedom. Life goes on. Maybe no one else knows. But *you* know!" He tapped his sunken chest. "In here. It eats at you—one little piece at a time." He looked around the vault and shook his head. "Worthless if you've lost yourself. Worthless. Better to be rid of them."

This was not the conversation I had anticipated. I stared at him, but he no longer saw me. He was focused inward. A proud man, staring down the throat of whatever regrets he had so fiercely embraced. We sat like that, silently opposite each other, for what seemed a very long time.

Finally, he pocketed the lighter, pushed back his chair, and slowly stood. As he did, his face blanched. He steadied himself, grabbing the back of the chair.

I jumped up and hurried to his side. "Are you okay?"

He glared at me. "If I was okay, do you think I'd look like I do?" He took my arm. "It's my back. Damned vertebrae are as soft as chalk. Help me back upstairs. We'll talk about how to handle the collection later."

The color slowly returned to his face as we shuffled out of the vault. But he was clearly in pain.

"I took a run on the beach this morning," I said as we walked toward the stairs. "Caught some kid spray-painting your seawall, but he was too fast for me."

He stiffened and asked me to describe exactly what I'd seen.

I did.

"I expected—" He stopped himself in mid-sentence. "Did he say anything? Did he speak with an accent?"

"No. I just caught a glimpse of him. We didn't speak."

"I've been afraid of something like this," he mumbled. "But not so soon."

"Do you want me to call the police?"

There was a second's hesitation, a flicker of indecision. His right hand drifted to the pocket that held the silver lighter. Then he shook his head. "No. I'm sure it was . . . nothing."

But his moment of doubt, that narrowing of the eyes and stiff-ening of the body, spoke louder than his words. He was spooked, but not to the point of calling the authorities. Whatever that kid had been doing, it was more than petty van-dalism. And Stevenson knew it.

Together, we took the stairs one at a time, Stevenson leaning hard against me. When we reached the top, he was out of breath. He pulled away from me. His left eyelid twitched, his face all flushed anglcs and loose skin. He stood, slightly bent at the waist, clutching the top of the banister with one hand, sup-porting his back with the other. He was ancient now, stooped under the pain of his illness and some other misery, having, I supposed, to do with honor lost. He pushed his face at mine.

"I may want you to do something for me," he said, his voice a hoary whisper. "I'll pay well. It could involve some risk." He closed his eyes and some of the chill left his voice. "They would never suspect you. The danger would be minimal."

There was no proper response. I just starcd at him.

"Go—finish your breakfast. I've got to think. Later, we'll talk."

"Are you sure you don't want me to call the police?" I asked again.

"Do not call anyone." He slowly pushed away from the banis-ter and went into his room, quietly closing the door behind him.

I stood there for a long time.

Then I went back downstairs and cleaned up the dishes.

12

By two o'clock I was ready for a break. Andrew Stevenson's offer to pay me well to do something risky had haunted me all day. The graffiti meant something, but what? I'd started the appraisal with the vault door wide open, listening for any sign that the old man was up and about. If Amanda was around, I hadn't seen or heard her either. I wanted an explanation, but it didn't look like I was going to get one anytime soon.

I grabbed a beer out of the refrigerator and stepped out into the midday heat, headed for the seawall, the cold bottle sweating in my hand before I'd walked ten paces.

It was the kind of hot that made lazy seem smart. The air was heavy, but charged—simmering with a somnolent energy that seemed on the verge of wakening. The sky was the color of pewter, the light harsh, directionless. A swirling breeze set the palm fronds clattering; the beach was empty.

The cold beer was bitter and good. I swallowed some, fantasizing about the marketing of the collection. An extensive catalog. A tie-in with a major charity—a black-tie fund-raiser that would attract a few Hollywood types. A well-known scholar to write the forward to the catalog—someone with the haughty condescension that most people expected in an art expert. How else would they know the stuff was any good? Maybe Philippe de Montebello from the Met. A man who could out-condescend the best of them. He'd—

"Can I have a swig?"

I turned and found M.K. coming toward me across the lawn. She was dressed in a businesslike pantsuit, but barefoot, carrying her shoes and purse in one hand, shielding her eyes from the glare with the other.

"Can you believe this weather?" she asked, joining me on the seawall.

"It's not what the television ads promise," I agreed.

"I think I'm going to melt. You mind sharing?" she asked, reaching for the bottle.

Tipping it, she swallowed deeply. "Last night was . . ." She hesitated. "I'm sorry."

"Last night you acted like a daughter who cares about her father. That's nothing to apologize for."

She took another swallow. "My father loved beer. He can't have it now. But when I was little, he would take me to the club for lunch—I remember sitting across from him, watching him pour beer into his glass. He wouldn't fill it up. He'd pour in an inch or two at a time, look at it, then drink it down. He made it look like the best-tasting thing in the world. I loved those lunches."

She handed me the bottle. "He's been such a big presence. It's hard to imagine life without him. He and my mother are inseparable. I don't know what's going to happen to her when he's gone."

"They're still in love—after all these years—aren't they?"

M.K. cracked a small smile. "Like no two people I've ever known."

"It must have been a good way to grow up."

"Yeah. Too bad it's not genetic," she said, looking out over the ocean.

I offered her the beer.

Frowning, she took it and drank some. Then she shook her head ruefully at some thought she didn't share with me.

"As bad as that?" I asked.

"Worse," she said.

"London?" I asked.

That gave her pause. She turned and looked at me, her face flat, as though she wasn't sure whether to get defensive or angry or both. "What do you know about London?"

I held up my hands. "Easy. I don't know much. Your mother mentioned that you'd come back from there a little worse for wear."

She arched her eyebrows. "Worse for wear? My mother said that?"

"Not exactly in those words. I don't think she meant physically."

"I hope not."

I couldn't help laughing. "If whatever happened to you in England damaged your looks, thank God I didn't meet you before. I'd probably be blind now."

She hesitated, then smiled. "Go ahead—ask what happened."

I shook my head. "No. I don't think I will."

She looked at me curiously. "That's a first."

I didn't say anything.

We stood there watching a couple of crabs dart around the little waves slapping the beach.

Finally she said, "Anyway, it's over and I'm goddamn tired of talking about it."

I agreed. "I've had enough trouble of my own. I'm not looking for more."

She took another sip of beer. "Maybe we'll trade sad stories one day, Wil."

I shook my head. "No way. I'm through with sad stories. I want some happy endings."

"That's not a very *New York* attitude."

"Call me unsophisticated."

She laughed. "Fuck sophistication," she said, draining the last of the beer. "I want some happy endings too."

Our eyes met and something clicked into place.

We stared at each other, then she looked away.

But the moment had held a thrill I didn't want to let go of.

"I've got to go into town." She handed me the empty beer bottle and stepped off the seawall.

I watched the sway of her hips as she walked away, wondering what *had* happened in London. Then I decided I didn't care.

Halfway across the lawn, she turned and looked back at me. "Trouble usually comes when you're not looking for it."

I nodded. "But if you're lucky, it comes in a nice package."

She laughed, and I laughed with her.

"You want to try and start over tonight?" I asked.

"What time?"

"Seven-thirty—I'll meet you by the pool. Don't be late."

"Not a chance," she called.

Then she was gone.

13

THE NEXT TIME I LOOKED at my watch it was five-thirty. Spread on the table in front of me were the Cézanne watercolors. It would take at least an hour to catalog them. My eyes burned. The vault felt cramped. I was tired. I wanted to get outside into the light of day, no matter how oppressive the temperature. Maybe a swim. The Cézannes could wait until morning. Stevenson hadn't shown. I assumed he'd been in bed all day—knocked out on whatever pain medication he was taking.

I returned the Cézannes to their solander box, then slid the box back into the right drawer. Then, for some reason I couldn't explain, I bent and opened the drawer Amanda had described as containing the "miscellaneous" things. Just a quick look, then the pool.

Inside the drawer there was no solander box, just a stack of unmatted drawings of various sizes and subjects. I carried them to the refectory table, sat down, and spread them out.

Amanda was right. Andrew Stevenson had bought his mystery drawings with catholic taste. There were drawings of people and ruins, still lifes of flowers and fruits, animals, sailboats, windmills, even a couple of hunt scenes. But, oddly, there were almost a dozen drawings of burning buildings—a damned strange subject to buy again and again. I wondered what that said about his psyche. Some of the drawings had been executed on clean, modern paper, but most were on tattered, brittle material. Stained and discolored with age, they appeared at first glance to be old masters. Some were real, others obvious fakes. Nothing struck me as special until I got to the bottom of the pile. There I found an old, coverless sketchbook that had been roughly stitched together. I picked it up and opened it.

An hour later I was still staring, afraid to blink. Afraid I might be dreaming.

If I was right—and somehow I knew I was—I held in my hands an incredibly complete sketchbook by Velázquez. *Velázquez* . . . I rolled the name on my tongue. Said it out loud just to hear it. Fourteen pages filled with drawings of dwarves and horses, all notated in what appeared to be old Spanish. I thumbed through the book again. Not one, or two, or eight . . . Fourteen pages of drawings by arguably the greatest painter who ever lived. But it was the last four that left me dumb with wonder. Detailed sketches and color notations for the head of Juan de Pareja, one of Velázquez's most famous portraits. A painting I knew well from the Met, where I had, over a number of years, spent hours and hours studying it.

The first time I'd seen the portrait, I'd stood enthralled. The voices and footfalls of tourists and other visitors echoing through the Met's second-floor galleries faded from my consciousness and I was alone in a crowded room, unable to tear my eyes away from the brooding Spaniard Velázquez had immortalized. It was a few ounces of oil paint laid down on less than a square yard of canvas. But it caught my attention and refused to let go of my imagination. Pareja stood, dark and handsome, bearded chin held high, wearing a rich cloak and lace collar, his intelligent eyes fixing the viewer with a look as penetrating as any he was likely to ever receive. Calling this masterpiece a portrait was like calling the Cathedral of Notre-Dame a church. According to the Met's catalog, the painting, executed in 1648, had been exhibited in Rome, at the Pantheon. There, in 1650, one expert had said that while "all the rest was art, this alone was truth."

I searched Pareja's face for what truth. What thoughts fueled that piercing gaze, that arrogant throw of his shoulders? Something smoldered in Pareja, and Velázquez had captured and displayed it for all the world to see. Was it anger? Ambition? Lust for the kind of fame and fortune, the very talent that his master and teacher Velázquez himself possessed? Pareja seemed to look out through a window in time, the answers to my questions written on his face, decipherable if only I concentrated hard enough. He knew something I wanted to know. And it was that very wanting to know, wanting to understand, that lay at the root of my love for art. How had Velázquez seen Pareja so clearly? How was he able to capture the very nature of humanity in a thin skin of pigment? Pareja understood. And although I didn't, I knew there was grace in merely understanding the questions.

Now I held the master's preliminary sketches for *Juan de Pareja* in the palm of my hand. I was directly connected to Velázquez, his thoughts laid bare. Pareja himself had looked at these sketches. Had he liked them? My hands shook, but I couldn't put the book down. I turned again to the last four pages. The studies were each slightly different from the actual painting. Pareja, both studio assistant and servant of Velázquez, smiled in some of the studies, looked fiercely dismissive in others. The master had drawn him from a number of perspectives—higher, then lower, right side, left side—orbiting the sitter like a moon, working to find the right angle. Working to uncover and decipher the true face of Juan de Pareja. Velázquez! I said it out loud again, the very sound of the name conjuring up a thrill. I wasn't sure how to prove their authenticity, but these sketches were nothing short of miraculous. They had heat and blood, the power to fire the imagination.

I flashed on Henry Harper and the single drawing he'd sold the Getty for over three million dollars. What did that make this book worth? Ten? Twenty? Did the amount matter? I started to stand, then I sat back down. Then I stood.

Circling the table, I tried to decide what to do next, who to call first. My mind raced, thoughts and images jumping in and out of my head. My banker was in for a shock.

I fell back into the chair, clutching the book to my chest. It was the discovery of a lifetime. Priceless. There were only a hundred or so Velázquez paintings known to exist in the entire world. Henry Harper had made waves with a single drawing. And here was a book full of them, each at least as important as the one Harper had sold so successfully. Stevenson was going to be ecstatic.

I racked my memory for the name of an expert in Spanish old masters, someone to authenticate the sketchbook. Then it came to me—why not call Harper? He'd know as much about the Velázquez market as anyone.

Pulling out my notepad, I began to scribble my impressions. Then I measured each page individually and noted it. I loaded the Polaroid and started firing away. But somehow the camera jammed on the sixth picture. I shook it. Banged it with the heel of my hand. Shook it harder, to no avail. The damned thing was locked tight. In my haste to clear it, I opened the base and exposed what remained of the film.

Cursing, I tossed the exposed cartridge onto the table and dug through the camera bag for a fresh one.

There were none.

I'd brought only one cartridge of film. Idiot! I picked up the shots I'd taken and thumbed through them. Good—but not great. I needed more.

Henry Harper would know who to contact, which expert could give an authoritative opinion of the authenticity of the sketchbook. I checked the time—not quite six o'clock. If I hurried, I could FedEx Polaroids to him in New York for Monday morning delivery. I'd use my office for the return address—no reason for Harper to know where the drawings had been discovered. I didn't want him on a plane.

The sketchbook lay open on the table. I realized I didn't want to leave it, not even for a minute. I put the Polaroids into my camera bag. Then I closed the sketchbook, thinking briefly about hiding it under the other mystery drawings, feeling foolish for even considering it. Publix would have film. I could be there and back in less than half an hour. FedEx stayed open till eight. Plenty of time to take all the photos I needed and still get the package out to Harper.

I turned out the lights and carefully closed the vault door.

Then, feeling a little silly, I went back in and picked up a catalog of Impressionist drawings, thinking I'd hide the sketchbook under the thick catalog.

I'm no thief. But looking down at that little sketchbook, I couldn't stop thinking about how easy it would be. A Velázquez sketchbook—the key to my future, a big, fat, bright, shimmering, glittering, golden future. A future small enough to fit into my pocket.

And no one would know.

The thought grew claws. It twisted and turned and refused to let go of my brain.

I flashed on Peter Jacobs. And that sobered me. For a moment.

But the sketchbook wasn't really part of the collection.

It wouldn't be like stealing.

No one would even miss it.

I was reaching down to touch it when the quiet of the vault was shattered by a loud thump, then a terrified scream.

14

ANOTHER THUMP. AND I WAS on the stairs, taking them two at a time, the heavy catalog still in my hands. I hesitated outside the Stevensons' suite of rooms.

"No! You can't wake him. Can't you see, he's sedated—he won't wake up!" It was Amanda, her voice edged with desperation.

There followed a gasp—the smack of flesh on flesh—then something heavy hitting the floor.

I was moving again, down a short hall to what had to be Andrew's bedroom. It had been arranged like a sickroom. Only the floor lamp beside the desk was lit, the lampshade tilted at a crazy angle, casting an uneven pool of light onto the carpet near the oxygen tanks at the foot of the hospital bed.

Leaning over Andrew Stevenson from the far side of the bed, holding him up almost in a sitting position and shaking him by the collar of his robe, was a dark, heavyset kid wearing black sweats. "Wake up!" he hissed. "*¡Viejo tonto!* Wake up, you old fool." His shoulders knotted and flared each time he shook the old man.

I glanced around the room for Amanda. The place had been turned upside down. I couldn't see her.

"Wake up! Now! Wake up!" With every shake, Stevenson's head snapped back and forth on the thin stem of his neck.

I had to do something.

"Stop!" I demanded, stepping into the room. "Let go of him! Now!"

The kid looked up at me, Stevenson dangling like a broken doll in his hands. In the dim light I recognized him. I'd seen him on the beach, spray-painting the seawall. Now he was sweating, his face streaked, as though he were wearing makeup and it had run. He couldn't have been eighteen.

His eyes flicked over me. Then, calmly, almost as if he had expected this interruption, he dropped Stevenson back against the pillows and picked up a kitchen knife from the bedside table. He wore surgical gloves. The blade of his knife, curved and honed to a wickedly thin edge, caught the light.

My heart climbed into my throat. "Amanda? Are you in here? Talk to me." I didn't take my eyes off that blade.

The kid moved toward the foot of the bed, the knife held lightly, competently, in his right hand.

You don't live in New York as long as I have without getting mugged. The number-one rule is to give them what they want, no matter how much you want to keep it. "Easy," I said. "Go easy. Don't do anything crazy. Where's Amanda? What do you want?"

"Crazy?" He grinned and took another step so that the bed was no longer between us. "Why it is you think to tell me I'm crazy? You the one crazy. Don't be no fucking hero—just come in here. You do what I tell you, everybody is going to be fine, no?" His voice was low, his accent Cuban or South American. My instinct was to keep him talking.

"What do you want?" I repeated.

"Get the fuck in here, or I kill this old man. Now!"

Chest tight, pulse thumping in my ears, I measured the distance, trying to decide what to do. The knife didn't leave much room for argument. Then I heard her.

"Stop!" she cried. "He's sick. Leave him alone."

I risked looking. She was on the floor on the other side of the bed, just inside the open balcony door. Shaking her head, as if trying to clear it, she rose to her knees. A bruise was already forming on her cheek; blood dripped from the corner of her mouth.

"Amanda!" I called.

The kid turned toward her.

Ignoring me, she gained her feet. "I don't know how you got in here—don't know what file you're talking about," she told the kid. "I *can't* give it to you. There's money! Take what's on the dresser. I can get you more. My jewelry is in the next room. Take it. Take these. Just leave him alone!" She pulled out her diamond studs and, stepping closer, threw them at the kid.

With a soft *thunk*, the earrings bounced off his chest, fell to the floor, and rolled into the oval of lamplight at the foot of the bed. There they reflected the yellow light, refracting it into ten thousand points of luminescence. A pair of glittering jewels worth more than most houses. The kid didn't give them a glance.

"I'm not here for any fucking jewelry, lady." Two quick steps and he was on her, spinning her around, the edge of the knife pressed hard against her throat. He looked at me. "*Escucha.* Nobody gets hurt. Come in here—lie down on the floor. Do it! Now! Or I cut this old lady."

"Easy," I said, the word sounding silly in my own ears. I stepped farther into the room, my mind groping for some way to defuse the situation. "Do what he says, Amanda. Give him what he wants. Tell me where it is—I'll get it for him."

Her eyes were wide, her face waxy. "I don't *know* what he wants."

He shook her, then dragged her back toward the bed, the knife still pressed against the soft flesh of her throat. "The file. I told you—I want his file. You think it's worth dying over?"

I took a step closer.

"She said she doesn't know about a file. Take the jewels, the money," I said.

Another step.

"¡*Alto!* Down! Right where you are." He drew the blade across her pale skin. A thin line of blood jumped out.

She gasped.

I froze, my chest a hollow drum, my mouth dry. "Amanda, think! What file is he talking about?"

"There is no file." Her eyes were huge.

Andrew Stevenson groaned, "*Guerra*. War," then fell silent.

The kid hesitated. He looked at Stevenson—at me—calculating.

Then, shifting the knife to his left hand, he shoved Amanda back and away and reached down to the foot of the bed. Picking up what looked like a black box on a stick, some kind of stun gun, he extended his right arm and pointed the thing at me. He spoke to Amanda, but he kept his eyes on me. "Don't lie to me, lady. Find it!"

The black box was aimed at my chest.

I tightened my grip on the catalog, and took a half step back. There was nowhere to go.

Amanda huddled against the wall behind the kid, looking at Andrew, who lay stiff and pale, eyes closed.

Suddenly, without warning, she threw herself toward her husband, placing herself between him and the intruder. "There is no file!" she screamed.

For a brief second, the kid turned toward her.

It was long enough. I heaved the book at his head, then dove at his knees.

Something popped.

A plug trailing wires shot past my ear and sparked against the floor.

And I was on him. We went down hard, grappling at the foot of the bed. He dropped the black box and swung at my face with the knife. I jerked back, almost quickly enough. The blade flashed, the point grazing my cheek. A beesting, no more. I caught his knife arm, pinned it to the floor.

We struggled, each trying to gain the advantage, straining. Weight of muscle and bone, pressing, pulling. Elbows and knees, grunting, sweating.

He rolled hard to the right, then wrenched his knife arm out from under me and stood. I threw a solid shot, catching him on the point of his chin, but he turned with the blow.

The blade glittered in the lamplight. But he was off balance. I grabbed his arm again with both hands. Slippery and solid, he bucked and twisted, raining ineffectual punches with his free hand that I caught mostly on my shoulders and chest. I had him by twenty pounds, but I couldn't get a clean grip. It was like wrestling a muddy bull.

I took a chance and tried to turn him around, get a lock on his neck.

As I did, Amanda swung something heavy at the kid's head. A statue of some kind. The glancing blow bounced off his skull with a dull crack, driving him to his knees.

I looked at her in wonder.

"Get him," she growled, brandishing the statue in both hands. It was a hunting dog.

The kid was on all fours. He grunted and shook himself like a wet dog, his eyes dull and unfocused.

I grabbed him, reached to take away the knife.

But he wasn't as dazed as I thought. He bellowed, came up fast, and managed to swing the knife. The steel bit into my left shoulder.

I lost my grip. With a wild shove, he sent me spinning, slamming headfirst into one of the oxygen tanks at the foot of the bed.

The world exploded, bright white. A wave of nausea clogged the back of my throat. Then I was slipping down a dark tube. Twisting. Round and round. So much waste water down the drain. Echoing . . .

I fought it.

He was shouting in Spanish.

I tried to get up. The floor slewed crazily to the left, then the right.

Amanda screamed—a scalding cry, braided red and as sharp as razor wire—a scream cut short before it could fade. But not before it burned an indelible mark on my addled brain.

Lurching to my feet, I searched for her. I started toward the kid, then stumbled on something soft, yielding.

I looked down.

It was her.

I gaped, unable to comprehend. She lay, crumpled, by the bed, her eyes barely open, only the whites showing. She was cut—on her arms, her neck, the knife buried to the hilt between her ribs. Blood shone wet in the crazy light.

I tore my eyes away. The kid stood near the desk, rubbing his head, surveying the room as if unsure of his next move. He was bleeding from scratches on his face and a bite, or gash, on his hand. His sweatshirt was torn at the neck. "*¡Hijo de puta!*" he spat out. "Bitch!"

Bending, he pulled a small but lethal-looking automatic from an ankle holster and pointed it at me.

"Don't you fucking breathe," he whispered, his voice hoarse.

Swaying on my feet, I didn't. I was bleeding from the face and shoulder—it was over. I was dead where I stood. A pair of icy fingers pinched my gut. It was all gone.

Everything.

A moth flew in from the balcony and fluttered around his head. My mouth formed the word no, but I couldn't tell if any sound came out.

Andrew Stevenson mumbled "*Guerra,*" then groaned and fell silent again.

His gun still leveled at me, the kid started back toward the bed. "Wake up, *Tonto!*" He slapped Stevenson with his bleeding hand.

Stevenson groaned, but didn't open his eyes.

"*Guerra what?*" The kid slapped Stevenson again. "What does it mean, this war? What?!"

He hit Stevenson harder. This time the old man didn't even groan.

Indecision flickered across the kid's face. But the gun didn't waver.

Somewhere in the house a door slammed.

He stood stock-still. Then, looking me in the eye, he raised the pistol till the muzzle was pointed at my forehead.

This time I heard myself say it. "No."

"Tell the old man we want the file. One way or another we are going to get it. He does anything stupid, people he cares about die. ¿Comprendes?"

I nodded.

"Tell him we don't hear from him, the daughter is next. You got that?"

"Yeah," I whispered. "I understand."

Lowering the gun, he smiled, his mouth full of gold. "You no look so good now, tough guy. Tell the old man. He knows how to reach us." Then, without another word, he stepped out onto the balcony, looked around, climbed over the railing, and dropped to the ground.

I couldn't think beyond my next breath. A minute passed—a year.

Forcing myself to my feet, I staggered to the balcony. Blood smeared the railing. I touched it as if in a dream. The deeply shadowed lawn was empty. No sign anyone had crossed it. He was gone.

Amanda lay as I had left her. I fumbled with shaking fingers at her neck, but felt no pulse. Nothing. Christ! Blood was everywhere. Feeling sick and dizzy, I knelt beside her. My shoulder burned, the cut on my cheek dripped blood onto the carpet, where it mixed with hers. Think, I told myself. Think!

I tried to straighten her out, make her more comfortable. I glanced at Andrew. The old man's face was pasty, his lips blue. But he was breathing.

I had to get help.

The phone had been knocked from the desk, but it worked. I dialed 911. The operator told me to stay on the line, but I didn't want to leave Amanda alone. I left the receiver off the hook, the connection open, and returned to her side. Reaching for her hand, I noticed that the palms of my own hands were stained brown with something like shoe polish. It was on my shirt and pants. Whatever it was, it wouldn't rub off.

I sat there beside her on the floor, trying not to be sick, holding her limp hand, willing her to breathe. How could I have kept this from happening?

A breeze stirred the curtains. It carried with it the first cool promise of rain. Lightning flickered far out over the ocean. Then another gust of air riffled the curtains. I shivered, then closed my eyes.

The ambulance was a long time coming.

15

A CHORUS OF SIRENS WAILED in the distant darkness. The curtains rasped, silk on silk, stirred by what had become a steady
breeze. I let go of Amanda's hand and stood. I couldn't tell if she
was alive or dead. The old man lay across his bed, stiff and
waxen, eyes closed, breathing audibly—a hoarse intake that
sounded shallow, but regular enough.

They were slow to arrive. At least it seemed slow to me. But
when they came, they came in force. EMTs, uniformed and
plainclothes police officers, firemen, a K-9 team, all descending
on the house within minutes of each other, their loud and sudden onslaught rupturing the quiet Palm Beach night.

After I'd let in the first of the EMTs, and directed them up the
stairs to Andrew's bedroom, I became superfluous, a spectator. I
watched in stunned silence as two separate teams of men in
blue coveralls frantically worked on Andrew and Amanda
Stevenson.

The first uniformed cop to arrive at the house, a middle-aged
man with a graying crew cut and a sunburn, surveyed the scene
and ascertained that I was the individual who had called in the
emergency. He asked my name, if I needed immediate medical
attention. When I said no, he wanted to see some identification.

After taking my driver's license, he insisted on patting me down. He did it efficiently, taking care not to jostle my cut shoulder, explaining that it was procedure. I was too numb to argue.

He kept my license, then moved to segregate me. I didn't want to leave the Stevensons, but he gave me no choice.

Taking a firm hold on my good arm, he led me back downstairs to the living room. As we passed through the vestibule, he shouted over his shoulder for another team of EMTs.

And still they poured into the house. Shoulder-mounted radios crackling static and disembodied voices. Men and women nervously calling out orders that no one followed. There were too many of them, badges displayed, guns drawn, their flushed faces tight, their nostrils flaring at the scent of blood. Each eager to be the one who cornered the perpetrator.

They went room to room, searching, turning on every lamp, every chandelier, as if the attacker could be anywhere. But in spite of the lamps and chandeliers, darkness loomed in every corner of the huge old house. This was not like those tidy crime scenes on television. No one seemed to be in charge. I half expected to hear gunfire.

I called out to a burly man in a dark suit wearing a gold badge on a chain around his neck, "He's gone! He jumped off the balcony and ran." But the detective seemed not to hear.

I tried to tell the cop with the crew cut, my self-designated escort, but he just nodded. "We'll get your statement. First we need to confirm that the house is clear."

Shaking my head, I watched it unfold from just inside the living room, as if I were watching it all from a great distance. A dull roaring filled my ears. My shoulder throbbed; my cheek burned. The uniform with the crew cut never left my side. I tried to swallow my fear, but the lump in my throat refused to dissolve.

The small army swarmed over the house and grounds. But their search was in vain. The kid was gone. And no one seemed interested in asking me the first question about what had happened.

"Come with me. Let's get you looked at by the EMTs." It was

my escort, pulling me farther into the living room.

He led me to a pair of facing couches near the Stevensons' grand piano. "Sit down, Mr. Sumner," he ordered. "First we'll get you looked at—then we're going to need your statement."

"Now? Now you want my statement? The kid is probably halfway to Miami." I glared at him. But if he was the least bit intimidated, it didn't show in his weatherbeaten face or his watery blue eyes.

"Sit down, sir."

I started to argue. But when I drew breath to give voice to my anger, my knees started to wobble. The throb in my shoulder had turned into a dull ache that traveled the length of my arm. My face felt hot, rubbery, and numb. My head hurt.

"Right," I managed. "Go ahead and take my statement." Cradling my left arm, I collapsed onto the sofa, wondering how M.K. was going to take it, if the cops were going to keep her out of the main house. I hoped so. She shouldn't see her parents like that. No one should.

I tried to slow down, put my thoughts into some kind of order, but the scene played over and over again in my mind's eye. I couldn't make sense of what had happened. What kind of robber passes up jewels like Amanda's earrings for some file? A file Amanda said didn't exist. Stevenson's strange offer to pay me well for something risky lay at the center of what had happened. But how? Was the collection involved? The more I thought about it, the worse my head hurt and the less I understood. At some level, I knew my part in it was finished. The appraisal was over. I flashed on the Velázquez sketchbook and quickly pushed it out of my mind. There were more important considerations.

Amanda lay, badly hurt, maybe dying. And Andrew, with his talk of honor—how bad was he? I looked down at my hands, sticky with blood, and my stomach twisted itself into an icy knot. Something had been taken from me as well. My insides had turned to water when the kid pointed his gun at me. I'd been terrified—prepared to beg for my life. Too scared to form the words.

Closing my eyes, I lay back against the overstuffed cushions of the couch and tried to turn off the noise in my head, stop the images crowding into my skull. To rest. Just for a second. The cop said something, but I wasn't listening. The madness moved through the house without me. Blood from my cheek leaked onto the upholstery. But it didn't matter—Amanda would understand. I sank deeper into the sofa's down clutch, aware of the push and pull of my own breath, the bitter taste of my fear . . .

I was looking into the blinding beam of a flashlight.

"Hold still."

An EMT quickly took my blood pressure, made a visual examination of my wounds, clucking as he unbuttoned the collar of my shirt and gently peeled the blood-soaked material away from the slash in my flesh. Using a pair of blunt-pointed scissors, he cut away the shirt, but had to lift my arm to pull off the sleeve. My shoulder went off like a Roman candle.

"Shit!" I gasped.

"Sorry, man. It had to come off," he said, wadding the ruined shirt into a ball and tossing it to the floor. He whistled while he bandaged my shoulder. His name tag read "Francisco." The name didn't match the rest of him—a stocky, red-headed kid with a rust-colored goatee and shoulder-length hair. He looked Irish and smelled like he'd been eating chocolate.

Francisco turned to the cop. "This shoulder's gonna need some work. Head looks minor—a contusion. We'll need to transport him over to West Palm, to Good Sam. Let those guys with the degrees decide what all he needs. I'll go get the gurney."

The cop nodded.

"I can walk," I told Francisco.

He frowned. "Nah, man. Regulations." He rolled his eyes and stood. "We gotta wheel you out on your back. Like it or not."

As Francisco walked out of the living room, a small but intense-looking man in a tan suit came in, followed by a second man wearing perfectly creased jeans and a blazer. The two of them walked over to where I sat.

The man in the suit looked at my escort. "This is the fellow who called it in, Al?"

The uniform said, "Yes, Cap'n. Name is Wil Sumner. I've been with him since I arrived."

"Good work, Al." The man clapped the uniform on the shoulder. Then he turned to me. "Mr. Sumner, I'm Captain Laspada." He pointed at the man in the blazer. "This is Detective Harris. We have a number of questions; are you up to answering them?"

I said I was.

Laspada nodded. He was a little man with a big head. His hair, thick and as white as talcum, was combed straight back from a square pink forehead. He wore a composed and sober expression. With his steel-rimmed glasses, he looked more like a televangelist than a cop. But he had cop's eyes. Brown and intelligent behind the lenses of his glasses, they looked everywhere at once, missing nothing. I guessed his age at sixty.

Harris was in his forties, thick and tall and built like a wrestler. His fleshy face was dotted with old acne scars. His hair was cut high and tight, military style. A bony shelf formed a chin like the prow of a ship. Everything about him was big. Even his scowl, which looked permanent. If he had a girl, he called her babe and she had big hair and a chest to match.

"What's happening with the Stevensons?" I asked Laspada.

He shook his head. "It's not good, Mr. Sumner. I wish I could tell you otherwise. Before they transport you to the hospital, how about giving Detective Harris an overview of what happened. Time is of the essence with these cases. And we know very little."

I nodded. "Of course."

"Then I'll leave you with Detective Harris." Turning to Harris, he added, "I'll send Tapsell down in a few minutes, Frank. If you haven't finished, both of you accompany Mr. Sumner to the hospital. I'm sure he'll cooperate."

Then he turned on his heel, nodded once to Harris, and was gone from the room.

The uniform coughed.

Harris pulled a small pad and a fancy gold pen from the inside pocket of his blazer. "Start at the beginning," he instructed. "Who are you? What's your business here?"

"My name is Wil Sumner . . ." As I spoke, I looked at Harris, but it wasn't a suspicious cop I saw. I was back in Andrew's bedroom, looking down the barrel of the kid's gun—pointed at my forehead—the muzzle as big as a full moon.

"Yeah?" Harris urged, his tone impatient. "Go on."

I told him what had happened.

He looked doubtful. "You were a hero, huh? But there were no other witnesses? No one else saw any of this?"

His tone was incredulous.

Something inside me clicked. The fear that had found a foothold in my gut turned into anger. "That's right, Detective. I tried to help. You have a problem with that?"

He shook his head. "I got a problem with everything—until I find out what happened. Let's go over the part where you first came in again."

A woman I presumed to be Detective Tapsell appeared just as Francisco and his partner finished strapping me down on a gurney. Harris had already led me through my story once. Interrupting often, impatient and gruff, making notes while asking me to repeat certain details that in my mind needed no clarification. Francisco spread a thin blanket over my legs as Tapsell strode into the living room, all business. She looked to be in her late thirties, a tall black woman with close-cropped hair and skin the color of seasoned oak.

"Is he clean, Frank?" she asked, glancing down at me.

Harris shrugged and looked at the uniform.

My escort nodded. "He's clean."

She frowned. "Bear with us, Mr. Sumner." She turned back to Harris. "You finish his statement?"

"Couple of points I'm not clear on," Harris answered, studying his notes.

She looked down at me, gauging my condition. "The ambulance is ready to roll. We'll follow and finish at the hospital."

As the two EMTs wheeled me out of the living room, the detectives close on their heels, a uniformed female cop led M.K. into the vestibule from the direction of the kitchen. Pale under her tan, she wore a short cotton sundress. When she saw me,

she stopped and stared, shock registering on her already frightened face.

I called out to her, "M.K. . . ."

Before I could say more, Harris moved between us.

I turned on him, but he shook his head. "You'll have plenty of
time to talk with her after we finish with you."

Ignoring him, I twisted on the gurney and looked back in
M.K.'s direction, wanting to explain to her what had happened—
that I had tried to protect them, but had failed.

She was gone.

16

THIRTY-FOUR STITCHES LATER, we started over for the fifth time with who I was and what I was doing at the Stevenson house. This time, Tapsell asked the questions. Methodical and precise, she rarely interrupted, and when she did, her questions were pointed and well thought out. When she seemed satisfied, she dropped her pad into her duffel-size purse and rubbed her face.

We sat around a fake walnut table in a small, windowless break room adjacent to the emergency room, Tapsell to my right, Harris across from me. The hard orange plastic chairs had been designed by a diminutive sadist. I wasn't sure which hurt worse, my shoulder, my back, my ass, or my head. It was after eleven o'clock. The doctor had strapped my left arm to my chest and given me a sling; two butterflies held closed the cut on my cheek. I wore a blue paper hospital gown instead of a shirt.

A two-year-old calendar hung skewed on one institutional-green wall. A dark reproduction of Henri Rousseau's *The Dream* stood guard over a December long past. The other walls were bare. The room smelled of disinfectant, sweat, stale cigarettes, and burned coffee.

Tapsell looked as wilted as I felt. Harris was sharp, as crisp as the creases in his jeans. He had short, square fingers, the nails glossed with clear lacquer. He tapped them incessantly on the plastic surface of the table. A strange energy flowed between the two detectives. Tapsell seemed nominally in charge, but Harris appeared to resent her authority. It wasn't anything he said out loud, just a strong undercurrent of unspoken animosity. Tapsell, who had to notice, chose to ignore it. Maybe they were playing the old good cop, bad cop routine. If so, they were a hard act to follow. Tapsell, understated and softspoken, Harris leaning into his questions and comments as though he were walking into a strong wind. Tapsell a pro, doing her job. Harris all scowls and frowns, radiating suspicion and ill will. I found myself relating to Tapsell, trying hard to ignore the big, aggressive detective sitting across from me.

"One more question, Mr. Sumner." She stood and looked down at me. "What's the brown substance all over your hands and arms?"

I looked at my right hand. "I'm not sure. I think it came off the kid when we fought. It's dry now."

She frowned. "I want it analyzed. I'll get someone to lift a sample. You mind giving us a set of prints while we're at it?"

"Of course not." Standing, slowly, I felt older and stiffer than I would have thought possible. "You can take a sample and fingerprint me after I check on Andrew and Amanda. Where are they?"

Tapsell shook her head. "She's dead, Mr. Sumner."

Her words stopped me cold. I knew Amanda had been badly hurt, but there had been hope.

I sat down heavily. "When?"

"At the scene."

"Andrew?"

"Still unconscious. He's upstairs in intensive care. They aren't sure yet." Her voice remained calm, but her eyes were brown ice.

I looked away, feeling as though I'd been kicked in the stomach. Amanda dead? For what? I thought about her brave smile.

A kid with a knife had erased that smile, reduced her vibrant presence to so much blood and bone. Dead? Because of a *file*?

I closed my eyes. The kid hadn't acted on his own. Someone had sent him. Who? When I looked up, Harris was staring at me, leaning back, his chair balanced precariously on two slender metal legs.

"We're talking murder," he said, not sounding particularly unhappy about the fact. "Murder. . . . And I still don't understand this bit about not reporting the kid when he spray-painted the seawall. How 'bout you take me through it one more time."

I looked at Tapsell. But there was no help there.

"I told you who did it and why. The kid didn't just appear out of thin air. Someone sent him," I said, trying hard to keep the anger out of my voice.

"Yeah . . . So you say."

Harris was ugly, blustering, and, I was starting to believe, stupid. But I wanted the police to catch the kid—quickly—and find whoever it was that had sent him to the Stevensons' in the first place. Maybe I hadn't explained it well enough. I tried harder. "After I ran—it was the same kid. By the seawall. First he delivered an old silver lighter—at least I think it was him."

"And you didn't bother to report either incident?" Harris asked, a hard edge to his voice.

"Stevenson wouldn't let me."

Harris snorted. "You're telling me you saw this kid, told Mr. Stevenson about it—but he wouldn't let you report it? Why?"

"For the hundredth time, I don't know." But my answer sounded weak, even to me.

Harris just shook his head. "And while this is going on, you were looking at drawings?"

"That's why I came down here." I was beginning to sound like a broken record.

"Yeah—but you're no stranger here. You know lots of people, right?"

At this point, Tapsell excused herself, leaving me alone with Harris.

I felt wrung out. Amanda was dead. I hadn't stopped it. All I wanted to do was find M.K. and check on Andrew. "I'm tired, Detective Harris. Why don't we give it a break?"

Harris sucked his teeth, thinking about it. He tapped his fingers on the table for good measure, then put his fancy gold pen and his notepad into the breast pocket of his blazer. "Okay. That's enough for now."

He stood and stretched. "We see burglaries, petty vandalism— once in a while a domestic dispute. Drugs, but that's mostly with the kids. Murder? Murder's rare in Palm Beach. When someone does get killed, you can bet it was either the husband, the wife, or the lover who did it. If it wasn't one of them, it has to do with money. Lot of money on the island. Big money. People get ideas." He shrugged, then attempted a smile. Just one of the guys doing his job. "Sometimes things go wrong. It gets out of control. If I set something up in a house like the Stevensons', I sure as hell wouldn't leave empty-handed."

I stared wearily at him. "The kid wasn't a burglar."

"Yeah. I wrote down what you said about the file. Seems a lot of trouble for some mysterious papers the wife had never heard of."

"I don't understand it either."

"Me, I never stayed in a house like that. Too rich for my blood. I wouldn't know what to take anyway—unless someone told me." He tugged at his jeans, adjusting the creases. His grin disappeared. "You, on the other hand, would know exactly how much all of that stuff is worth. Being an appraiser and all."

What he implied set my teeth on edge. I pushed up out of my chair and locked eyes with him. "I'm tired. Too goddamn tired to play games with you. The Stevensons are still in trouble. If you don't want to tell them it wasn't just a burglary, I will."

He sneered at me. Then, rolling those heavy shoulders, he leaned across the table, thrusting his ridge of a chin at me. "A woman is dead. Her husband may be dying. You don't like my tone of voice? *You're tired?* Well, ask me if I give a shit. You were there. You're the only one talking." He shook his head. "A load of crap, that's what you're trying to sell me. But I don't believe in secret files—not in a house that stinks of money. You'll

answer my questions, like 'em or not—till I start believing you.
So sit your ass back down. Now!"

"Mr. Sumner . . ." Captain Laspada had entered the room
without my noticing. "Would you excuse Detective Harris and
me for a few minutes?" Without waiting for a reply, he turned
and left the room.

Harris glared at me for a minute, then followed him.

17

Fʟᴜᴏʀᴇsᴄᴇɴᴛ ʟɪɢʜᴛs ʜᴜᴍᴍᴇᴅ. With each breath I drew, the room shrank. What about the drawings? I tried not to think about them, not now, but how can you not think about something so monumental? Over and over, a loudspeaker in the ceiling paged a Dr. Whitworth. Where the hell was he? I started to pace, drifting around the table, muttering to myself. An eight-step oval. Around and around, a hungry rodent trapped on a wheel. The thought disgusted me. I stopped in front of the calendar and straightened it. I stared at the reproduction of Rousseau's *Dream*. *This* I understood.

But the room was suffocating me. I turned from the calendar and stepped to the door, the kid's threat still echoing in my mind.

Harris and Laspada stood together down the hall from the break room, deep in conversation, Laspada speaking, making sharp gestures with his small hands, Harris nodding.

Harris glanced up and saw me first. He interrupted Laspada and started toward me. Laspada put a hand on the big detective's arm, stopping him mid-stride.

"Captain Laspada," I called out, walking toward the two of them. "I'm going up to check on Andrew Stevenson. You want me, you can find me in the ICU."

"Like hell," Harris growled, moving, in spite of Laspada, to intercept me.

Laspada froze him with a look.

The two of them stood blocking the hall.

I stopped in front of them, past the point of caring what they thought. "Either arrest me, or move out of my way."

Harris looked like he'd like nothing better, but Laspada spoke before he had a chance to react. "Mr. Sumner, Detective Harris has some ideas that I don't necessarily share. But all this talk about a mysterious file concerns me. Palm Beach . . . Well, you ought to know, this isn't the kind of place that appreciates loose talk. We value discretion down here. Especially when careless rumors can affect innocent people. The Stevensons have been victimized once tonight. Your story could be misconstrued, somehow cast a bad light on that family. Even a hint of such a thing could be taken the wrong way." He paused to be sure I was following him.

"I wouldn't do anything to hurt the Stevensons," I said. "But I think the file does exist, and that whoever wants it is going to try again."

He shook his head, looking disappointed. "I'm not going to let that happen. But think about what I'm saying. Unfounded allegations can be dangerous to a man's reputation—his family's reputation. There might be a file. I'm not dismissing what you're saying. *Anything* is possible. But as of now, that's all we have—an unfounded allegation. It makes no sense given Andrew Stevenson's good name. On the island, folks have a way of circling the wagons when the Indians ride in. Our people value their privacy, pay me well to protect it. I'd thank you not to discuss the details of our investigation—not to the press, not to anyone."

I looked at Harris, who was nodding at Laspada's words. "*He's* out there, Captain Laspada. Those *folks* on the island might want him caught before he kills anyone else."

Laspada's face hardened. He stood silently for a moment, arranging his thoughts. He looked like a man who liked everything arranged in exact order, including himself. Then he drew his lips into a stiff and formal smile. I preferred his frown.

He said, "Mr. Sumner, the ICU is on the fourth floor. Detective Tapsell's up there now. She's already sent for a technician to get a sample of the stains on your hands, and your fingerprints. I'll send him up as soon as he arrives." He pointed down the hall toward a bank of elevators, then turned back to Harris.

Broward Gaines Junior stood arguing with Detective Tapsell at the end of a long corridor on the fourth floor. They were nose to nose, directly in front of a pair of windowless green doors emblazoned with foot-high white lettering identifying the ICU. A uniformed cop sat in a metal folding chair to the left of the doors, carefully examining his cuticles. He looked up as I approached, a bored expression on his face.

I wondered who had called the lawyer, and when.

"How is Andrew?" I asked.

Gaines, his hair rumpled as though he'd crawled out of bed to get here, glanced at me, then turned back to Tapsell. He looked angry.

She frowned at him, ignoring me. "Let me do my job, Counselor. If you force me, I'll get an order from the court."

Gaines glared right back at her. "I suggest you talk to your boss before you threaten me."

I tried again. "How is Andrew?"

Gaines answered, his voice as tight as his face. "He regained consciousness about two hours ago. M.K. has been with him since then." He paused and glanced at the closed ICU doors, as if expecting her to appear at any moment. When she didn't, he continued. "She hasn't left his side. Dooley Hoffman—*Dr. Hoffman*—says it looks like a stroke, but he can't be sure. Not until the test results are in. Andrew was disoriented—delusional. Hoffman sedated him. He won't wake up until sometime tomorrow."

"Does he know?" I asked.

"About Amanda?" He shook his head, a number of conflicting emotions crossing his face. He was scared, I realized. Who could blame him? "I'm not sure . . . M.K. might have told him. I don't know. Hoffman is trying to talk her into coming home for the night. The tough part is still to come—her father's going to need her in one piece." He ran his hands through his hair, took a deep breath, then turned to Tapsell and demanded, "This burglar— where are you going to start looking? How soon should we announce a reward?"

"It wasn't a burglar," I said.

Gaines hesitated. "Of course it was. I've spoken to Captain Laspada. He says it was a robbery attempt. Something went wrong. It got out of hand."

"I don't care what he says. It wasn't a robbery. Not the way he means. I was there. If we don't find the file, he'll be back."

Frowning, Gaines backed up a pace. "I heard what you said about this mystery file. Until we know more, I'd appreciate it if you wouldn't mention it to M.K. She has enough on her mind without worrying about something that doesn't exist."

"I think it does exist. Maybe she can help find it."

He shook his head. "You're mistaken—"

"The hell I am—"

Tapsell interrupted me before I could finish. "Over here, Karl," she called to a bear of a man wearing a white lab coat. "Your timing couldn't be better."

He waved and ambled in our direction, an unlit cigar bouncing in his mouth, a heavy equipment case clutched in his right paw.

"Thanks for getting here so quickly," Tapsell said.

"Did I have a choice?" the big man grumbled. He wore a blue plastic name tag, MORTON, spelled out in large white letters.

"Not really," Tapsell said.

The four of us moved out of the fourth-floor corridor and into a well-appointed waiting room set up for the families and friends of patients in the ICU. The soothingly pastel room was empty. Gaines took the couch, a cell phone appearing in his hand. Karl Morton opened his equipment case on the coffee table, then rummaged through the carefully arranged tools of his trade. Tapsell stood near the open door.

Morton took samples of the stains on my skin, then fingerprinted me. When he finished, he said, "Go ahead and remove your trousers."

"Why?" I asked. "There's nothing on my legs."

Gaines, sitting on the couch, phone to ear, watched carefully. Tapsell said nothing.

"It's not your legs I'm interested in," Morton answered. "It's your trousers." He pulled his cigar out of his mouth and pointed the gnawed butt end of the stogie at my ankles, then my thighs. "The cuffs are stained with what looks like blood, there's more up and down both legs, there, and there, and the same brown substance I removed from your hands, just above both knees. That makes them evidence, Mr. Sumner. We'll get you some hospital greens to wear." Picking a shred of wet tobacco from his lip, he examined it as though it too might be evidence, then flicked it away.

I handed over the "evidence" to Morton in the waiting room's bathroom. He tossed me a pair of surgical pants and left me to struggle into them on my own, calling over his shoulder, "I'll bag these and give you a receipt."

"Thanks a million," I muttered, trying to tie the damned drawstring with one hand.

It can't be done.

By the time I came out of the bathroom, clutching the waist of the baggy greens to keep them up, Morton was through stowing his gear. He turned to say something to Tapsell, but fell silent when M.K. walked into the room.

She looked around, not saying a word, her eyes finally settling on me, lingering on the bandages plastered to my cheek, the sling. She wasn't crying. Not now. But she had been. Her eyes were red and swollen, the little makeup she wore smeared.

"Are you all right?" she asked.

I nodded. "Your father?"

She looked at Morton, then Tapsell, as if noticing them for the first time. Then back at me. "He's resting—he'll sleep until morning. They tell me there's no immediate danger. Dr. Hoffman is with him. He practically ordered me out of there. Wants me to get some rest." She stood erect as she spoke, but her hands trembled, a pair of pale and elegant birds in a gale.

"M.K. . . ."

She turned to Gaines, who had risen from the couch.

"I want to go home, Broward. I want to change." She cut her eyes to me. "I'm sure Wil does too. Would you drive us?"

It was then that I noticed the dried blood on the front of her dress. I knew without asking that it was her mother's. But I wasn't sure how or when M.K. had gotten that close to Amanda's body.

"Of course I will," Gaines said. He moved smoothly to her side, pressing one of his hands to the small of her back. "Do what Dr. Hoffman says. Get some rest, M.K. I'll take care of everything."

The gesture bothered me more than I wanted to admit. There was something imposing about the two of them standing side by side; their blond good looks seemed unfair.

Gaines pulled his wallet from his pocket and held out a card to Tapsell. "If anything changes, have Captain Laspada call me at home. My private number is on the back. I want a twenty-four-hour guard posted outside the ICU. Only medical personnel are to be allowed in to see Andrew. That includes your people, Detective. Written instructions to that effect will be delivered to Laspada in the morning. Andrew's had a severe shock. I want him protected, not disturbed."

Tapsell took the card. "I'm sure Captain Laspada is sensitive to your concerns."

M.K. started to say something to Tapsell, then smiled wearily at Gaines. "Thanks, Broward," she said. "I'm too—I can't think straight right now."

"Are you ready to go?" he asked gently.

She nodded, then looked at me. "You ready, Wil?"

I said I was, then tried again to snug the drawstring on the surgical pants.

M.K. stepped over to me.

Gaines frowned.

Her long fingers trembled as she pulled tight the drawstring and tied it into a bow.

"Thanks," I said.

"No. I should be thanking you—for risking your life trying to save them," she said, looking up at me. "I . . ." Her voice faltered.

Gaines cleared his throat.

M.K. drew a deep breath, turned, and walked toward the door.

Tapsell and Morton kept their thoughts to themselves as Gaines and I trailed M.K. out of the room and down the corridor to the elevators.

Then we were in Gaines's new Jaguar, driving silently through the night, back over the bridge onto Palm Beach. The Gold Coast. The Millionaires' Playground. Only no one was playing now.

18

Gaines slowed the car to a crawl as we approached the Stevensons' house. A female cop stood at the foot of the driveway, keeping one eye on the traffic, the other on a television news crew standing by their van drinking coffee out of paper cups. Sharp gusts of wind stirred the ficus hedges surrounding the property—coconut palms danced, casting odd swirling shadows across the blacktop, the air alive now with the threat of rain.

The WPTV van, satellite dish deployed, stood parked on the shoulder of County Road, almost blocking the Stevensons' driveway. But the cop seemed more interested in joining the news crew for coffee than ticketing them. She looked us over, her reflective vest Day-Glo orange in the Jag's headlights, but made no move to stop us, instead throwing Gaines a familiar wave as we turned in.

The television people dropped their cups and scrambled to get a camera on us. No such luck. Gaines left them behind in a spray of gravel. He muttered something about the "goddamn vulture press" to M.K. as we thundered up the drive.

"I'll have them removed," he promised her.

Another uniform, this one an older male, stood by the front

door, not doing much of anything. Until we pulled up. Then, recognizing neither the car, nor Gaines, he adopted an authoritative pose, hands on hips, aggressively protecting the house from bad-intentioned desperadoes foolish enough to storm the driveway in a hail of gravel, bright beams blazing.

A few haughty words from Gaines straightened him out.

M.K. hadn't spoken since we'd crossed the bridge. She sat silently erect in the passenger seat, looking neither right nor left, as though her mind's eye was focused within, seeing whatever it is you see when the loss is too big for words.

When we got out of the car, she said to Gaines, "I want to go upstairs—I want to see where it happened."

"I'm not sure . . . ," he began. But she was already headed into the house.

She stopped just inside the front doors. The men and women with clipboards, surgical gloves, and cameras, their dispassionate faces showing no soft emotion, had spread throughout the house. Evidence techs—Karl Morton's peers. Calling out to each other in too loud voices about steaks and seafood, time off, or Jack's new boat as they went about the grisly business of measuring and dusting for prints, photographing and documenting in writing each and every detail of the scene. Just another late-night call out, another faceless assault to document. Concentrate on the facts—the evidence. Otherwise the job would overwhelm, turn normal people into freaks. Who could blame them for joking and talking while the victim's body chilled in the hospital morgue and the killer, free, at least for the time being, laughed among friends over a blunt and a shot of *anejo*?

Their blamelessly loud and jaded presence was too much for M.K. I don't think they'd have allowed her upstairs anyway. She, Gaines, and I retreated to her apartment. We all needed a drink.

I followed the two of them around the pool. Lightning flared in jagged bursts at the edge of the horizon, far enough out over the gulf stream that no thunder accompanied the flashes. But the storm would hit before too long. And if the wind and the lightning were any indicator, it would be a good one. I glanced at my watch and discovered that yesterday had become tomorrow. Time had jumped the tracks. It felt as if a week had passed since I'd rushed out of the vault and up those stairs. It had been exactly seven hours and forty minutes.

M.K.'s apartment was dominated by a large, terra-cotta-tiled living room. A high-tech galley kitchen opened to one side. Beyond the kitchen a hallway led to a closed door, probably the bedroom. The living room was furnished elegantly. Two silk-upholstered chairs and a couch, a bronze-and-glass coffee table. Expensive antiques and bibelots, cut flowers in crystal vases. Good Persian throw rugs. One wall held a built-in entertainment center with a television set, a stereo, and shelves of books and video cassettes. There were silver-framed photographs of family and friends, architectural prints on the walls. The overall effect was sophisticated and expensive.

Once inside, Gaines confidently assumed the role of host while M.K. and I settled on the couch. Opening a cabinet below the television set, he revealed a well-stocked bar.

"Cognac?" he offered.

M.K. nodded.

"Yeah," I agreed. "Make mine a double."

Gaines, no stranger to this bar, splashed three generous measures of Martell into crystal snifters, then carried them over to where M.K. and I had plopped down. He handed us our drinks, then sat stiffly on the arm of the couch. The uproar in the main house seemed to have disturbed him. It was enough to disturb anyone.

M.K. shifted on the couch to make room for him, leaning against me in the process. She made no effort to move away.

Tipping the snifter, I drank deeply. The alcohol burned a welcome course from lips to gut. I sat there, waiting for the knots to loosen, feeling the steady pressure of M.K.'s hip against my own, listening to the sharp edge of the wind wrapping itself around the tiled roof of the apartment.

M.K. groaned, or sighed. It was hard to tell which.

Frowning at her, Gaines slugged back his drink. I couldn't figure out their relationship. One moment he acted like an old friend, a distant cousin, a benign protector. Then he would make a show of touching her hand, her back, circling her like a jealous lover. Now perched on the arm of the couch, he seemed both distracted by his own thoughts and painfully aware of how close M.K. and I were sitting.

M.K., however, seemed oblivious to his signals. Either too lost in her own misery to notice, or adept at the utterly feminine strategy of adopting the high ground by refusing to acknowledge the obvious.

I lifted the snifter. Maybe I was reading too much into a strained situation.

None of us spoke for a while. We sat drinking and listening to the building storm, the thrash of wind and distant rumble of thunder.

Eventually, Gaines stood and refilled his glass. He brought the bottle over and set it in front of us on the coffee table.

"Obviously we won't be continuing the appraisal," he said to me, apropos of nothing. "You'll need to prepare a bill for your time. It would be best for everyone if you went back to New York. Including you."

I looked at him, surprised that he would bring this up now.

"I'm saying I think it would be in your best interests to leave," he said. "Before you get too involved."

M.K. said, "Now isn't the time for this, Broward."

He frowned. "I'm just trying to head off any potential problems."

"It's a little late for that, isn't it?" she snapped.

He looked down into his cognac. "This isn't going to be easy for any of us," he mumbled. "I just thought . . ."

A strong gust rattled the French doors.

Gaines fell silent, brooding over his own thoughts, both hands wrapped around his snifter.

I raised my own drink to my lips and swallowed. The brandy slid down easily. M.K. made no move to change out of her bloodstained dress. All of her energy seemed focused on simply maintaining. I wondered if we should tell her about the file. Then I thought about what Gaines had said about going back to

New York. He had a point. This wasn't my problem. I'd walked into it blindly. There was no disgrace in walking away. Was there?

M.K. shifted uncomfortably on the couch, then settled back against me, glad, it seemed, for the contact.

"Why?" she asked finally, her voice raw. "Why did he have to kill her?"

There was no good answer.

"What kind of an animal does something like this? Why? It's so goddamned stupid—such a waste," she said bitterly. "He didn't have to do it."

I made some understanding noises. Gaines echoed them.

"She was . . ." M.K. moved away from me and wrapped her arms around herself. She rocked like a disturbed child. "I was drowning and she pulled me out of London. Just flew over there and didn't say a harsh word—just came to get me and brought me home. She was so beautiful, so strong—and I didn't tell her, I didn't thank her for what she did. I didn't tell her how much I loved her. I was too busy suffering, being the tragic victim . . ." She choked back a sob. Tears slid down her cheeks. She shook her head and hit her thighs with clenched fists, suddenly angry. "How could this happen? It doesn't seem possible."

"It'll be okay," Gaines promised, not sounding too goddamn sure of it.

M.K. stood, a little unsteady on her feet but no longer trembling. "I can't sit here like this. I can't. I have to go back."

"Don't do this to yourself, M.K. You heard Hoffman. You need the rest; so does your father," Gaines insisted.

Heading for her bedroom, she called over her shoulder, "I don't give a damn what Dr. Hoffman says. I need to be with him."

She changed quickly and came out dressed in a pair of jeans. "Wil, I'm going to have Broward take me back to the hospital. You stay here—take my room. They won't let you upstairs anyway. Get some rest. Whatever you need, just take. I'm not sure when I'll be back; just make yourself at home."

She sounded like her mother. I said so.

She smiled, a weary shadow of the smile she and her father shared.

Gaines started to say something, then thought better of it.

"I'll walk you two out," I said.

She nodded.

Gaines looked at me, black thoughts swimming in his eyes. Then, he turned away.

I stood outside the front doors of the house and watched Gaines manhandle the Jag down the driveway, an angry boy with a big boy's toy. A SALGO FOR GOVERNOR sticker was conspicuously plastered to the rear bumper. If the female cop still guarded the far end of the drive, I couldn't see her. I stood there long after the elegant sedan's red taillights had disappeared. I shifted my weight and rubbed my neck where the strap of the sling had begun to chafe. Too many images jumped and danced in my head. The brandy hadn't loosened the knots, hadn't loosened anything.

A clap of thunder shook the ground, followed by a spattering of fat raindrops.

Hurrying into the house, I took shelter in the vestibule under the watchful eye of the cop Gaines had had words with.

"You're the one witnessed the whole thing?" he asked.

"Yeah," I said, watching the storm. "I'm the one."

"Too goddamn bad," he said.

19

WITH A SUDDEN HUSH, THE wind died and the rain began to fall in earnest, sheets of water lit by strobelike flashes of lightning that froze the torrents in midair. Violent bursts of thunder punctuated the storm. But in the hesitant moments between the bursts, the world went quiet, the only sound the hiss and sigh of the falling rain. I stood beside the old cop, watching the spectacle from the shelter of the doorway.

"A gutter buster," he muttered.

"Cool things off," I said.

"So you'd think. Damn hot for October. Too damn hot. But that's Florida."

We were a regular farmer's almanac, waiting for the storm to let up. But it gave no sign of abating. When he started in on the coming election, "the goddamn Spic politicians," I knew it was time to walk away.

The evidence techs, equipment packed in neat aluminum cases, had gathered by the staircase, waiting for the rain to let up too. One of them, a tall, cadaverous-looking man with gold-rimmed glasses, nodded as I passed. "We're almost finished," he said. "A couple of things left to do—but it will be easier in daylight. I've taped off the upstairs landing. Stay down here until we're through. Probably around ten or so tomorrow morning. After that, it's all yours."

I thanked him. I'm not sure why. It was a little like thanking the cop who just wrote you a speeding ticket. Reflex more than manners. I was coming to find that murder has a blunt etiquette of its own. And I was seeing the process up close and personal. Too damn personally, if you asked me.

Walking through the living room, I was struck by how radically everything had been changed by a single inelegant thrust of a sharp blade. In a matter of seconds, the world had become a much darker place. Lives had been irrevocably altered. Nothing would ever be the same for M.K. or her father, assuming Andrew lived. The house itself seemed reduced, diminished in some way that had nothing to do with size or surface.

Without any plan to do so, I found myself headed for the vault. Maybe I just wanted to reassure myself that the collection was still there, that in spite of the violently surreal events of the past several hours, I hadn't imagined it.

The interior of the old silver safe gleamed, organized and spotless. I opened a few of the drawers. The drawings were as I had left them. Then I stepped to the table—to where I had left the Velázquez sketchbook.

I was afraid to touch it, frightened about what I would do in the face of such temptation once it was in my hands.

The vault was as quiet as a crypt. But this only intensified the maddening echo of my own thoughts. I picked up the sketchbook. The brittle old paper seemed to glow in the hard, fluorescent light. I wasn't a thief, I told myself. But as I stood there, the thought floated away. No one knew the damned thing existed. No one would ever miss it. It weighed a few ounces. Even so, my hand shook.

Pound for pound, it was as valuable as anything in the world.

How many other hands had held it since Velázquez had last touched it? How many momentous decisions and calamitous events had overtaken the men and women who had owned this little book over the last three and a half centuries? Had anyone else held it while standing at the precipice, staring into the

stinking pit of their own greed? Why was this so hard? I knew
the difference between right and wrong. But what great fortune
hadn't been built on the back of some long forgotten misdeed?
In fifty years the Cali cartel would be as legitimate as the
Kennedys. Winning was the point. And didn't winners make up
their own rules as the game progressed?

Fingering the rough-stitched cover, I thought about the life
that had been so brutally ripped out of this house. Another
tragedy to which the sketchbook had borne mute witness.
Another bloody bit of pedigree. No . . . That wasn't true.

Suddenly, intuitively, I understood that fifty years from now
Amanda Stevenson's violent ending wouldn't be associated with
this book. Not even as a footnote. Did that matter? Should it?

I flipped through the pages. Velázquez had imbued each of
his drawings with grace and power. But they had nothing to say
that the artist hadn't considered, then invented. No amount of
human suffering or joy—no triumph or tragedy—would ever
enhance these insensate pages. As great as they were, they
were indeed bits of paper, no more than ideas of ideas. Not
nearly so precious as those whose lives they had touched, however briefly.

I took a deep breath. And the sketchbook's hold on my imagination dissolved. Just like that. No bright light flashed, no bush
burned. But a strange, dry heat filled my chest. Some of my old
resolve returned. Going back to New York was no longer an
option. Not until Amanda's killer, and whoever had sent him,
were put away. I didn't know exactly what I was going to do. But
I knew what I wasn't going to do.

Instead of taking the sketchbook, I carefully made space for it
in one of the drawers. Then I gathered my notes, packed my
appraisal gear into my duffel bag, and left it on the table.

After a last look around, I turned out the lights and carefully
closed the vault door behind me. Not knowing if, or when, I
might return.

20

EARLY THE NEXT MORNING I pulled my rented Ford to the curb in front of the island's police station, a two-story, salmon stucco edifice designed to resemble a Moorish villa. It looked more like a small resort hotel than a police station. I half expected to be approached by a valet parker.

I'd been summoned at dawn by one of Laspada's officers, who'd banged politely on M.K.'s doors until I'd picked myself up off her couch and opened them. Handing me my suitcase, he'd said, "Captain Laspada told me to pack these up and bring them to you. He wants you down at the station to look through the mug books. Right away."

Now it was a little past seven on a Sunday morning and the streets were empty. I climbed out of the car, moving like a man who belonged in a geriatric ward. The sky had been swept clean by the storm. The air was cool and damp and smelled of ozone and the sea. I sucked down a lungful of the salt air. For some people it was going to be a great day.

Inside the station, a large woman wearing sergeant's stripes sat behind a bullet-proof partition, chomping gum and reading the sports page. She lowered the paper and fixed me with a suspicious stare, proving that a police station is a police station no matter how fancy its exterior.

"I'm here to see Captain Laspada," I said through the grille in her window.

"And who are you?" she demanded.

Once I'd identified myself, she pressed a button releasing an electronic lock, then directed me through a heavy door that led to a small elevator. "Second floor," she grunted before lifting the paper.

He stood waiting for me when the elevator doors slid open, a steaming mug of coffee in his right hand. The mug said GRANDPA in big red letters. I assumed correctly that it wasn't for me. Dressed in a fresh, olive green suit and a crisp white shirt, Laspada looked remarkably well rested. His tie was held in place by a tie tack shaped like little gold handcuffs.

"Rough night," he said, looking me over. It wasn't a question.

"Couldn't have been much worse," I admitted, pointing to his mug. "Got any more of that?"

He nodded. "Follow me. This shouldn't take too long. I appreciate your getting here so promptly."

He led the way down a narrow corridor, lined with closed doors, to a small conference room. If others were at work in the building, I didn't see or hear them.

I wore jeans and a loose-fitting dress shirt, the sleeves rolled to my elbows. And in sharp contrast to Laspada's pink-cheeked appearance, I felt as if I'd been run over and then dragged through the streets by a large truck.

I wasn't the only one. Tapsell sat waiting in the conference room, a stack of thick, loose-leaf binders on the table in front of her. She'd taken the time to change into a navy blue pantsuit. But if she'd slept since I'd left her at the hospital, you couldn't tell.

"Mr. Sumner." She nodded. "I see you've lost the sling. How are you feeling today?"

"A little stiff. Nothing too painful," I lied. Pointing to the binders, I asked, "Is that why I'm here?"

Laspada took the chair opposite hers. "Detective Tapsell has pulled together some photos we'd like you to look through," he said, hands neatly clasped on the top of the table. "Maybe we'll get lucky."

"Is it down to that? A matter of luck?" I asked.

"Mr. Sumner, never scoff at luck. Luck is a tool. You use it. You use whatever it takes to get the job done. I like the job. I do it well. And I use every tool at my disposal." He narrowed his eyes at me. "*Anything*. Understand?"

I said I did.

"Good. Now, about these mug shots—" He was interrupted by a young woman carrying a pot of coffee on a tray with a plate of bagels. She was blonde and cute and plump and painfully aware of Laspada's presence, trying hard to please the boss.

The girl poured for me, then freshened Laspada's mug. When she turned to offer Tapsell coffee, the detective frowned, took the pot, and poured for herself. This seemed to fluster the girl, who after rearranging the bagels on the plate, which made no discernible difference to the way they looked, set out some paper napkins. She took a last nervous look at Laspada, then left the room.

Laspada looked amused, but said nothing.

Tapsell shook her head, looking tired and annoyed.

I wasn't sure how to read the situation.

Laspada remained silent as Tapsell briefed me on how to use the notebooks. "Each binder contains several hundred photographs of men who roughly fit the description you gave us," she began. "They're each identified by a number. You see a familiar face, I'll plug his number into the computer. Our files are cross-referenced with the state's youth gang task force. The symbol painted on the Stevensons' seawall doesn't correspond to any of the gang tags we've seen before. We checked out the lead you gave us about a similar tag in Flamingo Lakes—but it's a tough neighborhood and no one's talking."

I wasn't surprised. Fortified by the coffee, I flipped through the first few pages of the top binder. Most of the photographs were grainy head shots, black and white, but readable.

I looked up at Laspada. "If it's luck we're relying on, what changed your mind about me?"

"How do you mean?"

"If you didn't believe my story, I wouldn't be looking at these. Would I?"

He stood. "I haven't crossed anyone off our list, Mr. Sumner. I'll let you know when I do."

He grabbed a cinnamon-raisin bagel on his way out. He paused at the door and encouraged me to take my time and do my best.

Encouragement was one thing I didn't need.

Three hours later, I closed the last book. I hadn't found the kid. Every time I'd pointed out a possibility, Tapsell had left the room, typed the information into the computer, then returned only to tell me that the individual was currently incarcerated, or in two instances, deceased. After the first hundred or so pictures, the images began to blur. Mug shot after mug shot—all dark, young, Hispanic, and not the kid who had knifed Amanda.

"You up to going through them one more time?" Tapsell asked.

I was ready to give it a try when Laspada burst into the room, his face flushed with excitement. "Something's come up. Andrea, I want you and Mr. Sumner to take a little ride with me."

"What happened?" she asked.

He looked at me. "Luck happened. I'm not sure yet if it's good luck or bad."

"How?" I asked.

"I'll explain on the way," he said. "Let's go."

21

THE BODY FLOATED FACEDOWN, wedged between the barnacle-crusted pilings of a private dock on the north end of the island, one arm extended, swaying in the current like a long last wave good-bye.

Built to accommodate a large vessel, the L-shaped dock, surrounded by similar private docks, jutted sixty feet or so into the intracoastal waterway bounding Palm Beach to the west. A paved bicycle trail provided the only public access to the dock, which belonged to a brick house, shuttered for the off-season. The single slip sat empty too—except for the floater, recognizable even facedown.

Now I understood why Laspada had insisted that Tapsell and I accompany him. He made a clicking sound with his tongue, squinting down at the body, an oddly displeased expression on his flushed face. "Why? Why serve him up? Might as well have stuck an apple in his mouth," he mumbled to no one in particular.

Two uniforms stood at the end of the dock, talking with Harris and two kids holding fishing rods. Apparently they had discovered the body. The group fell silent as Laspada surveyed the situation.

Then Harris directed the two kids off the dock and stepped to his boss's side. He cleared his throat.

Laspada looked up.

"Kids were snook fishing, almost fell in, they got so excited," Harris explained. "Ran home and called it in from their house—over on Orange Grove. Parents and sisters are at church, won't be back until noon. I told 'em to go home, that we'd call later if we need them." He glanced at the two kids, who stood on the bike path, not looking like they were in a hurry to go anywhere. "They think it's just like TV. Only cooler." Harris shook his head. "*Kids*." Then he walked off the dock after them.

Laspada checked his watch, but kept his thoughts to himself.

A speedboat roared by, its wake rocking the corpse. I stared down at it, bobbing in the dark water. "It's him," I said.

Tapsell nodded. "You sure?"

I was. But I felt none of the triumph I had anticipated at catching up with the bastard. I'd imagined a confrontation, a chance to redeem myself—to laugh as they shackled him and threw him into a cage. Instead there was only a cold sense of frustration, as though I had been cheated out of something important.

Face grim, Tapsell pulled a pad out of her bag and made a note. "Let's wait till they get him out. Then you can make a positive ID."

The day had bloomed. A cloudless sky, pleasure boats of all sizes and shapes moving on the glassy surface of the waterway. A little slice of paradise—if you could ignore the body. Across the water, West Palm Beach—cars, traffic, people going and coming—Good Samaritan Hospital. I wondered what M.K. was doing at that exact moment.

Harris walked back out onto the dock, laughing at something one of the uniforms said.

The three of them fished around with a collapsible pole and a length of rope, trying to pull the body out from under the dock. But it wasn't going to be that easy. The current had solidly wedged the corpse's left leg between two pilings and a partially submerged cross brace. Someone was going to have to get wet to lift him free. Harris found the whole thing highly amusing.

The younger of the uniforms volunteered. Stripping to the waist, he climbed down into the water, ignoring Harris's taunts about the barracudas.

While he splashed around, an old blue Cadillac swung in behind Laspada's car. Karl Morton, equipment case in hand, climbed out of it.

Tapsell waved to him.

He returned the wave, pulled a cigar out of his breast pocket, and pushed it into his mouth. "We're getting to be quite an item," he called out to her.

"Don't you wish," she said. "What are you doing here?"

He walked over, greeting Harris and calling encouragement to the cop in the water.

Putting down his case, he smiled and draped an arm casually around Tapsell's shoulders. "Never a moment's rest for the wicked of heart, my dear." He glanced at Laspada, still standing at the end of the dock, then he nodded at me. Lowering his voice, he said, "The boss had me paged. Doesn't want to wait for the county medical examiner to decide what went down. Wants us to develop the case on our own." He looked down at the floater. "This our boy?"

She shrugged. "Mr. Sumner thinks so."

He looked at me. "Those brown stains washed off, eh? Salt water probably washed it off *him* too." He glanced speculatively at the corpse. "Bound to be some residue on the clothes. A match will stand up in court. Not that we're headed to court now. Goddamned unusual though—looking forward to the lab results."

The cop in the water managed to get a rope around the body and pull it away from the pilings. Harris and the other uniform unceremoniously hauled it up onto the dock.

He lay on his side, the rope snug around his waist, dripping on the weathered boards of the dock. Hazy eyes open, but not seeing. He didn't look dangerous now, stiff with rigor mortis, his knees drawn up, one arm pointing at the sky. He wore the same dark sweats and one running shoe, the other lost. The exposed skin of his bare foot had pruned, like he'd been in the bathtub too long. He looked puffy. Pale and waxy, as if the water had bleached the pigment from his skin.

Laspada stepped over and squatted beside the body without touching it.

"Karl . . ." he called.

Grunting, Morton opened his case and pulled on a pair of latex gloves. He untied the rope, then began poking and prodding, paying special attention to the kid's scalp and hairline, front and back.

The two uniforms and Harris crowded close.

The kid's face was unmarked, almost peaceful looking. I fought the urge to lash out and kick the son of a bitch where he lay.

Morton spoke into a small tape recorder. "Some rigor—not full. No bloating. Estimate eight to ten hours immersion. Water seventy to eighty degrees—salt. Two entrance wounds—small caliber—behind left ear. No exit wound. Victim probably dead prior to immersion. . . ."

He conferred with Laspada, then began to search the kid's clothing. The pockets were empty. No jewelry or other identifying objects.

Laspada looked at me.

"Well?" he asked.

"I'm sure," I said.

Frowning, he walked over and put a hand on my good shoulder. "You're positive about this?" he asked. "No doubt whatsoever?"

"No question," I said. "That's Amanda Stevenson's killer."

His frown deepened. "Well, that's it then. One killer accounted for. Now all we have to do is find out who did him, and why." He looked at his watch. "Almost eleven. Press will be here soon."

He guided me out to the end of the dock. "Mr. Sumner, what I'm about to say I'd like to keep between the two of us. Okay?" The flush of excitement, so visible on his face back at the station, had faded to an expression of concern.

"Last night, I was one of the Indians," I said.

He looked surprised. "We're both Indians on this island. And last night the circumstances were different. Now, I'm damned close to believing your story about this file."

"And I'm supposed to be grateful enough to act like you people didn't all but accuse me of setting the whole thing up?"

"That's about right." He crossed his arms and watched a boatload of fishermen idle by. "We were doing our jobs. You want to take personal affront, fine. Do it later. Call a lawyer—everyone else does. In the meantime, I think you might be able to help us."

"How?" I asked.

He turned to face me. "Mr. Sumner, Andrew Stevenson's attorney has told us in no uncertain terms that it's hands off. I can't force his client to talk with us. And without some explanation of what's going on," he held out his arms, then dropped them, "I don't have a lot to go on. I could butt heads with young Gaines, but that isn't likely to get me very far. The Gaines family is old and powerful. So are the Stevensons. I'm sure the Gaines boy is just doing his best to protect his client. But I need answers to questions I can't ask."

"Surely Gaines understands the situation."

"I've spoken to him twice this morning. What he understands is that Mrs. Stevenson is dead, that Mr. Stevenson is gravely ill. He doesn't believe your story and he wants to protect his client from further damage—to both his health and his reputation. I can't blame a man for doing his job. Even when it conflicts with mine."

"Why don't you order him to let you see Stevenson?" I asked.

He shook his head. "I can't *order* him to do anything. Under certain circumstances I could squeeze. But it's not something I'd consider without damned good cause. These people are used to getting their own way. You don't push them around. Not if you want to keep your job."

"Not even when an innocent woman gets knifed in her own home?"

He glared at me, then his expression softened. "Listen, you find that file. A reference to it—something tangible. I'll run with it. I'll push any buttons that need pushing. But I need more than words to fight with. Give me something I can get my teeth into."

"*Me?*" I asked.

"Who's better situated to look around and ask questions? Mind you, you're on your own as far as the department is concerned. But you find something I can use, I'll back you to the hilt."

I looked out at the pleasure boaters enjoying a Sunday on the water, then back at Laspada. "So now I'm a tool?"

He met my eyes. "Let's just say I think you can be helpful. And I think it's in your own best interests to do so."

"It's in all of our best interests. Isn't it?" I couldn't help shaking my head at his lack of subtlety. "I'll do what I can. But not for the reasons you think."

He maintained his stern expression for a moment, then smiled at me. Not the formal grimace I'd already seen, but a wry look of genuine amusement. "I expected nothing less. If and when you turn up something, anything—call me. I'll make it a priority."

Without waiting for me to respond, he gestured for Tapsell to join us. "Andrea, this'll take another couple of hours, at least. Why don't you take my car and drive Mr. Sumner back to his? I'm sure he has better things to do than hang around here."

22

I DROVE STRAIGHT FROM THE POLICE station to the hospital. It looked sadder, smaller, and shabbier in the sunlight. The parking lot was jammed with cars, everything from Rolls-Royce convertibles to rusted-out Buicks. Death and disease don't give a goddamn about demographics.

I cruised the lot until I found a space to stick my rented Ford, a narrow slot facing the intracoastal waterway, about as far from the main entrance as you could possibly get and still be on the hospital grounds. I parked, cut the ignition, and sat gathering my thoughts, listening to the engine tick.

Palm Beach floated on the other side of the waterway, an emerald mirage, its secrets carefully locked up, hidden behind all that lush green gorgeousness. And Andrew Stevenson held the keys.

I got out of the car and hiked across the asphalt, wondering if he would be in any condition to talk to me. I knew what to ask. It wouldn't take long.

All I had to do was get past Gaines.

The uniformed cop outside the doors of the ICU had other ideas. "Sorry, sir. I can't let you in. I got instructions."

He was a tall, skinny man with a long, droopy face and ears

that had kept right on growing long after the rest of him had stopped. Somewhere north of his fifties, with a slightly distended belly, red-shot eyes, and a general look of exhausted persever-ance, he brought to mind an undernourished hound dog. He held his radio in his right hand, the antenna pointed at my chest like a little rubber sword. It shook ever so slightly in his grip.

His name tag read PAPROCKI.

He looked so sad and wrung out, I almost felt sorry for him as he explained how he wasn't going to let me in.

Almost . . .

"Listen," I said, staying calm. "All you have to do is buzz one of the nurses on the intercom—have her get Miss Stevenson, she'll authorize you to let me pass."

"Don't know Miss Stevenson," he said.

"She's the daughter," I explained. "She'll authorize you to let me in."

He shook his head. "I can't disturb the family for any reason. Those are my orders."

"She won't mind."

He shook his head again. "Got orders. You don't like 'em, take it up with Mr. Gaines. He's over there in the waiting room." He pointed with his radio.

I glanced in that direction. "Since when is Gaines giving the orders?"

"Since he started paying the bill."

"What's that mean?"

"Mr. Gaines hired his own security. I answer to him. Just do what I'm told."

"Why don't we call Captain Laspada, see what he has to say?"

"I don't work for Laspada. I'm with the West Palm Beach Police Department. And like I told you, I take orders from the lawyer."

I started to argue, then realized I was wasting my breath. Turning toward the waiting room, I said, "I'll take it up with Gaines myself."

"Good," he called after me, adding something about the damned air-conditioning.

■ ■ ■

Gaines had folded himself into a chair in the ICU waiting room, a cell phone pressed to his ear, the morning papers open on the floor at his feet. He wore fresh clothes, chinos and a blue chambray work shirt, but his face was puffy, his tired eyes swollen. He nodded at me when I walked in, but continued his conversation.

He sat there, drawing a chain of interlocking squares on a leather-bound legal pad propped in his lap, his little clamshell of a telephone wedged between his shoulder and his ear.

"Of course," he said into the phone. "No . . . Everything that can be done . . . Yes, I understand, but it . . . I know . . . Patience is the only thing I can suggest . . ."

He winced at the response this last comment earned him, then nodded as though the person on the other end of the line could see him.

"Yes, of course I understand," he said.

I moved closer, waiting for him to finish.

Ignoring me, he ran out of room on his pad for more squares, flipped to a fresh page, and started a new chain, his face serious, nodding occasionally as he listened and doodled.

Finally, he snapped closed the phone and looked up at me. "You made the papers. They did quite a number on you."

"What are you talking about?"

He bent and picked up the *Palm Beach Post* at his feet.

The headline read SOCIALITE MURDERED IN BOTCHED ROBBERY! Below the huge black letters appeared an old color photograph of Andrew and Amanda dressed in formal attire. The story covered half of the front page.

Gaines held out the paper. "Check out page three. You're famous. Or should I say infamous. Fifteen minutes—starting now."

I took the paper from him, and opened it. Below a small photograph of me, taken around the time the press picked up the story of how Peter Jacobs had taken money out of a trust account and used it to buy a folio of fake Dürers, appeared the following: NEW YORK ART DEALER QUESTIONED IN PALM BEACH SLAYING.

My stomach bunched into a small knot. I read the article.

Then I read it again.

The reporter got everything right but the facts.

I turned back to the front page and read the lead article. A lot of dramatic supposition about an interrupted burglary, questions raised about the only witness to the crime, New York art dealer Wil Sumner. *Lucky fellow.* No mention of the file. Just enough detail to make clear that someone was feeding misinformation to the press. And I had a good idea who it was.

I crumpled the paper in disgust. "Nice work, Gaines."

He frowned. "If you think *I* leaked this, you're wrong." He bent and picked up a second paper. "Here. The *New York Times* picked up the story too. Ran an even better photo of you. Great publicity. Ought to do wonders for your career."

"What career?" I snapped, grabbing the second paper.

He flinched, then shrugged.

The *Times* reporter had me all but convicted of murder.

I lowered the paper slowly, feeling sick.

Gaines watched me, the slightest hint of satisfaction lighting his face.

I stifled the urge to stuff both newspapers down his throat. "I'd like you to tell the cop out there that it's all right for me to go in and see Andrew," I said between gritted teeth.

"Andrew isn't in any condition to speak with anyone."

"Says you? Or the doctors?" I asked.

"I'd like what I'm about to say to stay between us. Okay?"

I'd heard that one before. I didn't answer.

"If you repeat this, it's Andrew and M.K. you hurt, not me," he said coldly.

"Go ahead. Spit it out."

"Andrew is sedated—heavily—he's out of it. M.K.'s totally freaked. She's a wreck. When Andrew has been awake, he's been delusional. He doesn't know where he is—thinks the building is on fire. Early this morning he started screaming about nuns. Scared the shit out of everyone. He's in no shape to be talking to anyone. He and M.K. need time and space. I'm going to see that they get it. That's why you're not going to see Andrew."

I stared at him. "M.K. needs help."

"You want to help M.K., the best thing you could do is leave. Go back where you came from." He glanced at the papers in my hand. "Seems to me you have enough to worry about without screwing up her life too."

I tried to keep my voice level. "I'm not going anywhere, Gaines. They found the kid's body about an hour ago. Floating in the intracoastal. He'd been shot—execution style."

The news didn't faze him. "I've heard."

"Who told you?"

He shook his head and smiled, an ugly twist of his mouth. "I *live* here. You're the outsider. Listen to me carefully, because it's the last time I'm going to say it. There's nothing here for you. Go home."

I tossed the newspapers onto his lap. "These stories are crap and you know it. M.K. is in danger. Maybe you are too."

He stopped smiling. "Are you threatening me?"

"Don't be stupid. I'm telling you that I'm going to see Andrew. Before this goes any farther."

Closing his pad, he stood and stepped to the door.

I followed him out into the corridor. "I'm serious, Gaines. Someone has to talk to Andrew. This jealousy over M.K.—it's gone too far."

Flashing me a look of utter contempt, he called out to the cop, "This man has just threatened me. I'd like you to have him escorted off the property. If he makes trouble, I'll swear out a warrant."

"Are you out of your mind?" I shouted.

The cop looked at me and shook his head. "You sure, Mr. Gaines?" he asked.

"I want him out of here," Gaines confirmed. "Arrest him if necessary. If you can't handle it . . ."

"I can handle him just fine," the cop said, looking like he wished both Gaines and I would simply evaporate.

I stared back and forth between the two of them. "This is insane."

The cop shrugged, a resigned expression settling on his long face. "You want to do it the easy way or the hard way?"

I tried again. "You're not thinking, Gaines. These people aren't just going to go away because you ignore them."

He looked at the cop. "Well? Do I have to call the chief?"

"Stevenson is the key to this," I persisted. "If you don't want me talking to him, talk to him yourself."

The cop stepped to my side. "Come on, fella." He pulled his radio out of its holster and pointed at the elevators with the antenna. "Let's do this the easy way, huh?"

Gaines glared at me, but said nothing.

"You sure this is how it has to be?" I asked him.

He didn't respond.

The cop tugged at my arm. "Let's go."

"Okay!" I said, angrily pulling away from him. "I'm leaving."

I strode toward the elevators, the cop on my heels.

Glaring back at Gaines, I punched the elevator button and called, "Think it through. Don't win the battle and lose the war."

He stood alone outside the ICU, his face a stiff mask.

The elevator doors slid open.

Gaines lifted his cell phone, hesitated, then called after me, his voice full of poison, "The war's over, Sumner. And we're all losers."

23

FLAMINGO LAKES LOOKED AS ugly as I felt. I parked the Escort in front of the deserted, graffiti-covered house where I'd seen the same mark the kid had made on the Stevensons' seawall, hoping the worst of the neighborhood's inhabitants would still be sleeping off the effects of Saturday night. I'd driven here in a rage, needing to do something, anything but go back to the Stevensons' house and wait for news. I hoped to find out the name of the gang the kid who murdered Amanda belonged to. Something the cops had so far been unable to learn.

Three little girls wearing dirty T-shirts were jumping rope in the street. As soon as I parked, they coiled up their rope and disappeared.

The first two adults I saw refused to talk to me.

Four teenage girls walked by wearing their Sunday best, but when I approached them, they crossed the street.

No one wanted to talk to me. I was a stranger asking questions in a neighborhood where silence ruled. I didn't belong here any more than I belonged in Palm Beach.

I walked back to my car feeling like a fool, thinking I'd come on a wild-goose chase. Leaning against the hood, I stared at the burned-out hulk of a house and tried to decide what to do next. Nothing came to mind.

I was about to leave when I saw Mrs. Ruder, out walking a mangy-looking little dog. She'd looked ancient when I was a kid; she hadn't changed much at all. A tiny old lady with bad dentures, wearing an overcoat and a knitted hat. Dressed for snow.

I called to her.

"I've got Mace," she screamed, brandishing a little canister of the stuff. "Keep back!"

"Wait! It's me, Wil Sumner."

"I'll use it. I'll spray your damn eyes out you come any closer, boy."

"Mrs. Ruder, it's me, Wil. Wil Sumner. I used to cut your lawn."

She squinted at me. "Wil? Is it really you? I thought you'd moved up north. Gotten out of this sewer for good."

"I did. I live in New York now."

"Well, why didn't you say so? What are you doing here? Moving back?"

I shook my head. "I need to talk to someone in the neighborhood—someone who knows something about this graffiti." I pointed to the gutted house. "The blue mark—that wavy line."

She squinted at the spot I'd pointed out, then shook her head. "Animals. They're all animals. Can't tell one from the other. Gotten so I can't even walk my little Punkin' without having eyes behind my head. I carry mace, you know."

She showed me the little canister attached to her key chain.

I commiserated with her, then asked again if she knew anyone I could talk to.

She pointed to a small green house, one of the only decent-looking houses left on the block, and said, "Go ask Mr. Salinas. He's a schoolteacher—he might know what you're talking about."

After thanking her, I walked over to the house and knocked on the front door. Footsteps, then an unshaven, middle-aged man wearing an unbuttoned guayabera cracked it open, security chain still in place.

"*¿Sí?*" he said through the crack. "*¿Que quieres?*"

When I told him what I wanted, he closed the door, removed the chain, then opened it wide. "Why you want to fool with those peoples?" he asked suspiciously. "You a cop? We could use more cops around here."

Behind him I could see that the interior of his house was brightly lit and spotless, the furniture covered in a clear layer of protective plastic. A television was blaring a Spanish-language show in one of the back rooms. I couldn't see who was watching it.

"I'm not a cop. I just want the name of the group that uses that tag."

He considered this for a moment, then shrugged. "I don't know anything. Ask Pico Nuñez. He used to live there." He pointed at the deserted house. "He was some kind of activist. They burned him out anyway. His brother died in the fire, but people say the lesson was for Pico."

"Why?"

Mr. Salinas shrugged.

"Where is he now?"

A woman's voice called out in Spanish from the back room. It sounded like a warning.

He narrowed his eyes, started to shut the door, then seemed to think better of it. Making a show of looking at the Timex on his wrist, he said, "This time of day, I like to go have coffee and a guava pastry at the Tulipan. They have a very good baker."

Then before I could ask another question, he closed the door in my face.

24

THE TULIPAN BAKERY ON BELVEDERE Road had been around for longer than I could remember. It was more than just a bakery. Catering mostly to the Cuban-American community, it was a place to meet and drink coffee, talk politics, and gossip. They also made as good a Cuban sandwich as you could find north of Havana.

But I had no appetite. I walked in thinking I was wasting my time. But until I figured out a way to get past Gaines and reach M.K.—until I convinced her she was in danger, that her father was the only one who knew the way out—it was at least a step in the right direction.

The place was almost empty, everyone still at mass.

I stepped up to the counter and waited for the girl to finish rearranging a tray of fancy pastries.

"Is Pico Nuñez here?" I asked when she looked up.

She smiled and shook her head like she didn't speak English.

"*Café, por favor,*" I said, trying another tack. "Without sugar."

She made me a cup of café con leche, without adding sugar. "Two dollars, please."

I laid a ten on the counter and said, "Keep the change."

She smiled.

"I'm trying to find Pico Nuñez," I said. "I'm not a cop. I'm not looking for trouble. I just want to ask him a question."

She studied her arrangement of pastries, thinking about it. "Maybe you take your coffee outside and come back in a few minutes. I'll ask if anyone knows this Pico person."

I thanked her and walked out to my car.

Ten minutes later I was back at the counter.

She nodded at me. "Pico is out back."

Thanking her, I took my coffee outside and walked around to the alley at the back of the building.

A stocky man wearing white uniform pants and a sleeveless undershirt sat on a garbage can, a Camel dangling from his lower lip. Thick tufts of hair grew on his shoulders, but his head was almost completely bald.

"Are you Pico Nuñez?" I asked, stepping closer.

"What happen to your face, man? Look like someone cut you, eh?"

I nodded. "You should see the other guy."

At this, he laughed. "I'm Pico. What do you want?"

I described the graffiti, explained to him that I'd been told he could tell me who this gang was, where they operated.

He met my gaze and slowly shook his head. "I don't know nothing, man. Don't fuck with no gangs."

I sipped my coffee. It was strong. "I'm not saying you do, but if there were such a gang, where would they hang out?"

He drew on his cigarette, then flicked it across the alley. As he did, I noticed that his hand looked raw and red, the skin boiled and puckered, scarred horribly with burn tissue. His other hand was worse.

I pulled my dwindling money clip out of my pocket and peeled off a twenty.

He looked at it and started to laugh, a bitter sound. "What you gonna do with that? Bribe me? With twenty fucking dollars? Are you fucking kidding me?"

I put away the money.

His eyes never left my face.

"I wasn't trying to insult you. I need help. I saw your house—I grew up around the corner. I know what they did to your brother. They killed a friend of mine too. I want to know who they are, where they operate."

He looked at me impassively for what seemed a long time. Then he shook his head. "You ask a lot, man."

"Give me something—anything."

He looked down at his feet.

I waited.

When he looked up at me, the hatred was burning in his eyes. "*Las Flechas Azúles*. Ain't no gang. At least they ain't like the Latin Kings, or the Crips or Bloods, or any a those crews. Call themselves the Blue Arrows. They don't hang in any one place—they got little cells all over Florida—and they pros, man. They doin' more to keep the people down than any bunch a crack-dealin' homies ever could. Spread money and hate wherever they go—look at Flamingo Lakes. If you grew up there, you know—it used to be a decent place. Tried to clean it up, me and my brother. Tried to put together a community center, a place for kids to get off the street. Teach 'em a skill—baking, construction. But they didn't want no place like that. Wanted the neighborhood just the way it was. So they burned us out. Hear the same story from Liberty City to Jacksonville. Don't want the people to improve their lives. They want it fucked up. Those *cabrones* workin' an agenda."

"The Blue Arrows? Why haven't I read about any of this?"

He scowled. "Not the Blue Arrows, the people tellin' them what to do. Pick up the paper, man. Any paper. All you see is news about the drug war. What war?" he snorted. "Ain't no war—just a bunch of victims. Try and show 'em a different way to solve the problem, you might fuck with the war chest—the money. Fuck with the money, you fuckin' with power. Can't win. No fucking way."

He hopped off the garbage can and brushed off the seat of his pants. "They got juice—and that's all I'm gonna say. It helps you, fine. But you didn't hear it here." He started to walk toward the back door of the bakery, then stopped and said, "Whatever trouble you think you got with them, long as you walkin' and talkin', it ain't bad as you think."

Turning his back on me, he walked into the bakery and pulled the door closed behind him.

The lock clicked. It sounded loud in the empty alley.

25

LAS FLECHAS AZÚLES. What could they possibly want with a man like Andrew Stevenson? What kind of file had he put together?

This time I didn't bother searching for a parking space.

I pulled up to the hospital's main entrance and left the car parked against the curb. Let them tow it. I was focused on getting past Gaines and into the ICU.

I hadn't reckoned on Detective Harris standing just inside the hospital's front doors.

The big detective looked up when I walked in, then stepped forward to intercept me. A manila file folder was tucked under his left arm.

"Gaines said you'd be back. Where have you been?" he demanded.

"Speak to your boss, Harris. You're barking up the wrong tree." I kept walking.

He grinned, more a malevolent sneer than a smile. "Don't even try and go up there. They'll arrest you on sight. Gaines swore out a warrant."

This stopped me. "When?"

"When you threatened him, that's when."

"Where's Tapsell? I have information for her."

"She's not your problem anymore, I am."

I didn't have time for this. "Are you going to arrest me or not?"

"When I arrest you, it won't be for threatening a goddamn lawyer. Listen, Mr. Appraiser, I'm getting sick of saying this. Captain Laspada's got one way of doing things, I got my own way. I'm not near as subtle. Tapsell crossed swords with Gaines, so now the case is mine. And the way I see it, what we got here is a parallel investigation. And you're smack dead in the middle of everything I come up with."

He opened his file and withdrew an old photograph of Peter Jacobs. Thrusting it at me, he asked, "Remember this guy?"

When I didn't answer, he lowered the photograph and shrugged his massive shoulders. "'Course you do. The way I see it, you two are still working the angles together."

When I failed to respond, he went on. "Oh yeah, I've done plenty of research on you—know all about the little scam you two tried to pull. When that body showed up under the dock, I got to thinking about how convenient it was he got clipped while you were easily accounted for. Till then, I didn't figure you for having more than one partner. But the kid was just a convenient helper, wasn't he? Ran his prints and came up with a sheet longer than you are tall. Gang activity—no known affiliation—mostly kid stuff, trying to get a crew to accept him. Nothing close to murder. This kid graduated fast, and I figure the punk had plenty of help along the way. When's the last time you saw or spoke with this Jacobs character? How'd the two of you hook up with the floater?"

I fished the car keys back out of my pocket and stepped around Harris. He made no move to block me.

"You gonna answer me or not?" he sneered.

"You start asking the right questions, I'll talk till you can't stand the sound of my voice. But right now, you're in the twilight zone." I walked out of the hospital, slid behind the wheel, and started the car.

Harris followed me. But he made no move to stop me.

He stood on the sidewalk, glaring at me. I got the idea that he had been given strict instructions about how far he could go with me. And I didn't like what that implied about Laspada's methods.

I sat there for a moment trying to decide what to do next. Then it seemed obvious. If I couldn't get to Stevenson, I could at least head back to the house and try and find the file myself.

I rolled down my window as I pulled away from the curb. "Harris, ask yourself one question. If I had planned this thing the way you seem to think, what the hell am I doing now?"

That one got to him.

He stood there, watching me pull away, looking confused.

But the dull light in his eyes gave me the shivers.

26

I DROVE ACROSS THE ROYAL Poinciana bridge to Palm Beach, thinking about Peter Jacobs, reflecting on how hard I had worked to distance my name from his and how utterly impossible that had proved to be. Where was he now? What was he doing? I was wrung out, on edge. Harris was a fool. But a fool with a badge. A badge and a temper. To hell with him. A green Porsche convertible blew past me, a flashy redhead wearing dark sunglasses in the driver's seat, a cell phone pressed to her ear. A little white terrier sat beside her in the passenger seat. I could swear the dog cocked his head and smirked at me as they passed. I blinked and drew a deep breath. Dogs don't smirk, I told myself.

I rolled down my window and let the fresh air blow in my face. But my uneasiness increased when a late-model white van appeared out of nowhere and seemed to follow me a little too closely. I slowed down.

The van slowed.

I sped up.

The van sped up too.

I drove carefully, one eye glued to the rearview. The glare on the van's windshield rendered the driver invisible. This was silly. First the dog, now someone was tailing me. Get a grip, I warned myself.

I turned up the radio.

In spite of the light traffic, the van stayed on my bumper all the way across the bridge.

On the island, I slowed to a crawl. But the van refused the opportunity to pass me. Instead, it slowed too and hung back a few car lengths. It occurred to me that it might be Detective Harris—a misguided show of police force, his way of letting me know he wasn't fooling around.

The thought pissed me off. I had enough to do without worrying about him.

The green Porsche sat parked in front of the pumps at the gas station on Royal Poinciana Way, the redhead out pumping her own high test.

On an impulse, I jerked the wheel to the left and pulled in behind her.

The van kept going.

Exhaling, I looked at myself in the rearview mirror, feeling both foolish and relieved.

A pimply teenager in khaki work clothes approached me. "You need some gas, sir?" His eyes never left the redhead.

"No thanks. Just needed to turn around."

He looked at me strangely, then shrugged and walked away.

As I pulled around the Porsche, the redhead gave a little wave.

I waved back.

She frowned behind her shades.

The guy pulling in behind me tooted the horn of his shiny black Humvee.

She waved again, this time making it clear that it wasn't for me.

I eased the Escort out of there, thinking a Humvee in Palm Beach was only a little less useful than a tractor in Manhattan.

That didn't seem to bother the redhead.

A few blocks later the van was back on my ass.

No doubt about it—it was the same van.

What the hell was Harris up to? The more I thought about it, the angrier I got.

Just before the Stevensons' driveway, I'd had enough.

I pulled to the side of County Road to see what he would do.

The van slowed and came to a stop some twenty yards behind me.

Shaking my head, I got out of my car, planning to tell this misguided cop exactly what I thought of his childish games.

Just then a blue Volvo pulled to the end of the driveway across the street from the Stevensons' and stopped. A girl in shorts hopped out and started fooling with the mailbox.

The van started moving, rolling toward me.

"What the hell do you want, Harris?" I yelled.

But it wasn't Harris behind the wheel.

The driver—a thin man wearing white coveralls—steered the van around me without ever looking directly at me. ALONZO'S LAWN SERVICE had been stenciled in careful block letters on the door of the van. No sign of Harris.

Just a sharp-faced, dark-skinned man who smiled ever so slightly to himself as he rolled by . . .

It was the smile that got me, a cold and knowing little grin.

My heart started to pound.

I stood there and watched until the van disappeared around a bend in the road.

"Everything okay?" the girl at the mailbox shouted from across the street.

I told her everything was fine, then got back in my car and sat there awhile longer, trying to convince myself that everything *was* fine. That the man was a gardener, cruising around the island instead of working. Sight-seeing. It beat the hell out of trimming hedges—didn't it?

But my paranoid self wasn't buying it.

I waited until I was sure he hadn't doubled back, then turned into the Stevensons' driveway and parked next to an empty police cruiser. No sign of any cops. Which didn't surprise me.

Before I went inside the house I opened the Escort's trunk, removed the jack handle, and put it under the driver's seat.

Paranoid or not, the heavy iron bar was now within easy reach.

27

THE FRONT DOORS WERE UNLOCKED. A uniformed cop I hadn't seen before dozed in a mahogany chair he'd pulled out of the dining room and placed in the vestibule. A former jock, he was as wide as Harris, but older and taller.

He came awake when I entered, scrutinized me from where he sat, then said, "Cap'n Laspada told me to expect you."

I started to say something about the white van, then realized I didn't even have the license-plate number.

"The evidence techs are finished?" I asked, glancing at the stairs.

"About an hour ago." He lowered his voice. "Don't envy whoever's going to be cleaning up that mess."

"Bad, huh?"

He nodded. "Pretty goddamn nasty."

Maj sat at the kitchen table, reading the Sunday papers, one huge mitt wrapped around a coffee cup.

Charteen stood at the stove, her back to me, cooking what looked like enough food for a regiment. There was a roast, fried chicken, rice, yams and mashed potatoes, green beans, a chocolate cake. I didn't know who was going to eat it all. Maybe in her world, cooking was what you did when someone you loved died. Eating wasn't the point. It was a matter of sharing grief, not nourishment.

"Smells good in here," I said.

Maj looked up from the paper. Charteen continued stirring.

"Charteen . . . ," he called.

She turned. "Jesus Lord! What you doin' sneakin' up on us?" she snapped. "You been to the hospital?"

I nodded. "Yeah, but I didn't get in to see Andrew. The doctors have him doped up in the ICU."

She pressed her lips into a sharp frown. "Wish to God I could do somethin'. Help that good man somehow. But it's in the hands of the Lord."

She sighed.

"Say *here* you was there," Maj interrupted, jabbing a finger at the front page of the *Post*.

I met his gaze. "I was there."

"You get a close look at this robber?"

Charteen stepped from the stove to his side, a large wooden spoon clutched in one hand.

I looked from her tired face to Maj's. "It wasn't a robber."

"But the paper say—" Charteen began.

"Since when you believe what they print?" Maj interrupted again. He looked at me. "Wasn't no robber, then who done this? Why they kill Miz Amanda?"

"I wish I knew," I said, feeling suddenly as tired as Charteen looked.

Maj narrowed his eyes and studied me. The skin of his face was so smooth and shiny it could have been molded of wet, black clay. "The police, they been to see both me and Charteen. Came in the middle a the night. Rainin' to drown the dogs a hell. Didn't bother them none. Kept at it for hours. Sayin' nothin'. Just fill the air with stupid damn questions. Thinkin' maybe me or her had somethin' to do with this." He looked like he wanted to tear someone in half.

His eyes bored into mine. "Me and Charteen want to know what happened. Why? How? These papers wrong—you explain it to us."

They deserved that much, so I went through it again.

When I finished, they both looked at me, confused.

Charteen said, "But the boy did this is dead. Don't that mean it's over?"

"They'll be back. They want the file. Next time they'll be better prepared," I answered.

Maj asked me to repeat the threat against M.K.

I did.

Then I asked if either of them knew anything about the file.

Maj snarled in disgust, "What I look like to you? A lawyer? Some niggah Mister Andrew confide his business to? The mon been good to me. This whole family been good to me." He stood and leaned over the table, his huge hands splayed across the newspaper.

"Don't know nuthin' 'bout no secrets." He paused. "But I know one t'ing—muthafucka' threaten M.K. come 'round here again—he be wishin' he never saw ol' Maj."

He meant it. But something else he'd said struck me even more powerfully.

He wasn't a lawyer . . .

Of course Andrew didn't confide his business to Maj.

But Gaines *was* a lawyer . . .

And now he was the self-appointed keeper of the gates. No one could see or speak to Andrew without Gaines's permission.

Except for M.K.

And he'd asked me not to mention the file to her . . .

Painful thoughts trickled into my head.

What kind of game was Gaines playing?

It made no more sense than getting followed by a van belonging to a lawn service.

I looked up and found Charteen staring at me.

"These secret papers—what exactly we talkin' about?" she asked. "Letters? Legal papers? Some kind a formula?"

I shrugged. "I have no idea. I want to search Andrew's room. We see the file, hopefully we'll recognize it."

Charteen hesitated, then turned back to the stove. "The

police already up there—the ones in the white coats. If there's papers like you say, they gonna find 'em."

"They're gone, Charteen. And they weren't looking for the file. They were collecting fingerprints and evidence related to the killing."

"He right, girl," Maj said. "Police only see what they want to see."

She turned from the stove, looking stricken. "What you mean they left? Come in this house—my kitchen—like they owns it. Lookin' at my food, talkin' like they gonna starve to death any minute I don't stop what I'm doin' an feed 'em. They tell me I can't go upstairs. That I got to stay out from up there . . . Then they just up and leave? Not so much as a word? Not even the courtesy to let me know they done finished?" She waved the spoon at me, eyes wide. "What wrong with this world? Is everyone gone crazy?"

A shudder traveled the length of her body.

Maj stepped to her side and gently took the spoon out of her hand. "Gone be all right, girl. Every t'ing gone be all right."

She allowed him to put his arm around her and stroke her shoulder. But after a moment, she pushed him away. She frowned at me. "Don't seem right to go pokin' through Mr. Andrew's things. Don't even know what we lookin' for. Maybe we should wait on M.K."

Maj shook his head. "You heard the mon. M.K. be next, we don't find out why this killin' happen. We don't find this file, we ain't gone to know. Is we?"

She looked less than convinced.

"He's right, Charteen," I added. "These people won't just go away."

At that moment, the cop from the vestibule poked his head through the kitchen door. "Sure smells good out here," he said. "How much longer before we eat?"

Charteen shot him a look that would curdle milk.

He retreated in a hurry.

"If them po-lice did they jobs, 'stead of . . ." She glanced at the stove, then stepped over and shut off all the burners.

"Come on," she said, turning her back on her feast. "Let's see we can find those papers. Ain't cleaned this house all these years without peekin' now and again. Can't do no harm to take a look now."

Maj started to say something, but one sharp look from Charteen shut him up.

I was still thinking about the white van. "Before we get started, where's the phone book?" I asked, wanting to know more about Alonzo's Lawn Service.

But when I tried to look it up, I found no such listing.

28

ANDREW'S BEDROOM WAS A DISASTER.

Charteen, standing in the doorway, drew in a sharp breath and whispered, "Jesus Lord."

Maj stood silently behind her, shaking his head and flexing his hands.

I stared over their shoulders, measuring the reality of the room against the nightmare of my memory.

The three of us stepped in and gingerly picked our way around the mess.

A sooty coat of gray fingerprint powder lay on every hard surface. The air smelled metallic, and underneath, something cloyingly sweet. A large section of carpet at the foot of the bed had been cut away and removed. Areas of the carpet that remained were crusted with dried blood and stained with odd brown smudges that matched the color of the stuff that had marked my hands and clothing. Each of the stains had been circled with a black marker. Little numbered cards were strewn around the room in no particular order. The desk chair and floor lamp had been righted and stood together near the balcony doors. The lamp's crushed silk shade lay in the middle of the floor, as though forgotten. Andrew's bed had been stripped, the linen removed from the room. A pile of bloodied gauze pads and a couple of used syringes were scattered across the night table. One of Amanda's shoes stuck out from under the bed. The other was nowhere to be seen.

The catalog I'd thrown at the kid lay against the baseboard of the far wall. But my eye kept coming back to the blackened blood on the carpet, dried now to the color of dark cherries.

Closing my eyes, I could feel the kid's bulky strength, hear the rasp of the breeze on the silk curtains, Amanda's last, terrified cry.

Maj mumbled something, snapping me out of it.

I blinked at the sunlight streaming into the room and shivered.

Charteen whispered, "Jesus Lord," again.

And the frisson of fear melted away.

I'd never given much thought to who cleaned up after a murder. But one look at Charteen's wide-eyed expression as she surveyed the room and I knew I would never again watch the evening news without wondering who had sponged the blood off the walls once the cameras had been turned off.

Her mouth a tight line, her eyes blinking rapidly, Charteen shook her head once, then started out of the room. "Can't do no searchin' till I clean this up. Got work to do here. You two need to get out my way. Miz Amanda see this room lookin' like this—" She stopped in her tracks, frozen by her own words.

For a second or two she stood swaying in the doorway, her back to the room.

Maj moved toward her, but she reached out and steadied herself against the door frame before he could reach her.

"Come out this room," she whispered without turning around. "I got work to do."

Maj followed her into the hallway.

On my way to the door, I stopped to straighten the drawing over Andrew's desk. It had been knocked crooked, and looking at it now, I wondered how I could have failed to notice it sooner. A brilliantly executed black-and-sepia-toned study for *Guernica*'s screaming horse—signed "Picasso." The painting depicted the murderous bombing of the town of Guernica during the Spanish Civil War. This study, large and heavily framed, didn't seem to want to hang straight. I leveled it as best I could without taking the time to rehang it, then stood back and stared.

Picasso had captured the horse in quick, slashing strokes—far different from the smooth surface of the finished painting—its muscular neck contorted, bulging eyes looking skyward, mouth wide, teeth bared, tongue a pointed dart—terror and pain and outrage exploding upward in an equine scream. A scream aimed at the unseen planes, bellies full of death and destruction. It was a powerful drawing. Staggering in its raw energy, full of horror. An odd choice to hang in the bedroom, so that it was the first thing Andrew saw in the morning and the last at night.

I stood before it, transfixed. Picasso had distilled war and fear and violence into a single image of a screaming horse. A horse whose hideous cry echoed Amanda's at the moment of her death.

If Maj hadn't called for me, I would have stood there all day.

29

The sea shifted under a cloudless sky, an astringent blue against the softer, warmer blue of the horizon. Blue sky, bluer water. Too many shades to catalog. Indigo. Turquoise. Sapphire. Cerulean. Teal. Lapis. Prussian blue. Cobalt blue. Cornflower blue. I stood on the seawall beside Maj, thinking the blue of the afternoon was almost sharp and clear enough to wash away the image of blood dried to the color of dark cherries. But not quite.

Maj said, "Ain't a damn t'ing I know to do."

I made some noise about helping Charteen clean up Andrew's room.

Maj dismissed the idea. "Just be in her way. She done told us to leave."

He grunted and slid his foot back and forth across the sand-dusted top of the concrete wall, the scrape and grind of his work boot strangely soothing.

Fishing boats, large and small, rolled on the gentle swell. Three gulls spiraled on the breeze.

"Mon just flesh and blood, you know. Don't just fly away," Maj said, watching the birds.

"He was there. Then he was gone. Like that." I snapped my fingers. "Don't know how he did it."

"We figure out how he come and go, maybe we learn somet'ing important."

"There was no sign of forced entry. The kid knew what he was after. Somebody gave him directions."

Maj nodded. He squinted out at the world just over the horizon.

Whatever he saw there, he kept to himself.

I went back to cataloging the colors of the ocean.

"Maybe him come from the beach," Maj said, eyes still focused on the point where the sea and sky blurred.

"How?" I asked, thinking about the graffiti.

"Don't know," Maj allowed. "But it could happen."

"How would he get past the gate?"

"How he know to be lookin' for this file?"

I had no answer.

"Gone see somet'ing," he said, stepping off the ten-foot-high seawall the way most men would step off a city curb.

He landed catlike, one hand brushing the ground, his feet gouging deep divots into the soft sand.

Looking up at the wall, his smooth face unreadable, he walked back and forth, his boot prints the only man-made marks on the rain-dimpled surface of the beach.

"Not one t'ing . . . ," he shouted, moving up the beach toward the gate, pausing in front of the graffiti.

He studied it carefully.

"Come see this," he finally called, waving for me to hop off the wall and join him.

Measuring the distance to the sand, I shook my head. "I'll use the gate." I took off my shoes and wedged it open.

Maj pointed to the graffiti. "This what you be tellin' me 'bout?"

I nodded. "The Blue Arrows."

"Ain't heard the name. And I ain't never seen this mark. Why me be seein' it now?"

I didn't understand.

He kicked at the sand, looked out at the sea, then back at the wall. "Damn gang don't be paintin' this for kicks, mon. This mark here for a reason."

It took a minute for it to sink in.

"He came by boat? You think he came by boat?"

Maj frowned and pointed at the wall. "Be simple . . . Mon don't know the island, houses all look the same from the beach. Mon see the mark, he know which house to hit."

I studied the graffiti.

The blue paint stood out in sharp contrast to the weathered surface of the wall. A beacon. Damn near impossible to miss.

Maj and I walked to the edge of the water. But last night's storm had washed away any sign a beached boat might have left.

I turned and studied the graffiti again.

Who the hell were the Blue Arrows?

30

AN HOUR LATER, CHARTEEN called us upstairs. "Won't never really be right, but the worst of it's up. Let's get this over with. The file here, we find it. If not . . ." She shrugged, a lifetime of resignation in the gesture.

At first it felt odd, a breach of some unspoken trust to paw through another man's possessions—the accumulated detritus of his day-to-day life—while he lay helpless, unable to defend his history. But we had reason to be thorough. So we were.

We started with the desk. Bills and receipts; investment proposals and charitable solicitations; postage stamps curling at the edges; a green jade letter opener, the hilt carved into the likeness of an eagle's head with tiny ruby eyes; business correspondence; stock reports and property appraisals; old photographs of Andrew and Amanda and M.K. on a sailboat; a Patek Philippe pocket watch, the hands frozen at precisely 11:14; three loose buttons; a sterling Dupont lighter with a matching cigar guillotine; nail clippers; a Rolodex I suspected to be worth its weight in gold—a who's who with home addresses and private phone numbers. No secret file. Nothing vaguely sinister.

An Empire bureau stood against the wall across from the desk, the top decorated with precious bibelots and found objects. Small bronze animals—horses, lions, and elephants; seashells and bits of coral; silver-framed family photographs. The top drawer was filled with underwear, dozens of pairs of plain white briefs, under which lay a handful of Krugerrands scattered like so many pennies. The bottom drawer held socks. A box of Cuban Cohibas nestled under the socks, one of the bad habits I assumed Amanda disapproved of. But no file.

Andrew was a clotheshorse. His closet smelled of fine leather and expensive cologne. It housed a startling number of hanging and folded garments and shoes. Bespoke suits and sporting out-fits. Twenty or thirty colorful cashmere golf sweaters, displayed on their own built-in shelves. Secreted behind the tweeds and sport coats, I found a wall safe. My pulse quickened. But it was unlocked and contained nothing more incendiary than ITT div-idend statements and insurance policies. A lot of them.

Disappointed, I stepped out of the closet and looked around the room.

The very rich accumulate pretty much the same clutter we all do. Only there's more of it. And it's shinier. But if Andrew Stevenson collected secrets as well as art, he didn't commit them to writing and hide them in the obvious places. The file could be anywhere.

"Ain't no secret file in this room. Time we left it be," Charteen declared as if reading my thoughts.

"You." She gestured to Maj. "Help me move these books—'fore I break my neck trippin' over 'em." She pointed to a pile of a dozen or so books stacked just inside the closet doors.

"Don't need to be shoutin'," Maj said, bending to pick them up. "Ears be workin' just fine, girl. Always have, you know."

"Wait!" I'd stepped around the books at least a half dozen times and not paid them the slightest heed. Now I knelt and took a closer look.

Most of them were of modern vintage. A few were bound in expensive-looking leather. Some were thick, scholarly tomes, others photograph-laden coffee-table histories.

I examined each of them, riffling the pages. But no secret file fluttered out into my hands.

The books had two things in common. Each was about the Spanish Civil War, and each, according to the fancy engraved bookplates pasted on the inside covers, had been purchased from Galen Tessereau, Fine Books and Objets d'Art, 188 Via Parigi, Palm Beach, Florida.

"These important?" Charteen asked.

"Maybe," I said. "Just maybe."

31

GALEN TESSEREAU'S SHOP OCCUPIED a small storefront halfway down the Via Parigi, a brick-paved alley lined with exclusive boutiques running north off Worth Avenue. The alley was meant to remind well-heeled shoppers of Rome's Via Condotti.

Tessereau was late. On the phone he'd promised to meet me at seven-thirty. It was almost eight and his shop was dark, the windows curtained. The entire alley was blanketed in shadows.

I paced the narrow street, peering into every dark corner. Nothing stirred. I had the place to myself. *Palm Beach*. I shook my head. Some playground. My shoulder ached—I was tired, exhausted. My brain was a worthless wad of rusty steel wool someone had wedged between my ears. I wanted to lie down and sleep for a week.

Without warning, the lamps in Tessereau's shop went on and Galen Tessereau was standing in the doorway surrounded by a halo of light.

I waved and called, "Hello."

"Come in. Come in. Hope you found us easily enough. Sorry to keep you waiting," he apologized. "I was working in the back room." Dressed as though he were headed out for an evening's entertainment at Rick's in Casablanca, Tessereau wore a white

silk shantung suit over a pale blue shirt and a dark silk tie. He
was tiny, his bald head as furrowed as a walnut.

He held the door open, looking past me, surveying the empty
street behind me with his quick brown eyes. "There's a good fellow," he said as I stepped inside.

Then, he closed and bolted the door.

We stood in a room about thirty feet square, with high, cypress-
beamed ceilings, finely figured hardwood floors, and walls fitted
with polished mahogany shelves sagging under the weight of
books, old and new, stacked two and three deep. Recessed low-
voltage lighting cast a warm glow on everything. Large glass cases
built into each of the four corners of the room held an incredibly
rare and varied inventory, not at all what I had expected. There
were Egyptian amulets and stone carvings, Indian ivories and jew-
eled daggers, Khmer statues, a Benin bronze head next to an
ancient bronze astrolabe, mythical Chinese animals carved of
white and green jade, a two-foot-tall emerald-encrusted gold crucifix, Greek and Roman marble busts, Celtic and Etruscan gold
jewelry. That didn't describe a tenth of what was there.

The place smelled of dust and old leather bindings and the
perfume of some mysteriously spicy incense I couldn't place. A
tobacco-brown leather couch facing a carved teakwood desk
occupied the center of the room. The desk's top was buried
under piles of books and catalogs and stacks of papers and correspondence.

Tessereau stood quietly as I stared, wide-eyed, at the scope
and quality of his inventory.

"Amazing!" I said, shaking my head in wonder. "You haven't
left much out, have you?"

"Do you see the pattern?" he asked, obviously pleased by my
reaction.

I nodded. "All the great cultures under one roof—a private
museum of human history." I glanced at the shelves. "I'm not
sure about the books . . ."

"The written word," he explained. "The record of who we are
and where we've been. Perhaps the greatest achievement of
all . . ." He paused and regarded me carefully. "Not everyone

recognizes what I've tried so hard to accomplish. They see lovely knickknacks, expensive collectibles."

"You can't blame them—it's beautiful, all of it."

He beamed.

"Come in and sit down, Wil," he said, taking my arm and leading me toward his desk. "You were a bit vague on the telephone—I'm not sure I understand how I can help you."

I followed him and took a seat on the couch.

"Nika, come out here, please," he called.

Turning to me, he explained proudly, "Nika is my granddaughter—the only family I have left—and the brains of this operation. She's planning to attend medical school after I close the shop next spring. After I retire." He smiled again, the lines of his face unfolding, coming alive.

"Retire? Why?" I asked, looking around the shop. "What are you going to do? Go fishing?"

He laughed. "Fishing, indeed. No, my boy, I have plans." His smile faded and his voice grew serious. "Life is a tenuous proposition, at best. The longer you live, the rarer and more precious it all seems. What happened to Andrew and Amanda drives home my point. I'm going to travel—everywhere I meant to go and didn't. Andrew would understand."

"What will you do with your inventory?"

He hesitated, fixing me with those curious eyes. "I haven't decided . . ."

Then he called again for his granddaughter. "*Nika* . . . Come up front, dear. You can finish unpacking those boxes later."

I stood when she came out of the back room. She was a tall girl, Eurasian. Her skin was so pale and clear it was almost translucent—her face thin, her brow high, framed by a silky fall of hair so dark it looked blue. She wore a sleeveless, celadon-green silk shirt over black shorts. Aside from her eyes, as clear and as piercing as her grandfather's, the two bore little resemblance. She looked about twenty-four or twenty-five.

"I'd like you to meet Wil Sumner, Nika. He's the one who called about Andrew Stevenson's books," Tessereau said.

She hesitated, studying me. Then, she stepped over and

offered her hand. "Anika Tessereau," she said as we shook. Her grip was firm, her hand strong and dry, her gaze direct. "I hope we can help you find the answers you're looking for."

"I appreciate you and your grandfather meeting me on such short notice," I said.

"It's the least we can do. Mr. Stevenson has been a very good friend to us."

Tessereau directed Nika and me to sit down on the couch. He stepped behind his desk.

"Now, what exactly can we can do for you?" he asked, settling deep into the cushions of his chair. "If we are in a position to help Andrew, you can count on us."

I explained what had happened the night of Amanda's murder. I told them about the file, the threats against M.K.

Tessereau asked a couple of questions and shook his wizened head.

Nika listened in silence.

"The stack of books Andrew purchased from you were all about the Spanish Civil War. . . . Why?" I asked. "Did the topic merely interest him? Or was there more to it?"

Tessereau shook his head. "I'm afraid I don't see how any of this could be connected to my books."

"Not the books," Nika interrupted. "The war itself. But how could something that happened so long ago have anything to do with this?"

Tessereau thought for a moment. "Andrew was interested in the events leading up to the outbreak of the war. Particularly the fascist youth gangs operating in and around Madrid. The Falange. Something of an esoteric subject. He was there, you know."

I nodded. "What, specifically, was he trying to learn?"

"It's actually rather interesting . . ." Tessereau sat a little straighter in his chair, his eyes glittering now. "Andrew never would say exactly what he was looking for. But he was always very focused. It was something specific . . ."

He leaned forward. "Nika, did the package from Mr. Gulabayani in London arrive?"

"It came in on Friday. I haven't unpacked it yet," she said.

"Do so, child. Unpack it at once."

She unfolded her legs and left the room.

Tessereau stood and walked around to the front of his desk. "Andrew wanted firsthand accounts of a series of provocations perpetrated by the Falangist youth gangs operating in Madrid in pre-civil war Spain. Hundreds of acts of vandalism and violence were committed, then made to look like the work of leftist peasants in order to stir up the wealthy landowners." He scratched the back of one hand, warming to the topic. "Not a new idea, you know—do something so brutal that the population cries out for revenge, then make sure your enemies, in this case, the reds, are blamed. You become the solution—the savior of the people. But Andrew knew all of this. He didn't want general information. No, I got the feeling Andrew was looking for corroboration of something he already knew too well."

He paused to catch his breath and I thought about what Pico Nuñez had said about the Blue Arrows working an agenda. But it seemed too farfetched, not at all related to Andrew Stevenson.

"Some of these provocations were quite vicious," Tessereau continued. "It's a minor footnote to the war—nothing compared to the carnage that eventually took place. But Andrew was extremely interested in these gangs. He instructed me to buy everything I could put my hands on. Especially photographs. No matter the price." Tessereau shrugged. "Unfortunately there isn't very much of this material available. A few weeks ago I located an unusual memoir in the London shop of the Gulabayani brothers. Quite offbeat. Nika's unwrapping it now."

"Do you think it has anything to do with the file?" I asked.

He crossed his arms and shook his head doubtfully. "All of this is interesting. Fascinating, I suppose. But it happened sixty-odd years ago—not exactly the stuff of murder and intrigue. Not these days, eh?"

I said I didn't know.

"Well, someone obviously thinks Andrew knows something important," he said.

He fell silent while we waited for his granddaughter.

"Is this it?" Nika asked, hurrying through the door at the back of the shop holding a small, blue, leather-bound book.

"Let me see, dear." He held out his hand.

Clucking, he thumbed through it, then handed it to me. "Nothing too incendiary here. Actually, I think most would find it boring."

The book was heavier than it looked, the leather binding in almost perfect condition. The title was embossed in gold lettering on the spine: *Una Historia Personal—La Vida de General Manuel Rodriguez*.

I looked at Tessereau. "I don't speak or read Spanish."

He nodded. "Allow me to translate. 'A Personal History—The Life of General Manuel Rodriguez.' By Manuel Rodriguez." His voice held a note of irony. "A subject of little interest, unless you're Manuel Rodriguez—or Andrew Stevenson."

I opened the memoir and riffled through the deckle-edged pages. There were a number of photographs printed throughout the body of the book. But the writing was in Spanish. I couldn't understand a word.

"Is it expensive?" I asked, closing it.

Tessereau shook his head. "A hundred dollars."

"I'd like to look through it. May I borrow it?"

"Of course. You may have it if it will help Andrew."

I opened the book and flipped through it again. Then I did a double take. My mouth fell open.

"What is it?" Nika asked.

"What?" Tessereau echoed.

I pointed to the open book and spluttered, "Here. It's right here."

Under a caption I couldn't read appeared a photograph of a banner bearing the image of a stylized yoke, pierced by five arrows. It resembled the graffiti on the Stevensons' seawall. No, it didn't resemble it—the banner matched the blue spray paint almost exactly.

I tried to rein in my excitement.

"Hold it so that I can see it, Wil," Tessereau instructed.

"There!" I jumped up, stabbing at the page with my finger. "Right there!"

Tessereau leaned close.

"What does it say?" I asked. "What is it?"

Tessereau took the book out of my hands and read the caption under the photograph.

"*Las Flechas Azúles*. The Blue Arrows." He looked at me, his expression curious. "According to this, it's the name and the symbol adopted by one of the Falange gangs in Madrid. Rodriguez devotes a chapter to these gangs."

I reached for the book. "This symbol was spray-painted on the Stevensons' seawall. It marked the house for the killer. I've got to get this in front of Andrew."

"I can translate the chapter. It would take an hour or so, no more," Tessereau offered.

I tried to keep my voice calm, but my hands were shaking. "Andrew will understand it," I said, heading for the door.

Tessereau and Anika followed me.

"Good luck," she called as I strode down the alley toward Worth Avenue.

I hesitated and turned. "Thank you. Thank you both. I'll call as soon as I know something."

She and her grandfather stood framed for a moment in the door of their shop. Then the lights dimmed and they were gone.

I hurried back to the car, my thoughts racing.

The Blue Arrows . . .

A fascist youth gang from pre–civil war Spain? Operating here? Now? In Florida? It sounded ridiculous.

Out of the corner of my eye, I saw him approach. One of a handful of window-shoppers strolling the wide, well-lit sidewalks of Worth Avenue. I should have recognized him. But I'd only seen him once, and then, only for an instant. I was anxious to get to the hospital, my mind on the book, not my surroundings. Were Pico Nuñez's Blue Arrows related to the gang in Madrid? And if they were, how were they connected to Andrew Stevenson? I fumbled my keys out of my pocket and tucked the memoir under my arm.

One minute I was unlocking the Escort, the next, he had a

gun pressed hard against my belly. He didn't smile and he wasn't wearing his coveralls. But I knew. Even before the white van eased up next to where we stood.

"You!" I said, unable to keep the surprise out of my voice. "What the hell do you want?"

"*Oye—consolte—*into the van. Now." His voice was high, almost feminine, his face as thin and sharp as the blade of an ax.

"What do you want?" I repeated.

"One thing at a time. Move!" he said, shoving me toward the van.

The side door slid open, revealing two figures crouched inside with the garden tools.

I looked at them and hesitated.

Something very hard hit me behind the right ear.

Sheets of flame crawled under my skull and spread, a burning black wave breaking behind my eyes. The book fell from under my arm and fluttered to the ground. I wanted to pick it up, but my arms were numb. The man was smiling now. Then all of me went numb and the black asphalt rushed up and kissed my cheek.

32

I WOKE WITH A START IN the back of the van, flat on my belly between two lawnmowers, hands tied roughly behind my back, nostrils full of gasoline fumes.

My head felt heavy and misshapen. Someone was mewling.

It was me.

"*Mira*—he is awake, Kiki. I tell you I no hit him too hard."

A voice from the front of the van shouted, "*¡Callate la boca, Carlito!*"

I twisted onto my side to see who was talking. The move took my breath away.

The thin man who'd hit me, Carlito, had put away his gun. Maybe he didn't think he needed it anymore. He was ugly, long and lean, his sallow skin pockmarked, dark bags under his eyes. His long hair was pulled back in a ponytail; he wore tight black jeans with pointy black boots and a bright yellow T-shirt. Underneath the shirt he was all stringy muscle and bone.

Regarding me with flat brown eyes, he smiled. "You no move too fast, maybe you need some exercise."

I started to tell him to go to hell, but the van hit a bump in the road and the jolt made my eyes water.

Steadying himself on the cooler he was using as a bench,

Carlito shook his head. "Don't say nothing. Just keep your fucking mouth shut—you might live a little longer."

I stared at him, trying to look braver than I felt.

He shrugged and pulled a piece of monofilament out of his pocket and started tying complicated knots along its length.

"¿Qué pasa, Carlito? He too big for you to handle?" The same authoritative voice from the front of the van.

I craned my neck, but couldn't see who the voice belonged to. Only that it came from the passenger seat.

Carlito answered in Spanish, a jeering tone in his voice.

I opened my mouth intending to tell him to speak English, but before I uttered a sound, he was kneeling over me, his knee in my back, the fishing line looped around my neck, snugged so tight I couldn't breathe.

I could feel his sour breath, hot on the back of my neck as he hissed, "I tell you, no? Keep quiet." He gave the line a jerk for emphasis. "Understand?"

I managed a slight nod and he loosened the line.

Sucking down a deep breath, I lay on my belly, gulping air.

Carlito returned to his perch on the cooler, smiling, obviously pleased at his handiwork. Then he went back to practicing his knots as though nothing had happened.

I promised myself that I would make him eat that ugly little grin, assuming I lived through the night. Whoever these guys were, they made the kid who killed Amanda look like the sloppy amateur he was.

The van bumped and swayed and no one said a word.

A lump of hard ice grew in my chest. I closed my eyes, hoping my pounding skull wouldn't actually split open and spill whatever was left of my brains onto the greasy floor of the van.

The gasoline fumes combined with the yawing motion of the ride began to sicken me.

I fought it and nearly lost.

We drove for what seemed a long time. We might have been driving in circles, but I had an uneasy feeling they were taking me far out into the swamps. Why? What would they gain by killing me? Nothing . . . Nothing at all, I told myself.

I took comfort in the thought that if they'd wanted me dead, I'd be dead. I gathered this hopeful rationale around me like a blanket and tried to stay alert while Carlito tied his knots.

Later, I was thirsty.

"Can I have some water?" I asked him.

He sat on his cooler, looking at me the way a hungry snake looks at a mouse. "You like my little necklace? Not too tight for you? Maybe you no understand the word 'quiet'?" He shook his head. "Maybe you need me to teach you some manners."

He started to rise.

"Easy, Carlito," the voice in the passenger seat called out. "He's not worth shit, you fuck him up. Teach him some manners *after*, no?"

A third voice, the driver, piped in saying something about not needing manners, not in the fucking Everglades. Then, laughing, he opened the van's windows.

My carefully considered rationale dissolved.

And there was only the motion of the van and the rush of night air, smelling now of turned earth and stale water and rotting vegetation.

We were a long way from Worth Avenue.

33

AFTER AN ETERNITY, THE VAN slowed, then came to an abrupt halt. For a moment I lay there, grateful for the cessation of motion, my head a throbbing mountain of pain. Then the driver cut the engine. The front doors of the van opened and slammed shut. Voices outside, moving around.

This was it. My heart started to pound. I rolled onto my side.

"¡Alto!" Carlito glared at me, then looked in the direction of the voices.

Looking back at me, he said, "You want to stay alive, you stay still. No talking. Understand?"

I nodded.

He stared at me for a moment longer, then climbed out of the van, leaving me alone.

The three of them stood near the open door, conferring in Spanish. I listened through the thin metal shell separating us, understanding only the tension in their voices, struggling with the ropes binding my wrists, straining to no avail. The knots were snug—not quite tight enough to cut the circulation but tight enough to keep me from sliding out of them. I tried harder, pulling till the stitches in my shoulder began to burn.

Seconds ticked by, seeming like hours.

Then the three of them moved out of earshot.

I stopped wrestling with the ropes and strained to hear—tilting my head, trying to track them—desperate to know what they were doing. Mosquitoes whined hungrily, lighting on my cheeks and neck, biting, stinging. Sweat ran down my face, burning my eyes. The air in the van too close, vibrating with the voices of a thousand million insects whirring, buzzing.

Then, dogs barking. Large dogs. The night was suddenly alive with noise—seething, reverberating off the interior walls of the van, echoing inside my head.

Eventually Carlito returned and ordered me out into the darkness.

I sat up, terrified, moving too slowly, legs trembling. He grabbed the front of my shirt and jerked me up to my knees. I struggled to my feet, feeling as if I were watching events unfold from a distance, as though this were happening to someone else. I should do something, I thought. But what eluded me. I was a goddamn deer in the headlights.

We stood waiting for the others in front of an open shed that butted up against a little matchbox of a house. The two buildings were the only man-made structures visible in a large field of low scrub at the edge of what appeared to be a vast swamp.

A pair of large rottweilers, chained to a corner of the shed, growled and barked, sniffing the air. Behind them, the house was dark, the closed jalousie windows silvered by moonlight. The shed, a makeshift mechanic's shop, was lit by bare bulbs strung from the ceiling by thick orange extension cords. Clouds of insects swarmed around the lights. Three or four motorcycles lay inside in various states of disrepair.

But it was the night itself that dominated the landscape. The hungry howl of insects, larger, unseen creatures crying, shrieking, splashing and honking. Out there in the dark behind the house and the shed, where solid ground gave way to sucking mud and the black and fetid waters of the swamp.

Suddenly, I was more afraid of the swamp than of my abductors. I didn't want to die out there.

"*Oye*, let's move. Let's go," the biggest of my kidnappers

called, striding around the back of the van carrying the book Tessereau had given me.

I recognized his voice; he'd been sitting in the passenger seat. He was thick and tall, not much older than Carlito, maybe thirty or thirty-one. He wore a flashy silk suit over a T-shirt, and fancy alligator-skin loafers. His dark hair was cropped close. In spite of his size, he moved with the weightless grace of a well-trained athlete. "Come on," he repeated. "Move it! Let's go!"

"*¿Qué tal*, Kiki?" Carlito asked, pushing me toward the house.

Kiki smiled at him. "We're on schedule, Lito. But you got to quit with this teaching manners thing. How we going to do business, you keep fucking up the merchandise, eh?"

Carlito laughed, a short, high bark.

The rottweilers slavered and threw themselves against their chains as we approached.

Kiki walked ahead to calm them. "*Tranquilo . . . Tranquilo. Good dogs. Vengan a Papi.*" He sounded like a father quieting small, excited children.

I stared at the animals and forgot all about the swamp.

"*¡Ándele!*" Carlito said, poking me in the back with his pistol.

"Andoolay yourself!" I said, not taking my eyes off the beasts.

Kiki looked up from his pets and grinned at me, his mouth full of gold. "Easy, Lito. He isn't going anywhere."

The rottweilers nuzzled Kiki's legs. "Right, *pendejo*?" he spat out derisively.

Tearing my eyes off the dogs, I stared at him. I was tired of being pushed around and frightened enough to hate myself for letting them scare me so badly. "Wil . . . My name is Wil."

We stood there, eyes locked, the sweat gathering at my temples.

Finally, he shook his head, looking more amused than impressed. "I ask you a question, tough guy—Weel. Why you no answer me? You making a move? Or can Lito put his fucking gun away before he shoots you by accident?"

I glanced at Carlito. "Tell him if he touches me again, I'm going to make him wish he'd shot me when he had the chance."

Carlito stiffened beside me.

But Kiki just laughed. Which set the dogs off again. "Shhhh! Shhhh! *Trunquilo*," he said, stroking the flank of one of the big animals. "You are one tough-talking *hombre*. I'm thinking you watch too much goddamn television."

He turned to the third member of his crew, who stood in the shadows at the back of the van, a fat man with a shaved head and baggy jeans that buttoned well below his belly. "You keep watch, Turo. Let me know soon as you see the headlights, eh?"

Turo stepped away from the van, a sawed-off twelve gauge dangling in one meaty hand. "Shit, Kiki. Goddamn bugs gonna eat me alive," he complained. "Why can't Lito watch? 'Squitos don't bother him none. Don't even know the skinny fuck is there."

Kiki glared at him.

Scowling, Turo hiked up his jeans and did as he was told.

Kiki, Carlito, and I entered the dark house through the kitchen.

A platoon of palmetto bugs the size of small mice skittered away as Kiki flicked on the lights and we stepped inside.

The place smelled of stale sweat and tobacco, marijuana and booze, and something darker, uglier. It looked a little better than it smelled—but not much. Sagging plywood cabinets and gouged laminate countertops, a rusty stove and a dented refrigerator that might or might not work, a dinette table with three legs and four chairs. Flies buzzed and flitted over a rusted fifty-gallon drum overflowing with beer cans, empty bottles, and crusted food containers.

"You guys *live* here?" I asked.

Carlito whacked me on the back with the gun. "*¡Chingado pendejo!*"

I turned on him.

Kiki moved quickly. Stepping between us, he took the gun from Carlito and stuck it in the waistband of his pants. "Open some windows, Lito. Air this fucking place out. Then wait with Turo in the shed."

Carlito did as he was told, first fixing me with a look of pure malice.

Kiki grabbed my elbow and steered me into what nominally could be called a living room.

"What the hell was *that*?" he demanded, walking to the nearest window, turning the crank to open it. "You want to get shot? Got your hands tied behind your back and still you acting all macho. What you going to do? Bite *Lito*? Crazy motherfucker! What's wrong with you? I didn't know better, I'd think you were *Cubano—Marielito!* You got that bad attitude."

I wasn't sure whether or not it was a compliment.

"What now?" I asked, looking around.

"Now, we wait," Kiki said.

The bare concrete room was furnished with a couple of couches upholstered in stained Herculon, a table made out of an empty cable spool, two greasy-looking velvet reclining chairs, and a brand-new Mitsubishi big-screen television set with a high-tech VCR, Surround Sound speakers, and the most elaborate remote control I had ever seen.

The place didn't seem to fit Kiki and his flashy clothes and smooth moves. Not the graffiti scribbled on the walls, not the *Hustler* magazine centerfolds tacked up over the graffiti. Not the filthy couches or the overflowing garbage can.

But the dogs had seemed to know him well enough . . .

He plopped down onto one of the reclining chairs, a slight sheen of sweat on his face, the only sign that he wasn't here to watch a ball game. Gesturing toward one of the couches, he said, "Sit."

"What are we waiting for?" I asked, not wanting to sit.

He tossed Tessereau's book onto the cable-spool table without so much as glancing at it. Then he pulled a long switchblade out of his suit-coat pocket and snapped it open. He held up his hands and began working the tip of the skinny blade under his fingernails.

He was through talking.

I sat on the couch. "How about cutting me loose?" I asked.

No response.

"Come on, where am I going to go? You guys have the guns."

He looked up from his hands, but said nothing.

"At least tell me what this is about?" I asked, trying to draw him out.

"You don't shut up, I'm going to give Carlito permission to take you out in the swamp and teach you some goddamn manners," he growled.

I shook my head. "I don't think so. You wanted me dead, I'd be dead."

"Maybe you think too much." He frowned and dug at his nails. But we both knew I was right.

"Who killed your friend?" I asked, breathing a little easier.

He stared at me. "You talk too fucking much too."

"Why kill him?" I persisted. "Did they kill him because he blew it?"

"Shut the fuck up!" he ordered.

"Maybe they'll kill you too."

His face grew dark. "*¡Tú no sabes ni mierda!* You don't know shit!"

"I know that the kid you sent to get the file—your friend—is dead. Shot in the back of the head."

In a flash, he was on his feet. I didn't have time to react. One second he was sitting, digging at his fingernails. The next, he'd coiled and moved—the tip of his switchblade pressed hard against the hollow of my throat.

I felt a trickle of blood run down my neck.

"No friend of mine, *cabrón. Ése chivato pura mierda.*" He grinned wickedly, then spit on the floor, his eyes glittering, his knuckles white on the handle of his switchblade. "They should have sent me. Not some kid trying to earn his bones. I come for the file, I leave with the fucking file. Anyone gives me trouble— I kill them. Not just the woman. Everyone. But first, they going to tell me where it is. They *going* to tell me or I burn that fucking mansion to the ground with everyone inside. Nobody has to clean my mess. Nobody!"

I shuddered, knowing Kiki and his crew were capable of doing it just the way he said.

"What's wrong, tough guy? You got nothing to say now?" he taunted, pulling the blade back from my throat.

When I didn't answer, his face split into a huge smile, gold teeth flashing. He sat down on his recliner, and poking his thumb at his chest, he said, "I do business, *pendejo*. I take a job, I finish it, *Meester Weel*. Now you are going to do what you're told. You don't fuck up—and maybe you don't end up in the swamp, no?"

Before I could say anything, Turo shouted through the kitchen door, "*Oye*, he's coming, man. I can see the lights."

34

KIKI JUMPED UP, POCKETING his knife, his face flushed with excitement. "Stay here!" he ordered, shouting for Carlito to come into the room and watch over me.

I started to rise, then sat back down when Carlito hustled in, his knotted fishing line clutched in one long, thin hand. He was breathing hard. "Car's just pulling up, Kiki. Looks like there are three of them. The man, his driver, and a bodyguard. You want me to do anything?"

Kiki shook his head and pointed at me. "Make sure *he* stays put."

He turned and started for the kitchen, then stopped short and pulled Carlito's gun out of his waistband. Returning it, he said, "Lito—when I bring him in, don't say nothing, man. Just listen and learn. These people don't fuck around." Without waiting for an answer, he hurried out of the room.

Carlito stared after him, then settled into Kiki's recliner.

Their voices carried clearly from the kitchen.

I sat on the couch, listening to them talk in Spanish. Short, sharp questions from a deep, mellifluous voice I didn't recognize—followed by long, elaborate answers from Kiki.

Then, a whispered exchange I could barely hear.

I didn't understand a word.

After a while, Kiki came back into the living room to retrieve Tessereau's book from where he'd tossed it onto the cable spool. He looked down at me, his expression hostile, but said nothing, nodding to Carlito as he headed back to the kitchen.

More Spanish.

Laughter, followed by the sound of water running into the sink and the clink of glasses.

While this was going on, Carlito stared at me from Kiki's chair. A thin man with a very fat gun. A gun he sat stroking while his eyes burned holes in me.

I returned his stare, but it didn't make me feel very tough.

Finally, the conversation in the kitchen ended and Kiki ushered a tall, well-dressed man into the living room. He looked to be in his early fifties.

Carlito stood and eyed the man warily, then moved to a corner of the room, giving the stranger a wide berth.

The man looked around, a bemused expression on his clean-shaven, handsome face. He was dark, his thick hair longish, gray at the temples and combed back off his high forehead. He wore a good smile and a tan gabardine suit that looked like it had been cut by a tailor who knew the difference between style and fashion. He held Tessereau's book in his left hand, a long cigar in his right.

"You never heard of air freshener?" he asked Kiki, drawing on his cigar.

Kiki shook his head. "The place will air out in a few minutes," he said, not sounding too sure.

The newcomer nodded. Then, he looked at me, slapping the book lightly against his thigh. There was something lazy in his heavily lidded eyes. Something cruel. "Mr. Sumner, it was very nice of you to take the time to meet with me."

He said it straight, not a hint of a smile despite how ludicrous the words sounded.

I met his steady gaze. "What do you want with me?"

Smiling, he drew on his cigar and blew out a cloud of rich,

blue smoke. He eyed the couch across from me, then shrugged and sat down on it.

"Cut those ropes," he ordered Kiki. "We have business to discuss."

"'*Business*'?" I said.

"Business makes the world go round, Mr. Sumner," he answered, his languid eyes shining while Kiki used his switchblade to cut me loose.

I rubbed my wrists where the ropes had chafed them. "Maybe I don't want to do that kind of business."

Kiki muttered something threatening. But the man waved him off.

Chewing thoughtfully on his cigar, he blinked slowly. "Come now, Mr. Sumner. Given the situation, would you have responded if I'd picked up the telephone? Of course not. You'd have hung up on me and called the police. In any case, you're here. Have you been badly treated?"

I looked from Kiki to Carlito, then said, "I'll live."

"I certainly hope so," the man said, nodding and grinning. "Life is too precious to waste on matters of so little importance, no?"

When I didn't answer, he shrugged and continued. "I know this is an inconvenience for you, so I'll come directly to the point. We should be working together. Otherwise, you're wasting your time. This appraisal of yours is canceled. There's no way to know if you'll be asked to finish it. The collection *isn't* being offered for sale. You're not buying, you're not selling. You're not even earning an hourly fee. Not what I would call a profitable scenario." He sat back and crossed his legs.

He drew on the cigar until the tip glowed bright, then shook his head. "Unrelated to your predicament, we also have a problem. A most unfortunate problem. And, sadly, it also stems from the Stevenson situation. So far, our intermediary has been unable to deliver on his promises. So I have decided to help matters along."

He was so polished and self-assured, I wondered if he actually believed that Amanda's murder could be summed up as the "Stevenson situation." I tried to keep the anger off my face.

I didn't succeed.

He studied me through a veil of cigar smoke. Then he nodded. "I can see you are offended. That is unfortunate. Let me point out the obvious—maybe it will take the sting out of all of this. You want Stevenson's art collection. I can see that you get it."

It took a moment for what he was saying to sink in.

"Don't look so surprised. I represent a powerful group of men. Pragmatic men who aren't afraid to lead—to do what needs to be done. Stevenson isn't the only art collector in Florida. His collection is not beyond our reach."

I nodded dumbly. "Who are these men? What does Stevenson have on them?"

He ignored the questions. "We arrange for you to handle the collection, and in return you render us a simple service. A favor. That's all. Do as we ask, and you can be in Italy within a day or two. Attend the auctions, carry on with your schedule as if none of this had happened. We'll see that you have funds to operate—to buy inventory. Then, when the time comes, you will handle the sale of the Stevenson collection. Provided, of course, that you and I can come to equitable terms now."

I was speechless. How could he offer to deliver Andrew's collection? Who the hell *did* he represent? Something about going to the auctions in Italy tweaked a vague memory, but I couldn't put my finger on it. I rubbed my chafed wrists, trying to think of something to say to gain time while I tried to make sense of the whirlwind of thoughts spinning inside my head.

Kiki and Carlito stood watching, silently taking it all in.

"Well?" the man asked.

"Equitable is a damn *big* word," I answered, still groping for some pattern to his promises. It was there, but I couldn't get my hands around it.

"Big is also a relative term, Mr. Sumner." He paused. "May I call you Wil?"

I nodded. "What should I call you?"

He smiled easily. He was good at smiling, a born diplomat. "You may call me whatever you wish. It's unimportant."

"Why me? Why not someone else?"

"You are uniquely positioned to help us."

I'd heard that one before, from Laspada. "What, exactly, is this favor you're asking?"

He thought for a moment, rolling the cigar between his thumb and first two fingers. "I think you know what we want. The question is—are you willing to help us get it?"

I touched the tender spot behind my ear where Carlito had hit me. "I'm not sure I like your business methods."

He shook his head, looking disappointed. "That's too bad, Wil. Actually, you don't have that much choice after all." He leaned forward and pointed his cigar at my face. "You see, we want the file. Mrs. Stevenson's death was a mistake." He glanced at Kiki. "No one was to be harmed—but mistakes happen. The person responsible has been sanctioned. It's my wish, my sincere intention, that no more mistakes occur. It would be tragic if any-thing unfortunate happened to either Andrew Stevenson—or his lovely daughter."

I wanted to knock that confident look off his well-groomed face. But I wanted even more to get out of there. So I nodded and asked, "Are you sure this file really exists?"

Hesitating, he considered his next words carefully. "The file exists. We've been sent a sample of the contents—as a warning. Personally, I found it less than compelling. But my people aren't interested in seeing Stevenson's little vendetta made pub-lic. It's ancient history, but the timing is bad and the crowning achievement of an important man's life is at stake. I suppose that's reason enough to destroy the damned thing. You are going to help me."

"And if I don't?"

"Do not play games with me," he said sharply. "I haven't the time or the interest."

I looked at him.

He calmly stared back.

"*Las Flechas Azúles*. Who are they? What's their agenda?" I asked after a moment.

The question took him by surprise. He stiffened. For a second I thought I'd gone too far. Then he laughed, lifting Tessereau's book from where it rested in his lap. "More ancient history. Bad luck that you would find a memoir such as this. You recognized the old symbol, no? Years ago I told him not to use it. An arrogant bit of foolishness—a vanity. Another error in judgment. Trust me when I tell you it is the last."

He tossed the book to Kiki, who snatched it cleanly out of the air. "Put this in my car!" the man ordered.

Kiki nodded. *"No problema."*

The man glanced at his watch, a thick, gold Rolex. "Have you ever heard the expression *plata o plomo*?"

"No," I admitted.

"The Colombian cocaine cartels use this expression to convey a very simple idea. It means silver or lead. I think it fits our situation rather nicely. We're offering you a profit to help us. Silver, no? If you're foolish enough to refuse . . . Well, then I'm afraid we offer you nothing but a bullet. Lead . . ."

"And if I try, but fail?"

"No *ifs* about it. You will try, and you will succeed. It's that simple." Turning to Kiki, he said, "Go and get the rum. Mr. Sumner looks like he could use a drink."

Kiki disappeared into the kitchen, carrying Tessereau's book.

Carlito cleared his throat, then followed him out of the room.

The man looked at me. He drew on his cigar, then regarded it appreciatively. "You smoke, Wil?"

"Occasionally," I answered. Something about his face was tugging at my memory.

"Try this," he said, reaching into his suit pocket and pulling out another cigar. "I think you'll find it exceptional."

He tossed it to me.

I caught it, wondering about Stevenson's "little vendetta." How ancient was it? Gaines had to know more than he was saying. Why else was he keeping everyone away? I fingered the cigar, ready to find Gaines and get some straight answers. One way or another. First, I had to get out of here.

"You can't buy these . . . ," he was saying, ". . . made to my specifications in Havana. The rarest aged Cuban tobacco, production limited to two hundred a year—smoke them only on special occasions. Hand-rolled by a patriot who fought at the Bay of Pigs. Caught a mortar round, lost both legs. Wouldn't have happened if the air support Kennedy promised had arrived. But that's another story, isn't it? A matter of leadership. Someday I'll bring this man to Miami. Set him up with a little shop over on the beach. Until then, I'm forced to bring these in clandestinely. Go ahead. . . . Try it."

The cigar had a distinctive ring embossed with a gold lion against a royal blue ground. I nipped the end of it with my teeth and he flicked open a heavy gold lighter.

"Good, no?" he asked when I had it going.

Sitting back on the couch, I nodded and puffed and thought about his offer of *plata o plomo*. Did that make this a special occasion?

He seemed content to sit and watch the tendrils of smoke climb from the tip of his cigar.

Then Kiki came out of the kitchen with two large glasses half filled with dark rum. He handed one to the man, the other to me.

"*¡Salud!*" the man said, draining his glass in three large swallows. "To doing business."

I held my glass up and took a long swallow, then another. The rum was raw and burned a hole in my gut. My eyes watered.

"We understand each other, no?" he said, standing.

A question occurred to me, but it floated away before I could voice it.

"Why don't you just give Stevenson what he wants for the file?" I asked.

He shook his head. "The price he asks is too steep, my friend."

"How much?"

"It's not a matter of dollars. If it were, this would have been settled long ago. No, I'm afraid this is a matter of honor."

He smiled broadly at me. My new best friend. Bastard!

I smiled back at him and downed more rum.

Suddenly it seemed so simple. A rosy glow suffused the room. My smile grew. I'd just keep nodding and smiling till they let me go. Pretend to go along with the plan. I swallowed more rum, pleased at how cunningly clever I was being.

A thought hovered at the back of my brain, but it kept sliding away. I took a deep breath, shook my head to clear it. Too much rum too fast, I thought. The house seemed hot. My skin tingled.

Something was wrong.

The man pulled a pen from the pocket of his suit and wrote something on a piece of paper. "Call when you have the file. Understand? Leave word, and someone will come for it." He reached across the cable-spool table and dropped the paper into my lap.

I started to protest that I needed a name, that I might run into complications and need to speak with him, but the words came out jumbled. I gulped air and tried to think clearly. But there was a light fog dancing in the corners of the room. And whatever was wrong suddenly seemed very wrong.

But it was too late. The cigar fell out of my hand onto the couch. The room tilted on its axis and I was seeing everything through the wrong end of a telescope.

Then he was leaning over me and I was looking up at him from the floor, his face the kindest, wisest face I had ever seen.

"Wait," I gurgled, pawing at his lapel.

"It's late, Mr. Sumner. Get some rest." He tucked something into my pocket. Then he patted me a little too hard on my cut cheek.

It stung like hell and my vision cleared for a second. "Hey!"

"Call the number within twenty-four hours. Let it ring until someone answers. After that . . ."

He straightened up and his face receded, growing smaller and smaller. It was too small for his body. Someone ought to tell him.

I blinked and the fog thickened and I could hear music as if from a great distance. Opening my eyes, I saw that the music was Kiki speaking to the man in Spanish. Somewhere a woman called out. But I was too tired to listen.

Too bad . . .

Such a sad, sweet song . . .

Carlito and Kiki had me under the arms and were dragging

me into the kitchen. Kiki doused me with more rum. I giggled.

The fumes stung my nose. And that was funny too.

Then I felt sick. The light was too bright and somehow too dim, the air both hot and cold, the floor a living thing that rose up to meet my feet with each step.

"Bye—bye," I croaked.

Then the waves closed over me.

I was sinking down. Down to where it was blue and quiet.

My mother was there. Only it was Amanda.

Don't drink the rum, I screamed.

35

AT FIRST, I DIDN'T KNOW who was shoving his foot at me. Cracking open my eyes, I squinted up at the dark silhouette of a man framed against a brilliant pink sunrise. I lay curled at the foot of what looked like the Stevensons' seawall, my mouth full of grit, my head pounding, my clothes wet and stinking, wishing someone would turn out the goddamn lights.

"Stop," I groaned, closing my eyes. How I'd ended up on the beach was a mystery, but at the moment, it didn't seem important. All I wanted was to be left alone—to die in peace.

My tormentor had other ideas. He kept prodding me with that heavy work boot.

"Get away." I slapped weakly at his foot.

He just prodded harder, digging a steel-jacketed toe into my ribs. "Get up!" he commanded gruffly. "What wrong wit you? You gone stupid in the head?"

I recognized Maj's voice. Spitting out a mouthful of sand, I croaked, "Thank God. I need water."

"What you be needin' is a kick in the head. Now, get up! Dis no time for you to be layin' out. Me and Charteen been sittin' in that kitchen all night—waitin' on you, or some word from M.K."

I clawed my way up to a sitting position. Brushing sand and

sleep out of my eyes, I asked, "Layin' out? What's that supposed to mean?" My voice was steadier than my hands, but it sounded like it was coming from the bottom of a stone-lined pit. "I'm not layin'—"

"Why you do dis?" he interrupted. "Why you drinkin' now? Of all the stupid, bumbleclod . . ." He stood shaking his head, hands on his hips, a look of undisguised disgust twisting his features. "What be wrong wit you, mon?"

"I haven't been drinking," I whispered.

"Bullshit!" He hawked and spit. "You lookin' and smellin' drunk as a damn cane cutter on Saturday night. And that plenty damn drunk, you know."

I shook my head, drew the back of my hand across crusted lips. "It's not what it looks like."

He snorted. "And I ain't black and dis ain't daylight a comin'."

Shivering in my sodden clothes, I reached out a shaky hand. "Help me up. I'll explain."

He didn't take it. "Explain what? That you ain't drunk? You smellin' like hell, lookin' raggedy as a mango seed. M.K. gone and you layin' out all night wit a bottle a rum. Ain't nothin' to explain. Not one damn t'ing."

Closing my eyes, I breathed deeply.

Then his words penetrated the mist in my head. "Gone? What do you mean she's gone?"

He shook his head. "What I say? I say she gone. That ain't too damn hard to understand. She gone. Now, the mornin' passin'— you plannin' to explain this mystery? Or you plannin' to sit there moanin' like a kitten all day?"

"How do you know she's gone?"

"She gone alright. Mr. Gaines up there to the house now— tearin' up Mr. Andrew's room, searchin' for that damn file. Already tore up the library—he sayin' they called him, that they gone kill her if they don't get it."

I managed to climb to my feet, but the effort made my head spin. "I've got to get to the house. Need to talk to Gaines."

Wrinkling his nose, he grabbed my arm and steadied me. "Seem to me the time for talkin' be over."

I held onto him until the world stopped spinning.

"You ain't drunk, what be wrong wit you?" he asked, searching my face, suddenly looking concerned.

"They picked me up last night—outside Tessereau's place. Knocked me on the head and threw me into a van. Drove me out to a house in the swamps—then they drugged me."

I tried to bring the previous night into some kind of focus, but it was all a blur. "I'm not drunk, Maj. They drugged me. Gave me twenty-four hours to deliver the file. Gave me a number to call." I searched my pockets and came up with a soggy wad of paper; the number was barely legible.

He hesitated, looking at the paper in my hand. "Who? Who be doin' this?"

"I don't know. Doesn't make sense to take M.K. . . . Why call Gaines?" A sudden chill rocked me. I couldn't shake the feeling that somehow this was my fault, that I should have prevented it. M.K.'s face swam in front of my eyes, the sweep of her blonde hair. Then, Lito and his knotted fishing line. I shuddered at the thought.

Maj put his arm around my waist, his expression softening. "No tellin' what they done give you," he said, guiding me toward the beach gate. "Need to be seein' a doctor. Come on, I get you to the house."

"No doctors. Andrew's the key. We want the file, we have to see Andrew."

He nodded. "Sure we do. But now you best lean on old Maj. We gone take it nice and easy. Get you out a them wet clothes. Then we figure out what to do 'bout Mister Andrew."

I pocketed the phone number, and together we moved slowly down the beach.

We hadn't gone five steps when he stopped and let out a low whistle. "Look there, mon. Look what they done, Wil." He pointed at the seawall.

The graffiti, the blue yoke and arrows, had been sprayed over. What had been a decipherable symbol was now a jumble of meaningless initials and crude profanity.

36

MAJ AND I FOUND GAINES standing in Andrew's closet. He'd torn the bedroom apart. Clothing was strewn everywhere, drawers were upended, their contents spread in piles on the floor. Now, he stood surrounded by Andrew's cashmere sweaters, looking like he was going to scream.

Charteen sat on the edge of Andrew's bed watching the young lawyer through the closet door, her face sagging with exhaustion.

Ignoring Gaines, Maj convinced Charteen to go lie down in the guest room and get some rest.

He helped her up and escorted her toward the door.

She stopped in front of me and pinned me with her tired brown eyes. "Don't you let 'em hurt her. Don't let 'em do that girl no harm."

I nodded. "I'll do everything I can."

She stared at me a moment longer. "I be prayin' that be enough." Then, leaning on Maj, she shuffled from the room.

I turned to Gaines. "What happened?"

"I've looked everywhere," he explained, waving his arms. "It's got to be here. It's got to be somewhere in this house . . ."

"Tell me what happened," I repeated.

He opened his mouth, hesitated, then spoke brusquely.

"They took her. Grabbed her as she left the hospital. I thought she was here, but they already had her. They must have been waiting in the parking lot."

"When did it happen? How long ago?"

He began pawing through Andrew's sweaters. "Last night."

"Where were the police? Why wasn't anyone watching her?" I demanded.

He abandoned the sweaters. Then, ignoring my questions, he started pulling hats down from the closet shelves.

"It's not there, Gaines. We've already searched this room."

He turned and stared at me, his forehead beaded with perspiration.

"Well?" I said.

He didn't answer.

"Damnit, Gaines, say something! Where the hell were your police?"

He shook his head. "It's not my fault. None of this had to happen."

"Then why *did* it happen? Why didn't you see that she was protected? Where the hell were you?" I wanted to grab him, shake some answers out of him. But he didn't seem to have any.

"Out of my way," he said, stepping around me. "There's no time to argue about this. I've got to find that file. It's got to be somewhere in this house."

He headed for the door.

Maj, coming back into Andrew's bedroom, nearly collided with Gaines. Stepping out of the lawyer's way, he looked at me.

I shrugged. "Says it's not his fault."

Maj started to say something, then shook his head, frowning.

The two of us followed Gaines down the stairs and into the living room. He stopped in front of the window by the piano and stared out at the sunrise. "Where the fuck could he have hidden it?" he muttered, clenching and unclenching his hands.

I watched him for a moment, then spoke softly. "What exactly did they say?"

He stared out at the sea, a haunted look in his eyes. "It's out of control now."

"What's out of control?" I demanded. "What's this about?"

Turning on me, he snarled, "*It's* out of my control. Can't you see that? They'll kill her."

"Who are these people?" I asked, trying to keep my voice level. He just stared at me. "They gave me a phone number." I took the wet paper out of my pocket and shoved it at him. "Is it the same?"

He looked at the number, then at me. "How did you get this?"

I didn't answer him. "What's going on here, Gaines?"

"You don't understand one goddamn thing!" he exploded.

If I'd felt better, I'd have knocked him down then and there. Instead, I kept my voice flat. "Explain it to me."

He laughed, a bitter sound. "Time, Sumner. Our time is running out."

I stared at him for a moment, then the wet and the fatigue and whatever they'd doctored my drink with caught up with me. A shudder shook my body. Wrapping my arms around myself, I turned to Maj. "I've got to get out of these wet clothes. You call Captain Laspada—tell him what's happened. I'll change, then we'll go see Andrew."

"No!" Gaines shook his head violently. "There's no time. I sent the police away. They'll kill her if they find out the police are involved."

I hesitated.

"They'll kill her," Gaines repeated.

Maj spoke up for the first time. "Mon be right, Wil. Call 'em— them cops spend two days askin' us stupid damn questions. Best we find this file ourselves and give it up quick as we can."

I nodded. "Maybe . . ."

Gaines's face turned a heated shade of red. "Now the fucking gardener is calling the shots."

He turned away from us and ran both hands through his thick blond curls. "I'll handle this myself—you two stay out of my way. It's not your problem."

Maj kept his thoughts to himself, but his expression said plenty.

"You've already had your shot," I snapped at Gaines's back.

"Now they have M.K. We'll see Andrew, find the file. Then I'll decide about the police."

He whirled and stared coldly at me. "Why are you doing this?"

The question caught me by surprise. I stared at him. It was a question I'd avoided asking myself, one I didn't know how to answer.

"I'm going out to M.K.'s apartment," I said. "I'm going to change clothes, then you're driving us to the hospital to see Andrew."

He shook his head. "You're a fool, Sumner. I was at the hospital till three in the morning. He's still sedated. And if he was awake, I doubt he'd remember his own name, much less where he's hidden the damned thing."

"Then it's time to convince the doctors to unsedate him. And *you're* going to help me do it." I turned to Maj. "Bring Mr. Gaines with us. I don't trust him out of our sight."

Maj frowned, then nodded.

He stepped over to the lawyer and took him by the elbow. "We do it like the mon say."

Gaines moved to pull away, but Maj just tightened his grip and the lawyer winced in pain.

He stared hard at me for a moment, his face lit with hatred. "You're going to regret this. You're way the hell out of line here."

But the edge was gone from his voice.

Then his shoulders slumped, and he looked both defeated and strangely relieved as Maj led him out of the living room.

37

ANDREW LOOKED BETTER THAN I'd expected. Not great, but not nearly as bad as Gaines had led me to believe. He lay still in his hospital bed, a tangle of wires leading from his frail chest to a bank of monitors on the wall that glowed and beeped softly. IV tubes punctured each forearm. A scratchy silver stubble lay thick on his hollowed cheeks and a stale, sour smell rose from his wrinkled sheets. He had the pasty look of someone who'd been doped up for a solid month, but other than that, he seemed little changed by his ordeal.

His room, a glassed-in alcove, was one in a long row of similar glassed-in spaces circling a central nurses' station. The ICU was doing a booming business. Every bed was filled, but the crowded unit was hushed. An occasional moan or sigh, monitors beeping, the squeak of crepe-soled shoes on polished linoleum and the tap tap tap of a keyboard as a serious-looking nurse updated someone's medical chart.

According to the signs posted at the nurses' station, patients were allowed one visitor at a time for no longer than fifteen minutes, once every two hours.

No exceptions!

Fifteen minutes ... I hoped Gaines had exaggerated the decline in Stevenson's mental faculties too.

I leaned over the bed and touched his arm. "Mr. Stevenson— it's me, Wil Sumner."

He started and opened his eyes. "What?!"

I couldn't tell whether or not he recognized me. "It's me, Wil—the appraiser. I need your help."

He groaned and closed his eyes. "It's too late ... You're too late."

"Please. Try and wake up. It's about M.K."

He opened his eyes and drew a breath to say something, but before he could get the words out he started coughing. Mildly at first, but it got worse and worse. Deep, wracking, chest-rattling coughs.

Alarmed, I shouted, "I'll get the nurse."

But before I could turn away, he grabbed my wrist with a skeletal hand, his grip surprisingly strong. "No ... ," he sputtered, struggling to regain his breath. "No nurse. No more shots. Can't concentrate—they don't listen. Won't believe ..." He pointed a shaky finger at the nightstand. "Water. Some water. ... I'll be okay."

I poured him a cup from the plastic pitcher by the bed, then held it up to his mouth.

He gulped it gratefully, spilling only a little down the front of his hospital gown.

"The bastard killed her," he whispered, wiping at his neck with palsied hands. "What day is it? I feel like hell. It all runs together ..."

"Monday. We've been looking for—"

"Monday?" he interrupted, blinking.

I confirmed that it was Monday morning, then tried to ask about the file, but he interrupted me again, his voice stronger, but still hoarse. "Get the police. Go, now, and call them. I should have spoken to them first—before I sent him word of the file. But I thought ... God forgive me, I wanted to protect my own good name. All these years ... I thought the time had come, that he couldn't hurt me." He clenched a handful of the sheets, his mouth working. "I was a fool—now Amanda's dead."

I shook my head. "It's too late for the police. That's what I've been trying to tell you. They have M.K."

"What?" His eyes grew wide and he struggled to sit up. "When? When did they take her?"

"Sometime last night. They want the file. Once they have it, they'll let her go."

He grabbed my arm, his eyes wild. "But it didn't work. I should have known it wouldn't. It's not enough."

"What are you saying?"

"The file . . . I tried to scare him—to shake him up, make him withdraw. I wanted to put an end to it." He let go of my arm and sank back against his pillows. "Christ . . . What have I done?"

"Who? Who are you talking about?"

He stared up at me and whatever life was left in him seemed on the verge of leaking away. "You're an art dealer . . . It's not your battle. Call the police."

"They'll kill her if we call the police."

He turned his face away from me. "They'll kill her anyway."

"Goddamnit! That's not good enough. She's your daughter. Look at me! Tell me what this is about."

He faced me and I saw that he was crying.

"We have to fight them."

He closed his eyes. "How? How can we fight?"

"We'll use the file."

"What if it's not enough?" he said. "There is no smoking gun."

"They don't know that! They killed for it. But I have to know who we're dealing with. All of it."

He searched my face, then nodded at whatever answers he found there. "The bastard will be ready. He'll see you coming—he knows I know . . ."

"But I don't. So tell me."

He grabbed the shiny bars of his bed and tried to pull himself up, then fell back, his face twisted with pain.

"Easy," I said.

His eyes bulged and his mouth moved, but he couldn't speak.

He turned white and started to tremble. I thought the coughing was going to start again. Then the spasm passed as suddenly as it had begun.

"Do you need a doctor?" I asked, as stupid a question as any I'd ever asked.

He almost smiled. "No . . . No doctors. No more dope. We need time—time to talk," he rasped, reaching out for my arm with trembling fingers. "Pour me some more water. . . ."

I refilled his cup, thinking I should call the nurse anyway.

But he read the look on my face and shook his head. "No doctors," he repeated. "By the time they decide what to do with me . . ." His voice trailed off.

He managed a slight shrug, drained the cup, and handed it back to me. Then, using a control button pinned to the sheets by his head, he raised the back of the hospital bed to a more comfortable position.

"Sit down." He indicated a chair by the window. "You need to understand the history."

Staring past me, his gaze focused on the wall beyond the foot of his bed, he sat very still, his chest rising and falling in time with the monitor's beeping.

I waited, but it wasn't a hospital room Andrew Stevenson was seeing.

"There was a war coming . . . We all knew it . . . ," he began, his voice faltering.

I leaned closer.

His words are as follows, as best as I can reconstruct them.

38

THERE WAS A WAR COMING. We all knew it. But we didn't talk much about it and it didn't seem to worry my parents. Not at first.

"Modern war means business," my father used to say. "Profits and trade." The prospect of armed conflict didn't trouble him in the least. After all, he'd already had his war—the First World War. And from what he told me, it was a very good war.

Profits . . .

Madrid was the heart of the country. But by the mid-thirties, all of Spain was in turmoil. Including Madrid. It was about land reform, workers' rights, a matter of opportunity and sharing the wealth. But that smacked of communism and the natural backlash was already popping up all over Europe. Hitler, Mussolini— but we didn't see fascism for the evil it was. Not then. Not yet. Communism was the threat. Disrupting the flow of "profits," upsetting the centuries-old natural order of things, that was the big crime.

God knows there were profits enough to go around. . . .

My father was one of the first to recognize the enormous market for American technology in Europe. He moved the family to Madrid in 1930, just before the political left came to power and proclaimed the Second Republic. That was the beginning of the end. But politics was just a word to me. I was nine and I hated Spain. I didn't have the language yet. No friends. No baseball. The Yankees were hot—the Babe batted .359—and I missed it all. Over there it was soccer, soccer, soccer—football, they called it, but it was nothing like the football I knew about.

We lived in a large town house in the Salamanca neighborhood—not far from the Prado and the Retiro gardens. My parents entertained lavishly, parties several nights a week. Music, cigars, cards—this diplomat and general, that banker and his wife. Sometimes large parties of foreign dignitaries. If they counted, my father courted them. Even the Generalissimo— Franco himself. But I'm getting ahead of my story.

Eventually, it paid off. My father represented ITT in one of the biggest international trades they ever closed. Sold the Spanish government their first modern phone system. A nationwide system. Profits . . .

Still own ITT stock—a lot of it . . .

I remember the house like it was yesterday. Three stories, long, dark halls, the scent of leather and good tobacco in my father's study, thick Bukhara rugs and paintings of Arabs on horseback and in their harems by Edwin Lord Weeks. God, I loved those paintings. Servants and cooks. Two maids for every floor. Girls with names like Juanita and Rosa. Pretty girls from Saragossa in the north and Andalusia in the south—girls from the countryside with big hands and white teeth who giggled and made me wish I were older and could understand what they were saying. We had a courtyard with a tiled fountain and orange trees in huge clay pots.

The demonstrations came later. Thousands of factory workers and peasants crowded into the city parks for weeks on end. I would look at them on my way to school or my riding lessons; they were dirty and gaunt faced, and I remember wondering what they wanted, why they weren't working. Our servants were all clean and well fed—they seemed happy enough. What was wrong with this smelly lot? How little I knew. How precious little I understood.

At first there was hardly any trouble. The country people were on their best behavior. But you don't crowd that many hungry, homeless people into a city without conflict erupting. And when it did, it was always the fault of the communists. They were undermining the best of what Spain had to offer. Agitating, lawless—unruly animals. And the larger the crowds of these poor workers and farmers grew, the more virulent the rhetoric of the fascists became. But we believed them. The fascists. We wanted to believe them. It was expedient to believe them. You see, the communists weren't generating any business. Only trouble. And the socialists in power couldn't succeed with their policies of agrarian reform and appeasement. Not with the church lined up against them. And the church was quick to turn its back on these uneducated peasants and the leftist politicians who represented them—after all, it was perfectly clear to the clergy which side their bread was buttered on.

In the end, the church became the lever that turned it all upside down.

There were elections in 1936—the Popular Front, the left, came to power. And everything went to hell. Tensions between the right and the left—the aristocracy and the church on one side, the peasants and factory workers on the other—threatened to engulf the entire country in flames.

Spain was ripe for civil war.

But the middle class wasn't quite ready for the upheaval and bloodshed that was sure to follow. And without the middle class—the rank and file—civil war was too risky a business.

So the fascists set out to convince these bourgeois Spaniards that life with the communists was unlivable.

This proved easier than you might think. Provocation after provocation—some of them out and out atrocities—all blamed on the communists.

I know—I did my part.

And I'll live with it until the day I die. Maybe longer . . .

You see, my war started on a winter night in 1936. I was all of fifteen. Fifteen years old! Can you imagine?

One of my neighbors, a boy my age whose father was a ranking Spanish general, a fat and powerful man my father often entertained, came to our house with his parents for dinner.

Ernesto Caldero and I had met many times over the years, but he ran in a different, more sophisticated crowd than I. He was tall and haughty in that upper-class *madrileño* way. He had the swagger, the attitude. But his mother was American—he had dual citizenship—and he spoke English as well as I did. Only he pretended not to whenever it was convenient to distance himself from all things American. A not unusual sentiment in Europe during the thirties. He came from money on both sides of the Atlantic, but there was something dark in him, something cold and cruel that both attracted and repelled me.

That night, I just wanted to impress him. Show him that I wasn't just another ugly American.

It was February, cold and bleak. The winds swirled down from the high sierra north of the city and drove the party inside. All but Ernesto and I. We stood on the second-floor balcony of my father's study, looking out at the empty courtyard, talking, smoking cigarettes.

At least he had a cigarette stuck in his mouth, but he didn't have any matches.

Inside the house, the party was in high gear. We could hear them—muted snatches of conversation in a kaleidoscope of languages snared by the wind and carried up to where we stood on the balcony. Guitar music, bright laughter.

I pulled my jacket closer, trying to shut out the noise of the party and concentrate on what Ernesto was saying.

"We're organizing all over the country. Different groups—all part of the youth Falange, the Blue Shirts. I've started my own group," he bragged, his unlit cigarette bobbing between his teeth. "We call ourselves the Blue Arrows."

He paused and patted his pockets, looking again for matches. "You sure you don't have a light?" he asked.

I shook my head. "Tell me more about the arrows."

Ernesto scowled. "Not the *arrows*. The Blue Arrows."

"I know. I know. Can anyone join?"

He shook his head. "Get me a light. Then I'll tell you about our

group." He narrowed his eyes. "I might even let you come along—
we have something special planned for tonight. Something the
reds will think about for a long, long time. But first, get me some
matches."

I hurried off the balcony and into my father's study, looking
for a box of matches. I didn't mind doing his errand. You see, I
wanted to go along with the Blue Arrows. I wanted to be a Blue
Arrow. It sounded so exciting—so grown-up.

There were no matches in my father's study, so I grabbed the
silver lighter he kept on his desk.

Back on the balcony, Ernesto cupped his hands and lit his cigarette with great style. Then he pocketed my father's lighter.

I started to protest, but decided I could always get it back
later. Once I was a Blue Arrow.

"Come on," I said, badgering him to tell me more about the
youth Falange. I'd seen groups of them marching about the city
in their smart blue shirts, banners flying. But until that night, it
hadn't dawned on me that I might be able to become a member.

"Do you have to be a certain age?" I asked. "You know—to join?"

He looked at me with disdain. "Age has nothing to do with it."

"Then what do you have to do?"

He drew on his cigarette and frowned importantly. "You have
to prove that you have the balls to stand up to the communists.
They're like animals—dirty and dangerous—making life miserable for decent people. Women and children are afraid to walk
the streets. My father says we have an obligation to protect ourselves—our way of life. He has friends in high places. They all
say it's true. But these politicians don't have the will to do what
must be done. Only the Falange does."

"And what's that?" I asked. No one I knew seemed too terribly
miserable. "What has to be done?"

"They have to be stomped out. Don't you know anything?" he
said, shaking his head. "They're like scavengers, feeding off all
the rest of us."

A gust of wind rattled the eaves over our heads. I looked up,
wanting to go back inside, out of the cold, where the air didn't bite.

But Ernesto didn't seem to notice the weather. He stood

there, his cheeks flushed, his eyes glittering. "Don't let on I told you this," he said, winking. "It's a secret."

I moved closer, my eyes watering.

Ernesto looked at me, but said nothing, letting the silence grow until I couldn't stand it.

"Come on," I begged. "Tell me—I won't tell a soul. I swear it."

Finally he spoke. At first, his voice barely carried over the wind. "You've heard of General Franco. He taught those reds in Asturias a lesson. He's out of the country now, but when the time comes—when there's blood in the streets—he'll be brought home. He'll take over the armies and straighten this mess out. When he marches in with his troops, these red bastards will scatter like mice. You'll see. You'll see it's true." His voice rose as he spoke until his fervor was practically contagious. "First, my father says it's up to us to push the people into action. We have to force them to bring Franco back."

"How?" I asked, caught up in his patriotism. "How do you push the people to act?"

Ernesto squared his shoulders. "Fear. Fear is the only thing that motivates people. You have to scare the hell out of them. Then they'll do what's right."

I nodded, still wondering who it was that needed to be scared.

Ernesto was staring at me, waiting, I supposed, for me to say something.

I hesitated.

"Well?" he demanded.

"You're right," I said. "Fear. Scare them."

He smiled, a strange light in his eyes now. "You want to help me? You think you have the balls?"

My heart started pounding in my chest, but I tried to look cool. "How?"

"Be ready later. Four o'clock—sneak out of the house and meet us at the Alcalá gate. Wear something dark." He caught my arm and squeezed my elbow. "And remember. I'm in charge. You'll do exactly what I say—and you'll tell no one. Right?"

I nodded, trying to keep the excitement off my face. "I'll be there. Four o'clock."

He puffed on his cigarette.

I stood there planning how I would sneak out of the house without being caught, both the cold and my father's lighter forgotten for the moment.

The serious-looking nurse I'd seen earlier bustled into Andrew's room. She was an older woman wearing a starched white uniform and an expression that brooked little interference. Approaching the bed, she examined his various tubes and connections, humming to herself while she went about her task.

I stood and moved out of her way.

"Your time is up," she said, making a show of looking at her watch when she'd finished straightening his sheets. "You'll have to leave. Mr. Stevenson needs his rest."

I started to protest, but Andrew spoke first.

"Flo," he said, his voice strained. "Leave us alone. I need to speak with Wil—privately."

She clucked her tongue. "We have rules here, Mr. Stevenson. I was told not even the police were to disturb you. I'm afraid you and this young man will have to continue your conversation later. You need your rest."

Andrew lifted his head off the pillows and raised his eyebrows. "My money built this goddamn wing and I'll visit with whomever I want, whenever the hell I please. Now, leave us, Flo. I'll ring if I need you."

She flushed purple. "We'll see about that," she said, turning on her heel and stalking out of the room.

Andrew fell back against his pillows, the effort having drained him.

I refilled his cup of water, then sat down again.

He raised the cup, sipped at it, then handed it back.

"Where was I?" he asked, scratching at the spot where one of the IVs was taped to his arm.

"You were about to sneak out of the house."

He nodded. "It sounds so innocent. A boyish prank. You see, I had no idea what I'd gotten myself into. I thought it was all a lark. A great adventure. If I'd known innocent women were going to die . . ." He sighed. "But I didn't know. How could I know?"

He looked at me, but I had no answer for him. Clearing his throat, he adjusted the height of the bed, then continued: "I waited until three-thirty in the morning; the house was quiet, everyone asleep, then I crept downstairs and unbolted the front doors. It was colder than hell . . ."

39

It was colder than hell. The wind came in short, sharp gusts—so cold my breath blew white clouds as I hurried down the Calle Serrano toward the park. In my haste to get out of the house, I'd grabbed the first jacket in my closet, a blue blazer that offered little protection against the bitter wind.

It wasn't far, less than a mile from my house to the wide circle of the Plaza de la Independencia, but by the time I got there I was shivering, my heart beating as hard as if I'd run a race.

The others had already gathered there, waiting under the central arch of the Alcalá gate. There were six of them milling about in the shadows, Ernesto pacing back and forth impatiently. He slowed when he caught sight of me and gestured for me to hurry up and join them.

Traffic was almost nonexistent at that hour. The few vehicles within sight, mostly produce trucks from the countryside, paid me no heed as I ran across the usually busy circle.

Ernesto greeted me with a curt nod. "You're late."

I wasn't. But I was too excited to argue. "Sorry. What do you want me to do?"

Before he could answer, one of the other boys said, "Jesus, he looks like a goddamn tourist, Ernesto. Look at him!"

The gang all wore a kind of uniform—a disguise. Dark wool watch caps and leather aprons over the kind of rough blue coveralls you used to see on the workers at the city market. Around their necks they'd tied red scarves—the trademark of the Red Lions, the most notorious of the communist youth gangs.

My blue blazer had been a terrible choice.

I stood out like a pigeon at a cockfight in my street clothes, but there was nothing I could do about it. I wanted to ask why they were wearing those red scarves, only Ernesto was staring at me. So I kept my questions to myself.

The same boy complained again, "Come on, Ernesto—anyone sees us, they're gonna think we're a bunch of pansies."

"Shut up, Jorge!" Ernesto glared at him, daring him to speak. But Jorge knew better.

The others nodded and muttered. For the moment, my outfit was forgotten. But none of them seemed thrilled to have me along.

I didn't recognize any of Ernesto's friends, and he offered no introductions. They looked older than me—all of them.

One, a fat boy with an acne-spotted face, wore an ancient-looking revolver holstered on a thick belt around his waist.

Two of the others—brothers, judging from their curly hair and pointed chins—each carried paint cans.

You could feel their excitement as they milled about, waiting for Ernesto to give the orders.

The pistol scared me, but it was too late to back out. So I stood there, trying to look older, cooler—unconcerned. But my breath came quickly and the palms of my hands were slick with nervous sweat.

"Tomas!" Ernesto called to the fat boy with the gun.

I couldn't quite make out what the two of them said next.

Then he turned to me—the fat one. He didn't smile and his voice was curt. "I'm Tomas." He untied and tossed me his scarf. "Put this on and don't take all night."

I tied the scrap of red cloth around my neck with trembling fingers. It made me feel dangerous.

Ernesto checked his watch, looked at the others, and grinned.

"It's time. Let's go. No talking. We'll give them a lesson they won't soon forget. Won't we?"

The other boys voiced their agreement:

"We'll show them . . ."

"Goddamn red bastards . . ."

"Yeah . . ." I echoed, caught up in their mood, glad to be one of them.

But I still had no idea what we were going to show those faceless red bastards, or, for that matter, where, or how.

If I'd only had the sense to ask . . . The guts to back out . . . But I didn't . . . I was too busy trying to be like them. Tough and worldly. Christ, they were only boys—we were all boys . . .

Except Ernesto. He was woven of a different cloth—knew exactly what we were about to do, and showed not the slightest bit of fear or apprehension. Not the slightest sign of any last-minute jitters. I'm convinced that evil isn't governed by the same rules of flesh. Not at all. Look at him now.

But I get ahead of myself again . . .

We marched quietly, single file, through the frozen cobblestone streets.

Where we were headed was a mystery to me. No one said a word as we traversed block after block of shuttered shops and shadowy apartment blocks. My breath froze on the air and my feet began to hurt. The initial excitement I'd felt wore thin. I began to feel apprehensive, a little frightened, but on we walked, silently, a small military unit. At least in our own imaginations.

After a while, I stopped being afraid. I was too cold and miserable to be scared. I wracked my mind for a good excuse to go home and get out of the freezing wind. Not even the cats that scavenged the alleys of Madrid's barrios were out on such a night. But no one else was complaining, and I didn't want to be thought of as a coward. So I kept my mouth shut, buried my hands in my armpits, and struggled to keep up.

I began hoping we would run into a policeman and have to abort Ernesto's plan, whatever it was. Visions of my warm bed floated in front of me. But the *Guardia* were at least as smart as the alley cats because not a single officer crossed our path as we trudged through the streets.

Eventually we reached the Plaza del Ángel—a small square in the Embajadores section of the city. A working-class neighborhood I'd visited before—Carlita, my mother's maid, and her family lived nearby.

We stopped in the shadows of a shuttered café, chairs piled on the tops of tables, looking forlorn on the dark sidewalk.

Everyone stomped their feet and rubbed their hands together to stay warm. Everyone but Ernesto. Nothing seemed to bother him.

"The chapel—the Capilla del Rosario—is halfway down this block," Ernesto stage-whispered. "I picked it myself, it's perfect. We're going to make this look like the communists did it."

He pointed at a tall, thin boy with a scraggly mustache, the one who had complained about my blazer. "Jorge, you have the bar, right?"

Jorge nodded and held up an iron crowbar.

"Good," Ernesto nodded. "You pry open the windows and help me boost the others up and inside."

"Right," Jorge said, hefting the bar.

Ernesto looked at the two brothers carrying the paint cans. "Be careful. I don't want you to spill any until we ransack the place. This has to look right. Otherwise it won't be believable."

They nodded as one.

Tomas patted his pistol. "I'm ready!"

The fifth boy, a quiet-looking teenager named Carlos, who wore thick, wire-rimmed glasses, whispered his agreement. "I'm ready too. But remember, it has to look like we hate everything about the church."

Jorge laughed. "No problem. Goddamn catechism class drove me crazy."

Carlos frowned, then crossed himself.

Ernesto shook his head. "You keep watch, Carlos. Anyone comes along, you shout. Don't be shy. Give us a good warning."

Carlos, looking unnerved behind his misted lenses, nodded.

No one asked me anything. But I felt caught up in the rising tide of their excitement. "What should I do?" I blurted out.

Ernesto frowned at me. His eyes were impossibly bright in that shadowy street. "You stick close to me. Everyone has a job. Yours is to do what I say. Understand?"

I nodded, my heart beating so hard now that I was sure the others could hear it.

"All right. Let's go," Ernesto said, leading the way down the narrow cobbled street.

The old chapel was in the middle of the block. A seventeenth-century facade of brick and stone, tall, iron-mounted oak doors, three crosses on the roof and a small bell tower. It was a poor church, distinguished by age, not wealth or artifacts.

The seven of us stopped outside those tall and narrow doors and stared . . .

"¡*Mierda!*" Tomas hissed.

Jorge shook his head. "Impossible."

At first I wasn't sure what was the matter.

Then I saw . . .

The Capilla del Rosario had no windows to pry open. Only the imposing, iron-mounted slabs of oak that formed a pair of doors that had stood solid for several hundred years.

I looked around at the others.

Carlos looked as relieved as I suddenly felt. Now we wouldn't have to actually go through with it. We could go home without shame.

"What now?" Tomas asked, using his apron to wipe his fat and bumpy face, moist with sweat in spite of the cold.

The two curly-headed brothers stood off to the side, talking quietly. Then the smaller of the two, the younger-looking brother, motioned to Ernesto and said, "This is fucked up. We're leaving, Caldero—going home."

Good, I thought, sure that Ernesto would agree.

But he studied the front of the church without answering.

Then he turned to face us. "We'll burn it." Ernesto's voice was barely audible.

No one said a word.

"Burn it!" he said, this time louder, his words swirling up and around us, carried spinning over our heads by the wind.

I stood there, rooted to the cobblestones, too shocked to speak.

"How—how can you burn such a building?" Jorge asked, clutching the crowbar close to his chest.

Ernesto glanced up and down the empty street. He took the paint can from the smaller of the brothers and pried it open with his pocket knife. Then he held it out for us all to examine.

"Jesus!" Jorge exclaimed, wrinkling his nose. "It's petrol. I thought we were going to paint a bunch of communist stuff on the walls."

Ernesto didn't answer—just that intense stare.

And it dawned on us that he had planned it this way.

He had never intended to pry open any windows. He'd chosen the church, scouted it . . .

"It's simple," he continued. "We pry open the doors, but we won't stick around long enough for anyone to spot us. In and out." He snapped his fingers. "Imagine . . . Communists—burning churches right here in Madrid! Think what the people will say! Enough churches burn and they'll have to act. They'll bring Franco and his men out of Morocco and back to Spain where they're needed. They'll give us goddamn medals for this."

We all just looked at each other.

"Burn a church?" the two brothers asked as one.

Tomas looked unsure.

"Leave and you'll be sorry—all of you," Ernesto said. "You'll wish you hadn't—you'll be out of the Blue Arrows forever. I swear it."

Carlos crossed himself again.

"Give me the bar, Jorge," Ernesto ordered.

He took it and wedged the tapered end between the two doors. He gave a mighty heave, but nothing happened.

The brothers took a step or two back.

Carlos, Tomas, and Jorge watched, wide-eyed, their breath steaming.

I wanted no part of this. No one had said a word about burning a church. But my legs had turned to stone. I stood there, too terrified to speak or move, my heart going like mad.

"Help me," Ernesto ordered the others.

At first no one moved. Then, Jorge and Tomas added their weight to the bar.

The door creaked, but didn't give an inch.

"Come on!" Ernesto called to the brothers.

They looked at each other, shrugged, then moved to help.

No one seemed to notice me.

The doors creaked and groaned, but finally, it was the lock that gave under the weight of five boys, not those ancient oak beams.

And from the moment the weight of those five boys in their peasant disguises threw open the doors of the Capilla del Rosario, everything went wrong.

More horribly wrong than I could have imagined . . .

And I stood and watched. Did nothing to stop it. Years later I watched as Ernesto Caldero became more powerful and his wealth grew—only he was no longer Ernesto Caldero. He had a new name—a new identity. And still I sat on it—refused to tell what happened that night—thinking my own reputation was more important.

Look at me now . . . Your conscience doesn't give a good god-damn about your reputation. Not in the end. No, in the end it eats you alive—a little piece at a time. It strangles the life out of you. Slowly . . .

Look at me. Look . . .

What good is my reputation now?

But that night, I didn't think ahead. I was too frightened to think at all.

The doors flew open and they were in.

I didn't follow, but I could see inside. It was a small chapel, dark, not more than twenty meters from the front doors to the raised altar. Rows of pews separated by a central aisle. A high, beamed ceiling. A small stone font and an old table holding offering candles.

Ernesto had brought a flashlight. He used it now to illuminate the polished walnut pews. Empty—the only sounds the scraping

footsteps of leather soles on rough-hewn stone as the two brothers, Jorge, Tomas, and Ernesto moved down the center aisle
toward the altar.

"What are they going to do?" Carlos, who'd stayed outside
with me, whispered, fear strangling his voice.

He looked nervously about, pushing his glasses up on his
slight nose. "Should we leave? Should we?"

I couldn't answer.

I stood frozen, watching the five of them ascending the low
steps to the altar. I can't really say what I felt, I'm not sure it's
possible to put it into words. My family wasn't religious, but
burning a church went beyond anything I'd ever imagined
myself capable of. All the same, I stood there, just outside the
church doors, not protesting, not running away, not helping,
but not hindering either. I was a boy too scared to move, my
nose full of the smell of dust and old wood soap, candle wax and
the quiet exhalations of a million unanswered prayers.

And we were about to destroy it all.

For what?

Ernesto stood on the altar, shining his flashlight on the gleaming reliquaries. He called out for the brothers to bring him the
paint cans filled with petrol. Then he set about dousing the
altar. Within seconds the sharp stink of fuel oil overwhelmed
the old church smells, stinging my nostrils.

After dousing the altar, they came down the aisle, Ernesto
and the older of the brothers splashing petrol on the pews as the
other three followed them back toward where Carlos and I
stood.

As they drew even with the last row of pews, they splashed
the last of the petrol and dropped the empty cans.

Ernesto had turned to say something to Jorge when the door
to the sacristy opened at the back of the altar and light spilled
out onto the pulpit.

Everyone froze.

"Who's there?" a stern female voice demanded.

My heart stopped.

A nun in full winter habit stood in the fan of light flooding from the sacristy. She walked out onto the altar, followed by two young novices wearing heavy brown woolen smocks, each holding a gleaming candelabra and the cloths they'd been using to polish them.

We weren't twenty meters apart. I can still see their faces—the old nun, unafraid, the novices pale, their hair pulled back under their caps, their eyes shining.

Carlos made a whimpering sound.

No one moved or spoke.

Then the nun, a wide battleship of a woman, put her hands on her hips. "What do you think you're doing. This is God's house! Out! Out of this church now!"

Stepping down from the altar, she sniffed the air like a hunting dog, the smell of petrol thick in the confined space of the small chapel.

The two novices followed her, still holding on to their silver candelabra. I could see now that one of them was very pretty, her skin smooth and her features fine against the coarse weave of her smock.

She stared directly at me, the pretty one, her eyes wide.

I wanted to disappear. But I stood and bore the weight of her gaze, trembling from head to toe.

"Who dares to desecrate this house of God?" the old nun demanded, her voice thundering off the stone walls. "What have you done? Out! Now! Before I call the *Guardia* and have you all arrested."

She was fearless.

Before her anger, we quaked.

All but Ernesto.

He raised his fist and shouted, "Stop, old woman. I'm not afraid of you or the *Guardia* or even your God. Don't you know who we are?"

"You're a delinquent who deserves a good beating," the nun answered, starting down the aisle. The two novices followed in her wake.

"We're the Red Lions," Ernesto shouted defiantly. "And we fear no one—God included!"

"Out! Out now!" The nun advanced on him.

Jorge, Tomas, and the two brothers backed out of the church, leaving Ernesto standing alone beside the last row of pews.

He didn't seem to notice their desertion.

Carlos joined them—and together, the five boys ran off into the night.

But I couldn't move. I was rooted to the spot, paralyzed.

"You heard me, boy! Out!" The old nun took another step toward Ernesto.

But he stood his ground, waving something clutched in his right fist at her.

At this she stopped and held out her hand, warning the novices to stay behind her.

Ernesto knelt as though to pray, whatever was in his right hand glinting in the uneven light.

Then I recognized what it was—my father's lighter.

The night slowed—it was like a grainy photograph.

I tried to scream NO! but my mouth wouldn't work.

He flicked the lighter, scrape of flint on steel.

One of the novices dropped her candelabra.

It rang like a bell as it hit the stone floor.

The nun raised her hand, pointing. Her mouth was moving, but all I could hear was the silver bell of the fallen candelabra.

The lighter flared in his hand.

The night exploded in sound and light.

With a whoosh, the petrol ignited and raced across the floor toward the three nuns. In the split second before it reached them, I could see the flames reflected in their terror-stricken eyes.

And then the screaming.

The flames wrapped them in red light.

And still they screamed.

Screamed and screamed and screamed.

And Ernesto had me by the arm and was dragging me away.

He jerked me back from the burning church as the wind fanned the flames.

And then we were moving through the streets, Ernesto pushing me along, saying nothing.

■   ■   ■

Andrew lay still, exhausted. Sweat and tears moistened his cheeks. "And now he has M.K. . . ."

I sat, transfixed by his story. But I wasn't sure I understood. "This Ernesto—"

"He no longer goes by the name Ernesto. Now he calls himself Roberto."

I still didn't understand. "Roberto who?"

He stared at me, his eyes flat and lifeless.

"Roberto Salgo."

40

THE EFFORT OF TELLING HIS story cost Andrew dearly. He lay stiff under his sheets, his face drained of color, his skin greasy with sick sweat.

But I still didn't understand. "*The* Roberto Salgo? The man running for governor?"

Stevenson nodded.

"How?" I asked him, unable to relate the horror story I'd just heard to the patrician-looking man I'd seen speak at the museum. "How can Ernesto Caldero be that Roberto Salgo? You must be mistaken."

"How doesn't matter. He has M.K., that's all that matters now."

I sat there, stunned, not sure I believed a word he'd told me. "How can you be sure?"

Andrew took a deep breath and gathered himself. He looked too exhausted to continue, but somehow he found the strength, his voice raw, his pallor alarming. "It's him. I'm as sure of it as I am of my own name. I've tracked him across the years—spent a fortune for information. This day had to come. It was only a matter of time. But I waited too long. Too goddamn long."

He shifted in the bed and coughed.

When I moved to pour more water, he waved me away.

"There was a civil war—a terrible conflagration. Records were kept—but nothing like today. There were no computers. Switching identities with a dead civilian was not unheard of. Deserters did it every day.

"In late '36, soon after the war started, Ernesto Caldero joined the Forty-first Infantry Brigade—Franco's shock troops. The *Brigada Diablo*. A year later he became a captain—one of the youngest officers in the army—fought all over Spain until the end of the civil war in '39. The record on this is clear. Then, by 1940, he disappears. In 1941, Spanish War Department records list him as dead. Only there were witnesses who said otherwise. Plenty of them. Mostly dead now themselves. But I have affidavits identifying him, placing him in specific locations at specific times. Before and after 1940. Sworn statements from men who served with him—firsthand accounts of his brutality. He was there—at the massacre in Providencia in '37. They lined up three hundred civilians in the soccer stadium and machine-gunned them. According to witnesses, a young officer from Madrid named Caldero gave the order. After the executions, Caldero's men raped and looted and ravaged the town. Then, in Najera in '39, seventeen boys, not one over the age of fifteen, all hung by their necks from telegraph poles in the center of the town. Left them to swing until their rotting corpses dropped to the ground—an example, a lesson from the *Brigada Diablo* to those who sheltered or fed Republican sympathizers. After the hangings, the *Brigada Diablo* were unleashed on the women of the town. Again, the orders were given by a young officer named Caldero. The killings were terrible, but it was the rapes, the brutality against women that angered Franco. This was a war crime even Franco would not tolerate.

"Then, in 1940 Caldero disappears—at least officially. I've checked—and I haven't been able to turn up one document proving his death. Only the war department's list of casualties. How easy do you think it would be for a man like Caldero's father, a general, to doctor army records? My best guess is that after news of the atrocities spread, his father used his influence to get Ernesto out of the country. In the process, he simply adopted a new identity. Not a fabrication—the identity of a real person, one of the tens of thousands of civilian casualties. Entire families disappeared. Who would know? Who would argue?"

He stopped talking, his breath coming in rapid gulps. But he wasn't finished. He swallowed some water, then continued.

"I picked up the trail here, in Florida, in the mid-fifties. Tracked down his mother's family. One of his mother's cousins, a respected banker, helped him get started with the first wave of Cuban émigrés."

"You can prove this? It's in your file?" I asked, still not sure.

He nodded wearily. "All of it . . . If you want to call it proof. Old photographs, affidavits, newspaper clippings of his subsequent activities. His involvement with the Cuban expatriates. He'd been through a revolution, knew how to handle himself in a bad situation. In the beginning, the Cubans provided the money, Salgo provided the security, the contacts they needed to get their wealth out of Castro's reach. These Cubans were smart—a hardworking bunch. Salgo was no fool. They used each other. As a result, Salgo became an even wealthier man, and the Cubans gained a foothold in South Florida. Hell, they've cornered the sugar market—own millions and millions of acres of cane. No one questioned his identity—why would they? It's the sugar money that's backing Salgo now. Clean money—even though Salgo's dirty. I guess this campaign of his is a reward for services rendered. A plum for Salgo."

I glanced at my watch. He'd been talking for over an hour. It was a monumental effort. I didn't know how much longer he'd last. "Is that what drove you to act now? His campaign?"

He nodded and cleared his throat. "I'd waited long enough. How much time was left to me? To see that bastard gain official power here—here in America—after what he'd done . . . I couldn't allow it. I wrote him, warned him to withdraw from the race and disappear—that if he didn't, I would come forward. I told him I'd assembled documents that proved who and what he really was. Swore I'd use them to force him out in the open—to spend the rest of his life in disgrace, looking over his shoulder, wondering when they were coming for him. But it was too little, too late. I underestimated him. You see the way it turned out." He rubbed a shaky hand over his face.

"Christ," he groaned. "I'd take it all back—all of it—if I could. Let him be governor. Let him be president."

I shook my head. "You couldn't have known. You—"

"Nonsense," he interrupted. "It was the obvious move. I've gotten old—I acted like a goddamn fool. Now he's holding M.K. It's all there—everything I told you—in the file."

I stood and began pacing back and forth at the foot of his bed. He followed me with his eyes, his face a frozen mask. I wished I'd been able to hold on to the memoir Tessereau had produced. I wondered what Andrew would have thought about the picture of the kid with the Blue Arrows banner. Was the boy in the photograph one of the boys who had burned the church? Was it Salgo himself? I thought about Pico Nuñez, his burned hands. Stevenson's drawings of burning buildings. The burned-out crack houses in Flamingo Lakes.

I stopped pacing and looked down at him. "The silver lighter?"

He nodded weakly. "All these years—he kept it. Sent it back to me. A reminder of my own culpability. As if I needed to be reminded."

He was telling the truth. As hard as it was to accept, Andrew Stevenson was right. I knew it in my bones. But that didn't mean I knew what to do about it.

"Maybe you didn't underestimate your leverage," I said. "He wants that file. I doubt he'll harm M.K. until he's sure it's been destroyed. We're going to have to play his game—set up a trade, the file for M.K. But I'm not sure how to keep the field level. He's dictating the rules."

Andrew's chin quivered. Tears flowed down his grizzled cheeks. "This is my fault. I want you to get my daughter back. Whatever it takes."

"I'm going to try. Now, where did you hide the file?"

He closed his eyes and whispered, "That night—I tried to tell him. Tried, but the words wouldn't come—I was doped up. I would have given him the file. If I had, Amanda would be alive. M.K. wouldn't . . . I . . . I just couldn't seem to get the words out."

"I was there. It wasn't your fault."

He shook his head, eyes still closed, lost in the fog of that night. "I'd have given him anything . . . It's behind the Picasso—in my bedroom. Behind the study for *Guernica*."

"Of course!" I slapped myself on the forehead. "War. That night, you said 'war.' *Guernica!* I should have understood."

He opened his eyes. "Go now. Go and get my daughter. If it becomes a matter of money . . ."

I stepped to his side. "It's gone too far for that."

He swallowed hard and reached for my hand. "Do whatever needs to be done. I'll say nothing about any of this until I hear from you."

It was an endorsement I neither wanted nor deserved. I started to say something about doing my best to keep M.K. from being harmed, but he cut me off. "Get moving, Wil. I've told you all I know. There isn't time to say more—not now."

I looked down at him and nodded. But I had one more question. "Why me? Why did you tell Gaines to hire me to appraise the collection?"

He hesitated. "Andy Height—you remember him—at the Norton?"

I nodded. "He helped me—taught me to look with my eyes *and* my heart."

Stevenson almost smiled. "He came to me—told me about a boy who loved art. The books he gave you—where did you think he got them?"

I was speechless.

"Well—it beats the hell out of cleaning cabanas, doesn't it?" Andrew asked.

I wasn't sure whether to laugh or cry.

I hurried out of the room.

Behind me, I heard him sigh, then only the beeping of his monitor.

41

GAINES DROVE MAJ AND ME back to Palm Beach in his Jaguar. On the way, I gave the two of them a condensed version of Andrew's story.

While I spoke, Gaines kept his eyes on the road, his knuckles white on the steering wheel.

I kept it short; the facts without embellishment were dramatic enough.

When I finished, Maj slapped a huge palm against the fancy leather of the backseat. "Mon got all that to lose—he gone do what needs to be done to protect hisself. No backin' him off with words an threats. He gone understand only one t'ing—"

"So we give him what he wants. Then we walk away," I interrupted.

Maj snorted. "He killed Miz Amanda, and you be t'inking he just let you walk away soon as he has dis file? Then what? He sit back an hope you don't change your mind and take it further? Ain't gone happen." He frowned. "Less you ready to go to war, we best call the law now."

"You actually think the police are going to believe you?" Gaines asked, his eyes flicking to the rearview mirror. "You think they're going to buy for one minute that Roberto Salgo is involved in something like this? By the time they get through shaking their heads and laughing at you, M.K. will be dead."

I stared at him. The Salgo bumper sticker on his car hadn't escaped me. "You have a better plan in mind?"

He glanced over at me, then back at the road. "We handle this without the police. Our first priority is to get M.K. back. Once we involve the authorities, we become spectators—and once Salgo's name surfaces, we're talking about the FBI and the Florida State Troopers and every other law enforcement agency that can think up a reason to share jurisdiction. Believe me, they won't all share the same agenda we do. Too many rules—too many careers to protect."

I shook my head. "You're right—but Maj has a point. We hand over the file, we give up the only card we hold."

Gaines looked at me, his mouth a tight line, his knuckles still white on the wheel. "This isn't a goddamn game. Anything goes wrong, she's dead. I say we give Salgo whatever he wants."

I didn't answer. He was at least partly right, still, something about his reaction to all of this was bothering me. I wasn't sure why, but I couldn't shake the feeling that something was off-kilter.

"Well?" he asked.

Things were moving too fast. We had to act—but Gaines was right. This wasn't a game. I wasn't qualified to make this kind of decision. Who was? Who could be trusted to put M.K.'s safety first once Salgo's name surfaced? Laspada? *Harris?* There was too much at stake. Too many angles I couldn't see, much less anticipate. I'd come to Palm Beach to do an appraisal—a shot at gaining back some of the ground I had lost in the art business. Not this . . .

I glanced at Gaines, but he was lost in his own thoughts.

Maj sat, stone-faced, in the backseat.

I rubbed my eyes and drew a deep breath. Then I made up my mind. "No police. We'll hand over the file—but not all of it. We'll keep back just enough to act as an insurance policy. As soon as we look it over and decide how much to keep, we'll call and set up a meeting. The file for M.K."

Maj grunted his approval.

Gaines said nothing, but his left hand strayed from the wheel of the car to his knee, where he began rolling the fabric of his trousers between his thumb and his forefinger.

I looked away, wondering how he was going to handle himself when it came time to deal with M.K.'s abductors.

It was not a reassuring thought.

42

WHEN GAINES PULLED UP IN front of the Stevensons' portico, Maj and I hopped out of the car before he'd come to a complete stop. He lagged behind, and we didn't wait for him. I was too anxious to get inside the house and find the file.

It was exactly where Andrew had said it would be, one of the first places anyone with any experience of searching a room would have looked. The paper backing the heavily framed Picasso had been slit and behind the drawing an inch-thick manila envelope had been inserted.

Maj whistled. "Damn fine t'ing we be finding dis, you know. Been worrying Mister Andrew's memories might not be reliable."

I tore open the envelope and spread its contents across the desk. As I did, the silver lighter fell to the floor. I picked it up and held it in my hand as I looked at Andrew Stevenson's file.

Just as he had described, it contained a handful of yellowed photographs, typed affidavits in Spanish with witnessed dates and signatures, news clippings, and handwritten reports. A number of recent articles had been clipped from the *Miami Herald*, most of them dealing with Salgo's past links to the sugar industry, both as lobbyist and spokesperson. Several of them had the same byline, a reporter named Raoul Hernandez. One in particular caught my eye, an article about a mysterious plane crash that had killed the leading proponent of the penny a pound sugar tax, a man named Jonathan Korn.

But as I picked up the article, another piece of paper caught my eye. A recent-looking list of names and addresses. But it wasn't the names that drew my attention—it was the repetitive chain of linked squares that had been doodled in the margins of the page . . .

They were the same squares I'd seen . . .

Then it hit me. Gaines had never questioned Andrew's story. What lawyer would listen to me recite the kind of allegations Andrew had made against a man like Salgo, and not ask a single question? Not one?

The answer was obvious. Gaines hadn't questioned the story because he knew it was true. Why then had he been so quick to deny the existence of the file? Judging from the little squares he'd doodled on that list of names, I had to assume he had at least some idea that Andrew was collecting information. Maybe he'd helped Andrew assemble the list in the first place.

Maj cleared his throat.

"What?" I asked, still looking down at the list of names, trying to decide exactly what they meant.

He cleared his throat again. "You best pay attention," he said.

When I looked up at him, he angled his head toward the door. "Got us a new problem."

Gaines stood in the doorway of Andrew's bedroom holding a large-caliber automatic leveled at my chest.

"Move away from the desk," he said, his voice tight.

I just stood there staring at him. "You knew all along, didn't you?"

He said nothing, his face a white mask.

"Why, Gaines?"

"Move, or I'll kill you where you are." The gun shook in his hand.

Maj and I backed away from the desk.

"Why, Gaines?" I asked again. "Why are you doing this?"

He glanced at the papers spread across Andrew's desk and took a step toward them. "I'm going to get M.K. *Without* you interfering. Now, move—move out there." He pointed to the balcony with his free hand. "Outside, now!"

"Don't do this. You don't stand a chance alone," I said.

But he didn't answer.

Instead, he raised the gun and pointed it at my face. His hand shook, but the muzzle never strayed far from my chin. "Get out on the balcony now!"

Maj took my arm. "Come on, mon. He serious."

Once we were on the balcony, Gaines shut and locked the French doors behind us.

I watched through the glass, dumbfounded, as he gathered up the contents of the file and tucked the papers under his arm. All but the lighter and the article I still held.

I stuffed them into my hip pocket and tried to decide what to do.

Gaines stepped back to the balcony door, the gun still gripped in his fist. He was sweating. "Stay where you are till I'm gone. Understand? Don't call the police. They'll kill her."

Then he turned and ran out of the room.

Maj reached for the door handle, but I grabbed his wrist and shook my head.

"Wait," I whispered. "Give him time to get downstairs."

"What I give him is time to wish he didn't pull no gun on old Maj. That's what I give him."

I looked down from the balcony. The drop to the ground was eight or ten feet.

Maj shook his head. "Ain't soft as the beach, you jump off a this balcony."

I climbed over the railing anyway. "We don't have much choice," I said, hanging by my arms, then dropping.

The impact nearly knocked the breath out of me.

Maj landed lightly beside me, rolled, and came up on to his feet, still shaking his head. "Now you bleedin', mon. Why you don't let me force the door?"

A bright red stain was spreading across the left shoulder of my shirt. Some of the stitches had let go, but there wasn't time to do anything about it.

"I left the keys to my car in M.K.'s apartment," I said. "Wait here. I'll get them."

"No time, mon." Maj pulled a worn sliver of a key out of his back pocket. "We take my truck, Wil. She parked right beside the back door. Got me a shotgun under the seat—might be a good t'ing to have."

Together we ran around the back of the house and jumped into the cab of a rusted-out blue Ford pickup.

As he got the key into the ignition, we heard Gaines's Jag roar to life and thunder down the driveway in a rattling spray of gravel.

"Hurry!" I urged, thinking we'd never catch him in this heap.

But Maj smiled. "Don't be needin' to worry so much. He want off this island, he drive the speed limit. Palm Beach cops don't be allowin' no speeders—not even when they be drivin' Jaguars."

He turned the key and the truck purred to life, the engine sounding smooth and powerful. "Put on your seat belt—that the law. And stop all that frownin'—damn lawyer don't get away from us. No way, mon."

He was right.

We pulled out onto County Road and Gaines was less than a quarter of a mile in front of us. Three cars separated the Jag and the pickup, and Gaines, easily visible from the high cab of Maj's truck, never even glanced in his rearview. He drove well below the speed limit, his car phone clamped to his ear, looking for all the world like a man out for a leisurely cruise.

But the image faded when Maj reached under the seat and pulled out a worn and ugly sawed-off double-barreled shotgun that looked old enough to have seen service in the civil war.

He laid the gun across his lap and broke the breech open. Then he pointed to the glove compartment, held shut with a twist of baling wire. "Grab me a handful of shells out a the box, Wil. Might as well be carryin' a rock, we don't load it."

I did as he asked, keeping one eye on Gaines's car. I'd put so much emphasis on finding the file, I had no idea what to do now that we'd lost it.

Maj whistled a pretty good version of Bob Marley's "I Shot the Sheriff" as we crossed the bridge into West Palm Beach, one hand on the steering wheel, the other caressing the old shotgun.

43

WE DROVE WEST ON OKEECHOBEE Road, following Gaines past the shiny strip malls and car lots, the fast-food chains and the multiplex theaters, past the point where the retirement developments with their cracked shuffleboard courts and faded sales pennants gave way to cane fields and old shell pits, then swamp and scrub. When the salt air of the coast gave way to the smell of freshly turned earth and then the dusky, fecund smell of the swamps, I began to think we might be headed for the same small house I'd unwillingly visited the night before. My stomach tightened at the thought of confronting Kiki and Carlito without a weapon of my own. I cursed Gaines and his bone-headed move. But there was nothing to do but follow him and hope for the best.

We passed a rattlesnake as thick as my thigh, sunning himself by the side of the road.

"Good eating," Maj said as he pointed the monster out. "Jerk snake taste almost like chicken, you know."

This was a Florida they didn't advertise on network television, a Florida that I couldn't equate with M.K. I thought about how little I knew about her—how much I wanted to know—and prayed that we weren't too late. I stared at the back of the Jag, Gaines's silhouette visible through the rear window, and decided to hurt him if anything happened to her. But the empty thought gave little satisfaction.

Gaines cruised along just under the speed limit, doing nothing to shake us, not acting at all like a man who thought he was being followed. Even so, Maj hung back, always keeping a vehicle or two between the pickup and the Jag.

After an hour, the Jag's brake lights flashed and Gaines slowed. He was looking for something.

Maj pulled the pickup onto the narrow shoulder of the paved road and stopped.

Half a mile ahead, Gaines turned right onto a dirt track winding north through a thicket of palmetto palm.

We gave him a five-minute start, then followed.

Maj drove slowly, carefully guiding the pickup over the rough track, until we came to the edge of a clearing.

We stopped and looked around.

"This is it!" I said, recognizing the tiny house and shed some two hundred yards across the clearing.

Maj nodded. "Nice place."

I couldn't tell if he was being sarcastic or not.

The Jag had pulled up in front of the shed. The white van stood a few yards closer to the house. No one was moving about—at least not within our line of sight.

While we watched, the driver's door of the Jag swung open and Gaines stepped out into the sunshine carrying a leather briefcase. Without looking around, he strode directly toward the house, looking more like an insurance salesman making a house call than a hostage negotiator entering the lion's den.

The front door of the house opened, and Gaines walked through it with a familiarity that set the warning bells in my head ringing.

If the rottweilers were around, they didn't show themselves.

"What you want to do now?" Maj asked.

"Let's hide the truck—go the rest of the way on foot," I said. "Carefully . . . Last night there were two dogs—big, nasty fuckers."

Hefting the shotgun, he said, "Take a mighty big dog to be eating this much thunder."

Then he backed the truck up and parked it, well hidden behind a thick tangle of undergrowth.

I didn't want to tell him that, in a fight, I'd pick the dogs over his old blunderbuss.

I thought it might hurt his feelings.

We picked our way around the edge of the clearing, careful to keep plenty of foliage between us and the house. The swamp was alive with noise, black water shining like pools of crude oil—dragonflies hovering, frogs croaking. But the mosquitoes weren't as thick as I remembered them.

Then again, it was still daylight.

The shed was empty—no sign of Turo and his twelve gauge. But two of the jalousie windows on the near side of the house were wide open, the interior dark behind fly-specked screens.

Moving quietly, we approached the house and took up positions flanking the open windows. From where we stood, we could hear voices arguing inside, but we were exposed—standing out in the open, visible to anyone approaching the house if they looked in the right direction.

"Why you no sit down and relax? I tell you, Guillermo is on the way." It was Kiki, sounding like he was trying hard not to lose his cool.

"There's no time," Gaines answered. "I've brought the file. Now I'm leaving with the girl."

"The girl stays put," Kiki growled.

"Damnit! I had a deal," Gaines said. "I spoke with Guillermo myself. I was told the girl could leave with me."

Kiki laughed. "You thinking I'm lying to you? Like some fucking lawyer?"

Gaines said something I couldn't understand.

But his answer made Kiki chuckle even louder.

Then his laughter stopped as abruptly as it had started. "No one is going nowhere," he said. "I don't give a fuck how close you and old man Salgo are—I got orders. So sit down—*Mister Palm Beach Lawyer*. You ain't no big shot yet. So shut your mouth and relax—before I relax you, no?"

Maj glanced at me, his eyes full of angry questions.

I shook my head in disgust. At least we knew where Gaines stood.

"Why?" Maj mouthed.

I didn't know and I was beginning not to care. Why Gaines had betrayed the Stevensons wasn't going to change the fact that he had betrayed them. What I wanted was to get my hands on him and make him pay for what he'd helped Salgo's people do. The fear I'd bottled up until that moment suddenly turned into the purest white-hot anger I'd ever known. I didn't want explanations. I wanted someone to pay—to pay for Amanda, for the pain they'd caused Andrew and M.K. I wanted blood—and not just Broward Gaines's.

I nearly jumped when his voice came from just inside the window, inches from where I stood.

"I don't have time to wait for Guillermo. Sumner and the god-damn gardener will be calling the police any time now. If this is going to work, if I'm to be of any use in the future, I can't sit around and wait for that to happen."

"Fuck Sumner and fuck the gardener," Kiki shot back. "No one is going anywhere until I say so."

"I have the file," Gaines insisted. "That was the deal."

Kiki grunted, unimpressed.

There was the sound of papers rustling.

I looked at Maj.

He stood there, his face hard, the shotgun clutched tightly in those big hands.

It was time to make a move. Somehow, we had to draw Kiki and Gaines out of the house. If we could free M.K., then get our hands on the file . . .

I'd closed my eyes, trying to remember the layout of the interior, when Maj tossed a pebble at me.

"Look," he mouthed, pointing at the clearing.

A black Mercedes bumped out of the tree line, headed for the house.

Without waiting to see who was driving, Maj and I hit the ground and crawled around the far corner of the house.

There was no way to tell whether or not we'd been spotted.

44

We lay flat on the ground, hidden in the tall grass at the edge of the swamp behind the house. We hadn't crawled far, but my breath came in hard, sharp gasps, my heart hammering in my chest.

Maj was sweating, his face as shiny and black as carved obsidian, nostrils flaring, lips drawn tight over those white teeth. He held his shotgun ready, but it didn't inspire much confidence.

At the front of the house, car doors opened and slammed shut, voices spoke in Spanish. I couldn't tell how many.

We waited, motionless, for what seemed an eternity.

I expected the dogs—slavering, growling, teeth snapping. But they never materialized, and no one came looking for us.

When it seemed certain that we hadn't been spotted, I motioned to Maj and we moved quietly back to the open windows. But the only voices we heard now were faint and seemed to come from the opposite side of the house.

We needed to know who was inside and where they were. Especially M.K.

"The windows on the other side of the house might be open too," I whispered. "Wait here. I'll check."

He shook his head, but when he saw that I was serious, he pushed the shotgun at me.

"Take it," he said under his breath. "But hold her tight. She kick like a damn mule."

I cradled it in the crook of my elbow, hoping it wouldn't explode in my face. Then, I crawled back the way we had come—an inch at a time—sure the dogs would be on me at any moment.

I made the tall grass, then circled around the rear of the house, only to discover that the windows on the opposite side had been boarded shut.

I wasn't sure what to do next. The shotgun weighed a ton. Wiping the sweat from my eyes, I stood and leaned against the wall, waiting for my heart to slow before heading back to Maj. I wracked my brain for a plan. We had two assets; an antique shotgun that might or might not work, and the element of surprise. But how to use those assets? How many people were inside the house? How well were they armed? Where the hell was M.K.?

Cursing Gaines and Salgo and wishing we had called Laspada, I pushed away from the wall, then froze when I heard someone moving in my direction from the front of the house.

Holding the shotgun against my chest, I flattened myself back against the wall and held my breath, trying to become one with the concrete block.

Turo stepped around the corner of the house, carrying a semi-automatic pistol in one hand, a can of Coke in the other.

Unaware of my presence, he stood a few yards from me, looking off toward the tree line, sipping his soda.

I could smell him, hear the gurgle as he swallowed the Coke, count the beads of sweat on the can, the hairs on the back of his hand.

There was nowhere to go—nowhere to hide. I had the shotgun, but if I fired it, I'd bring whoever else was in the house out in a hurry. I might get one more of them with the second barrel, assuming it worked, but that would be it. We'd be finished—it would be over before it started.

Turo took a long pull of the Coke, his Adam's apple rising and falling as he swallowed.

It seemed as if time stopped. The rest of the world ceased to exist and there was only Turo and me. I could sense his rhythm, the beat of his pulse. And something new rose up in me. I could feel my own blood ticking hot through my veins. A swelling in my chest—a tightening and at the same time a loosening. A darkness coursing thick through me, urging me to strike.

The urge built, the blood ticking hotter. The anger burning, a red haze at the edge of my vision.

"Turo," I whispered.

Startled, he turned, his eyes wide.

Gripping the barrel of the gun, I swung it like a club, catching him square on the forehead with the butt. The impact was a satisfaction, vibrating up my arms and down my spine.

He dropped his pistol, tried to point the can of soda at me.

I drew the shotgun back to strike again.

Then he fell, blood pouring from a gash over his right eye.

He moaned once, started to roll over, then went limp.

And I wanted to swing again, to pound the heavy butt of the gun against his skull.

Fighting the urge, I picked up his pistol and shoved it into the waistband of my pants.

Then, breathing hard, the red mist thick in my head, I leveled the shotgun at the corner of the house and waited to see who would be next. I was ready.

Let them come.

I waited.

Minutes passed . . .

It might have been hours. But no one came. Maybe no one heard us.

Turo was breathing, but he wasn't going anywhere. So I left him where he lay and made my way back around the house.

Maj's eyes locked on mine when I stepped around the corner, then his gaze traveled to the pistol shoved into my waistband. "You okay?" he whispered.

I nodded. "One down—soon they'll miss him. We've got to

make our move. Now, before they know we're here—it's the only advantage we have."

He looked doubtful. "How we know how many be in there? We don't know where they keeping M.K.—go in and start shooting, we might hit her."

He was right, but as he whispered, a thought occurred to me. A fire had started this mess sixty years ago. Why not end it with a fire?

"We don't go in, Maj. We make them come out. We torch the Mercedes and wait for them to come to us. You have any matches?"

He looked at me like I was crazy, but searched his pockets and handed over a pack.

Then he smiled. "You learn to be t'inking dis way in New York?"

I nodded, not wanting to tell him I saw it on an old episode of *Mission Impossible*.

45

THERE WAS NO GASOLINE IN the shed, only motorcycle parts and tools. But they'd left the white van unlocked, keys dangling in the ignition, a full, five-gallon gas can beside the lawnmowers.

Maj kept his shotgun trained on the front of the house, while I crawled around the far side of the Mercedes, dragging the heavy can behind me. They hadn't bothered to lock the Mercedes either.

The car smelled of fine leather until I doused the front seats, then the floor, soaking the carpet and upholstery with the volatile liquid. The fumes were thick enough to burn my throat. I moved around to the rear of the car and splashed more gasoline over the backseats. I was thinking I might be overdoing it when something wedged under the armrest of the rear seat caught my eye. It was Tessereau's book. Now I knew who had arrived in such style. But was he alone?

I grabbed the book and shoved it under my shirt, then backed away from the car, pouring a trail of gasoline behind me.

At my signal, Maj took up a position behind the van.

Dropping the empty gas can, I jacked a round into the chamber of Turo's gun and nodded to Maj.

He gave me a thumbs-up.

This was it. I drew a deep breath. Then, striking a match, I tossed it on the gas-soaked grass and sprinted to the corner of the shed.

The car went up with a concussive *whooomp!*, a bright-red ball of flame reaching high into the sky.

My ears popped. The front windows of the house blew inward.

For a moment, there was nothing but the scorching flames— then thick black smoke roiled up from the car like a storm cloud rising out of the ground.

No reaction from inside the house.

The heat from the fire warmed one side of my face. My ears rang.

I glanced at Maj.

Still no reaction from the house . . .

Then, the front door of the house was thrown open and two men I'd never seen before, both wearing suits, darted out, guns drawn.

The door slammed closed behind them, and my hands started to shake. I didn't have to do the math to know we'd made a big mistake.

The men approached the burning car cautiously, crouched low, guns ready. They didn't see us, but Maj had them covered.

No sign of Kiki or Gaines. They'd stayed inside with M.K. How many others were in there with them? I tried desperately to think of a way to draw them out.

"What the fuck's happening?" someone yelled from inside the house. "You see anybody?" he shouted through the broken windows.

It sounded like Kiki.

Neither of the two men answered.

Then one of them spotted the empty gas can.

"*¡Mira!*" he yelled, pointing to it. "We got company!"

His partner shouted something in Spanish and began circling the car, his gun held in front of him in a combat grip, scanning the tree line for a target.

My brilliant plan had come apart at the seams.

I tried to salvage it. "Kiki! Gaines! Out of the house! Now! You—by the car—down. On the ground! Both of you! Do it!"

The two men hesitated, then hit the deck hard, rolling in opposite directions and firing at me as they moved.

I ducked as bullets slammed into the roof of the shed, showering me with splintered plywood.

When the shooting stopped, I risked looking. But the two men had taken cover behind the burning car.

Then one of them stood and fired several rounds at Maj.

Maj touched off his shotgun and the shooter disappeared in the smoke.

His partner, still hidden behind the car, screamed and kept on screaming. Firing blindly at the van, he tried to pin Maj down.

It was moving too fast—spinning out of control. I slid across the dirt floor of the shed to get a better angle on the Mercedes. But before I'd gone three feet, Maj's shotgun went off again and the screaming from behind the car ceased.

When the blast echoed away, a voice inside the house shouted, "JoJo! Ramon! Where the fuck are you? What's happening out there?"

No one answered.

The front door opened a crack and Kiki shouted, "I know it's you, Sumner. You and the goddamn gardener. You fucked with the wrong people, asshole! Now you got to pay!"

"Come out of there, Kiki!" I yelled. "The police are on the way! Let her go and get out while you can!"

His laughter carried across the twenty yards separating us. "Cavalry better get here quick if they're gonna save you and the nigger!"

I shot at him, but the rounds went high and the door slammed shut again.

Just as the door closed, Maj, crouched low and moving fast, zigzagged from the van to the shed.

"You okay?" he asked, kneeling beside me, breathing hard.

I nodded. "Some party, huh?"

Nodding, he broke open the breech of his gun, shook out the

spent shells and reloaded. Then he wiped the sweat off his brow with the back of his hand.

He was bleeding from a three-inch furrow where a bullet had grazed his shoulder.

"You're hit," I said.

He glanced at his wound. "Good t'ing dey can't shoot worth a shit. What you want to do now?"

I looked at the house and shook my head. "Not much we can do. They've got M.K."

Then, as if they had heard me, a voice from inside the house called, "Hold your fire!"

A moment later, M.K., hands held loosely at her sides, appeared at the front door, a gun held to her head.

46

THEY WALKED OUT OF THE house slowly, M.K. leading the way. The man who had offered me a cigar stood close behind her, holding a short-barreled .38 against the back of her head.

"Step away from the shed!" he shouted. "Drop your weapons. It's over. We aren't going to wait for the rest of your party to join us."

I stood up, showing myself without leaving the limited shelter of the shed. But I kept my mouth shut, not wanting to tell him there was no rest of our party.

M.K. looked pale, but she appeared to be in one piece. She met and held my eye, trying to tell me something without speaking.

But I couldn't read her expression.

Then, Kiki and Gaines stepped out of the house.

Kiki held an Uzi. Gaines gripped his briefcase as if it were a weapon too.

If anyone was left inside, they didn't make themselves known.

Maj stood and showed himself, training his shotgun on the group. If he let go with both barrels he'd cut them all down. But he couldn't fire without hitting M.K. first.

I held Turo's gun ready, but there was no clean shot.

It was a stalemate.

The man holding the gun on M.K. calmly surveyed the situation. He was dressed for the office and looked strangely unruffled and out of place here.

"Lay down your guns," he said, caressing M.K.'s hair with the stubby barrel of the .38. "I won't hesitate to shoot her. Although it would be a great pity to ruffle such beautiful feathers."

I gritted my teeth and said, "Are you okay, M.K.?"

She started to say something, but a quick tap of the barrel against the back of her neck changed her mind.

I stared at her, trying to weigh the odds. But the odds sucked. They'd changed the moment the Mercedes had pulled up. I'd been too hyped on my own adrenaline to see it. Blood had been spilled and more was about to be spilled. I tried to think of a way to stop it. But how?

Maj eased forward a step. As long as he held that shotgun, we at least had their attention.

I decided to try and change the odds. "Let her go, Guillermo. You have what you wanted. You don't need her anymore."

"Guillermo?" He smiled. "How would you know my name?"

"Kiki told me. He told me a lot of things. Just let her go and we'll leave peacefully. No more shooting."

Ignoring me, Kiki edged toward the still burning car. Staring beyond it, he called out, "Both dead, boss. Fucking shotgun tore Ramon to pieces."

He took another step away from the group.

"Tell him he best stop where he is!" Maj shouted. "One more step and dis nigger gonna blow him straight to hell."

Kiki froze, then drifted closer to M.K., his Uzi trained steadily on Maj. But at that range he knew pulling the trigger would get them all killed.

Guillermo shook his head, his smile fading. "Gentlemen, we don't seem to have grounds to bargain in good faith. I'm afraid my father will be most disappointed."

"Your father?" I asked, not paying attention to his words, wracking my brain for a way out.

"He loved Ramon. Brought him here from Spain. And look what you've done . . ." He shook his head sadly. "No, I'm afraid things have gone too far to simply walk away. And you, my friend, share the blame. Miss Stevenson is innocent of any wrongdoing. I wish her no harm. Her father and my father may harbor certain enmities, but that doesn't make her my enemy. I would be inclined to let her go. But how can I do so with that gun your man is holding aimed at my chest? I think it's time we discussed value, no?"

"What value?" I asked, watching Gaines, the bile rising in my throat.

He seemed to be following the conversation with great discomfort. When the shooting started, I planned on taking him out first.

"I told you before . . . ," Guillermo was saying. "This is business, Wil. Nothing personal. As my father always says, 'It's a small man who puts his personal interests in front of the general good.' Wise, no?"

"Your father . . ." It took a minute for his words to sink in. "Guillermo Salgo? You're Roberto Salgo's son?"

He nodded. Then, without taking his eyes off me, he said, "Broward, you failed us. We promised you power and responsibility, a chance to be your own man. A chance to escape your father's shadow. All you had to do was deliver the file. Simple, no? Do you think I wanted *this*? Any of this? *You* forced me to get involved, and now look . . . Look what you've caused!"

I glanced at Gaines; he was shaking his head.

"What a team we would have made in Tallahassee," Guillermo Salgo continued, talking to Gaines. "My father in office, your family connections . . . All you had to do was control the situation—deliver the file. Instead, *this* is what you've delivered to me."

M.K. turned on Gaines, in spite of the gun. "Is it true?" she blurted out before Guillermo spun her back around.

"It's not what it sounds like," Gaines said.

"Oh my God, Broward!" she cried, her face twisted with pain. "You don't know what you've done. Why? Why?"

Gaines flushed.

He opened his mouth, but before he could say anything, Guillermo cut him off. "Enough conversation!" He pulled back the hammer of his pistol. "You have thirty seconds to throw down your weapons and step away from the shed. Otherwise she dies."

"She dies and you die," I said, my hand tightening on the pistol.

"No!" Gaines shouted. "Both of you—wait!"

He reached into his briefcase and pulled out the file. Then, before anyone could react, he darted toward the burning car and threw it on the fire. "It's over. No one can harm Roberto now, so let her go!"

"Stop him!" Guillermo screamed. "My father wants that file."

It was too late, but Kiki crouched and sprinted for the car anyway, firing a short burst from the Uzi as he ran.

The bullets sent up little geysers of dirt all around Maj's legs. But he didn't flinch.

His shotgun jumped and the blast lifted Kiki off his feet in a pink spray of blood.

He fell to the ground, bloodied and broken.

But before he'd come to rest, Guillermo Salgo had pulled M.K. hard against him. Keeping her between us, using her as a shield, he moved toward the van.

"I'll kill her!" he screamed, his veneer of fine manners shattered. "If you move, I'll kill her. I swear to God, I'll fucking blow her head off!"

I stepped toward him anyway, Turo's pistol held down at my side. "Let her go, Guillermo. Let her go and drive away. We won't try and stop you."

"No!" he shouted, eyes flicking from me to Maj and back again. "Stay put! She goes with me!"

I moved a step closer, but there was nothing I could do to stop him.

He dragged her toward the van.

Out of the corner of my eye I saw Gaines reach into his brief-case and pull out the big pistol he'd held on Maj and me. Dropping the briefcase, he raised the gun and took an unsteady step toward Salgo.

"Guillermo, let her go."

Startled by Gaines's voice, Salgo turned to look at him.

When he did, I raised Turo's gun and screamed, "Down, M.K.! Down!"

She hesitated, then dropped to the ground.

Guillermo spun around, but it was too late.

I fired twice.

M.K. screamed as he collapsed beside her, blood fountaining from two dime-sized holes in his forehead.

The pistol suddenly felt heavy in my hand. I ran to her side, vaguely aware that I'd just killed a man, but not ready to think about what it meant.

"Oh God! Oh God!" she repeated, climbing to her knees. "Get me out of here!"

Gaines, still holding his gun in his right hand, clutching his side with his left, stepped over and looked down at her.

"I'm sorry, M.K. So sorry . . . ," he whispered. "I just wanted something of my own."

She stared at him, horrified.

He took his hand away from the wound in his side and looked down at it as though surprised. Blood stained his shirt and trousers.

Part of the shotgun spread that had taken Kiki down must have torn into him too.

Without another word, he sat down hard, the pistol falling from his right hand.

"No one was supposed to get hurt . . . ," he stuttered, his face white with shock. Then he collapsed onto his side, curled in the fetal position.

M.K. looked at him, unable to speak.

Maj bent and picked up Gaines's gun. "Best I be checkin' dis place out. Don't need no more surprises," he said gruffly, moving toward the house.

I put my hand on M.K.'s shoulder. "It's going to be all right now," I said softly. "Just hang on for a little while longer, we'll get you out of here."

She swallowed hard and nodded.

Turning to Gaines, I asked, "How bad is it?"

He looked up at me, comprehension fading from his eyes.

"I—I want to go home now," he said, his voice small and barely audible. "Don't tell my father. Please just take me home, I'm late."

I started to say something, but M.K. spoke first, her voice a strained whisper. "It's okay, Broward. We'll take you home."

Moving slowly, she crawled to him and lifted his head onto her lap. Stroking his thick blond curls, she whispered, "Just rest. It'll be okay, Broward. We'll get you home."

Then she looked at me, tears streaming down her pale cheeks. "Get help. Please get him help."

But it was too late.

47

M.K. SAT ON THE GROUND, Gaines's head still in her lap. She seemed frozen in place, pale and stiff, her hands covering her face. A shiver ran through her in spite of the warmth of the afternoon. I couldn't tell whether or not she was crying. She hadn't suffered any physical injuries, but she'd been shaken to the core. And that kind of hurt could be slower to heal than any number of broken bones.

I stayed by her side while Maj checked to see that the house was empty. The full brunt of what had happened hadn't hit me yet, but I felt loose inside, a cold, watery hollowness in the pit of my stomach. Looking around the devastated yard, it was a miracle that we'd come through it in one piece.

The fire had died down, but smoke still rose from the burned-out hulk of the Mercedes, casting a dark shadow over the house. Torn and bloodied bodies lay in impossible postures. It was a war zone, but none of the dead wore uniforms. Neither did the living. The flames had consumed Andrew's file, but I still had Tessereau's book, its hard angles and sharp corners snug against my belly.

Maj didn't take long. Except for the three of us, everyone on the property was either dead, or in Turo's case, seriously incapacitated. But Guillermo Salgo hadn't operated alone. For all we knew, Lito had taken the dogs to the vet and might return at any time. I forced myself up onto my feet. No telling who he might bring along for the ride.

M.K. refused to move. Maybe she couldn't. I remembered how my legs had turned to putty the night Amanda was killed. They weren't exactly steel posts now.

We gave her a few minutes to gather herself. But it did no good.

Finally Maj and I coaxed her up off the ground and practically carried her to Gaines's car. We folded her into the front seat. Then I faced the unpleasant task of searching his blood-soaked pockets for the Jag's keys.

I started to use Gaines's car phone to call 911, then changed my mind and dialed Laspada's number.

Maj, still clutching his shotgun, kept an eye on the tree line, just in case.

Laspada answered on the first ring. He reacted with cool professionalism, advising me to stay put. If he was surprised by my call, he didn't show it. He asked who was involved—if anyone needed immediate medical attention. When he heard Salgo's name, he cut the conversation short, saying he would notify emergency services himself, not wanting to talk any longer than necessary on a cellular phone.

"Stay where you are and don't talk to anyone until I get there," he instructed before hanging up. "The world's going to know soon enough anyway."

Three state troopers, two sheriff's deputies, and a Palm Beach County fire rescue team arrived, sirens screaming, within ten minutes.

The sheriff's deputies separated Maj and me as soon as they'd had a chance to survey the situation. They demanded ID, and weren't shy about searching us for weapons. Standard operating procedure—I was all too familiar with the routine. I started to argue when they took Tessereau's book away from me. But I held my tongue. Laspada would get it back soon enough.

The fire rescue team split up, one EMT tending to M.K., the

other roaming the property with the state troopers. Three tense-looking men, guns drawn, faces tight.

By the time Laspada reached the scene, almost forty-five minutes later, M.K. and Turo had been transported in separate ambulances to the hospital. State, county, and local police were crawling all over the property. A coroner's van bumped down the dirt track, followed by a news crew. Two helicopters hovered overhead. Members of the county's SWAT team milled around a black truck, looking vaguely disappointed, there being nothing left to shoot at. It was controlled confusion, a repeat of the swarm of law enforcement personnel that had descended on the Stevensons' house.

But it didn't have the same effect on me. Maybe my perspective had changed.

The deputy who had taken Tessereau's book escorted me to his patrol car and installed me in the rear seat. "We'll need your statement, sir," he said. "Just give me a few minutes, then I'll run you over to the sheriff's office."

I nodded, saving my breath. There would be a lot of questions and I wasn't sure I had all of the answers. I watched through the windshield as another deputy escorted a disgruntled-looking Maj to a different car. I wanted to tell him to stay calm, but it was impossible.

The patrol car I'd been placed in was a portable cage—no handles on the insides of the doors, thick wire mesh between the front and the backseats. The windows were cracked, but it was hot and close and smelled of sweat, French fries, and fear. I was beyond tired. I closed my eyes and tried to relax. But it didn't work. That watery feeling in my gut climbed into my chest. I was worried about M.K. This wasn't over. Not yet.

Finally, Laspada arrived with Harris in tow. Once he spoke to the sheriff's deputies, Maj and I were released into his custody.

Harris conferred briefly with the coroner's people, then disappeared into the house.

Laspada waved to someone, then took me by the arm. Maj followed.

"This is some shit storm you walked into. You're both lucky to be alive," he growled, leading us to his car. "Why didn't you call *before* you started shooting? You have some kind of hero complex?"

"There wasn't time," I said, trying to keep up.

He stopped in his tracks and stared at me. "Do you realize what's about to happen? Do you have any idea what the Salgo name means in South Florida?"

I stared right back at him. "I'll show you what it means. One of those deputies took a book from me. Get it back and I'll show you exactly what kind of people the Salgos are."

Laspada glared at me for a moment, then frowned. "You two have a lot of explaining to do. I want formal statements. You'll give them at the station. Get in the car—let's go."

"What about M.K.?" I asked. "She and her father may still be in danger. I want to check on her."

"Get in the car, Wil. We'll call the hospital from the station."

I didn't move. "I want your assurance that a police guard will be watching out for her."

His eyes went cold behind his glasses. He started to say something, but Maj interrupted. "Somebody assign a damn guard to her when dis foolishness start, wouldn't be no need to be takin' statements now. Would there?"

Laspada opened his mouth, then closed it and shook his head. "All right. Your point is well taken. You have my word that guards will be assigned to Miss Stevenson twenty-four hours a day until this matter is resolved."

Three hours and five cups of coffee later, Captain Laspada looked even less happy.

We sat on opposite sides of the table in the same conference room Detective Tapsell and I had used to go through the mug books. Maj was down the hall with another detective. I assumed he was having as good a time as I was.

"It's the goddamnedest story I've ever heard," Laspada said, turning off the tape recorder and rising from his seat at the table.

"It's true. All of it."

He stepped to the window. Then he turned and looked at me, his face grim. "'True' . . . I like that word. I hear it every day." He turned back to the window. "Now all you ask is that I go out and arrest a man like Salgo . . . without a shred of hard evidence. Just your word. Hell, we don't even have this file I've been hearing so much about. It's not going to happen. I can't do it."

"You have no choice," I said.

He stared at his own reflection in the window. "So you say. So you say."

I got up from the table and went to stand beside him. "Sometimes the truth is enough."

He started to answer me when a secretary burst into the conference room and said, "Captain Laspada, I think you might want to see this. Roberto Salgo is about to go on television—it's a live press conference."

48

LASPADA STEPPED OVER TO a built-in cabinet and opened a pair of doors, revealing a television monitor. He turned it on and stood back, hands on his hips, watching as Roberto Salgo took his place at a podium.

Salgo cleared his throat, a grim expression on his aristocratic face.

"I have a prepared statement," he began, his nearly accent-less voice deep and somber. The resemblance he bore to his son, Guillermo, was remarkable; I don't know how I missed it. But there was nothing lazy in this old man's eyes. They were as hard and sharp as shards of ice.

"Two hours ago I was informed that my only son, Guillermo Diego Salgo, was killed."

The reporters gathered in front of the podium let out a collective gasp.

Salgo quieted them with a gesture.

"A little past one o'clock this afternoon, my son called me in order to let me know that an acquaintance of his was in serious trouble. The daughter of Andrew Stevenson, one of our most successful industrialists, a man I have known and admired for many years, had been kidnapped and was being held for ransom. The timing of this reprehensible act led my son to believe it was related to the failed robbery that culminated in the death of Amanda Stevenson, Andrew's wife, just last week. Fearing there was no time to lose, my son, and his close friend Broward Gaines Junior, a respected officer of the court, accompanied by members of my own security detail, attempted to secure Miss Stevenson's safe release. All of the facts are not yet available, but it is my understanding that after safely removing Miss Stevenson from harm's way, my son and Mr. Gaines were brutally gunned down."

He paused and drew a deep breath, looking directly into the camera, his lined face the very picture of grave sorrow and strength.

Then he continued: "My staff and I are working closely with law enforcement officials to see that the men who engineered this tragedy are brought to justice. A ransom note and other pieces of incriminating evidence have been turned over to the Florida Bureau of Investigation. My son secured these items prior to joining Mr. Gaines in an attempt to rescue the Stevenson girl, a heroic attempt that succeeded at the cost of their own lives. It is with great sadness—the grief that only a parent can feel—that I come before you now in order to honor my son. As more detailed information becomes available, I promise to keep you informed. In the meantime, I ask that you pray for my family, and for those other families who have suffered such a grievous loss today." He stepped back from the microphone.

Pandemonium broke out among the reporters, who must have thought they were there to cover another campaign update.

A tall black man in the first row shouted a question. "Mr. Salgo, sir, how will this affect your run for the governor's office?"

Salgo, who had turned away from the podium, turned back to the microphone, an angry tear in his eye.

"My son was killed by criminals today. If my son can be killed so easily, so brutally, how safe are your children? You ask how

this will affect my campaign ... Well, I don't know how to
answer that question. But I can tell you this—if becoming governor will allow me to make this state a safer place for every single one of us, I won't quit. No, sir. I won't quit. Not while men
with guns think they can terrorize the rest of us. I refuse to let
the gangs and the drug dealers and the pimps and the thieves
have the last word. Not while the memory of my son lives on."

With that he turned and strode from the podium.

Laspada looked at me.

I stood there, stunned.

"What do you think of that?" he asked, shaking his head in
wonder as he turned off the television.

I stared at him. "You don't believe any of it, do you?"

Laspada took off his glasses and began to polish them. "No.
His story doesn't support the facts as I understand them. Now,
ask me if that matters."

"How can it not matter?"

Without his glasses he looked older, tired. "What I think or
believe won't matter at all. Not if Salgo can really produce those
documents. If he has a ransom note—a credible-looking piece of
paper that supports his version of events, and I can't believe it
would be too difficult to obtain such a document, not if what
you've told me is true—he succeeds in creating a scenario at
least as likely as the one you've presented."

"Wait a minute!" I protested.

But Laspada held out his hands. "Whoa! I listened to you—
now you listen to me. I believe you. But that's not the point.
We're talking about a powerful man—maybe the next governor
of Florida. Without a direct link between the thugs who took
M. K. Stevenson and the Salgos, we've got nothing to go on but
your word."

I opened my mouth, but he cut me off. "No! Without hard
proof it's not enough."

"You're forgetting about M.K. Guillermo held a gun to her
head. She'll refute everything Salgo just said."

He smiled bitterly. "M.K. must have been terrified—scared
half to death. Can she identify Guillermo Salgo as the man who

kidnapped her? He was probably a hundred miles away with a dozen reputable witnesses. Maybe she misunderstood what he was doing with that gun this afternoon. Maybe he was trying to protect her, and you and Maj inadvertently got in the way. Maybe it was all a tragic mistake. And speaking of Maj, what kind of witness do you think he'll make?"

"A damn good one," I snapped.

He pursed his lips. "Maj isn't going to be a witness. We looked into him as a possible suspect after Amanda Stevenson's murder. He's a good man—clean. A family man. No criminal record, not even a traffic violation. But he's been here for over ten years and he never bothered to fill out the papers for a resident alien card. No green card. Which makes him an illegal alien."

"You're not going to—"

"No." He shook his head. "We're not going to pursue the matter, I'm not going to let anything happen to him. Unless Salgo's people get hold of him first."

He paused.

"Wil, I've been around for a while—seen some crazy things happen. And one thing I've learned—in the criminal courts, you have the rights you can defend. And Salgo can afford to do a whole lot of defending. If I can make a pretty good argument on his behalf, imagine what his own people can do. He'll have the best lawyers and spin doctors money can buy. If I kick this investigation upstairs, what do you think is the first thing the DA is going to look at? He's going to assess his chances of winning. You saw Salgo's performance. The man's a master at creating an image. His son's body is still warm and Salgo's on television condemning the men who killed him and asking the public to pray for him. How do you top that?"

I said nothing, wondering whether he was trying to convince me or himself.

He pressed his lips into a hard line. "Without irrefutable evidence you don't touch a man like Salgo."

By the time Laspada finished talking, I felt sick to my stomach.

Judging from the sour look on his face, he did too.

We stood in front of the blank television screen for a few minutes, lost in our own thoughts.

Finally, he stepped back to the table and picked up his notepad. He studied it for a moment, then sat down heavily.

"What are you going to do now?" I asked.

"I'll tell you what I'm not going to do," he said, dropping the pad onto the table. "I'm not going to lay down and watch it happen. The Stevensons deserve better. But I'm going to move cautiously. Quietly. No reason to tread on any toes till I know where this is going to end up."

It wasn't the answer I wanted, but it was better than nothing.

"How can I help?" I asked.

He turned on the tape recorder. "Take me through it one more time—slowly."

49

OVER THE NEXT THREE DAYS I shuttled back and forth
between the hospital and the police station. M.K. was preoccu-
pied and at times withdrawn. But the energy between us had
shifted in some subtle way. Neither of us said anything—but it
was there. In the way she looked at me. In the hurried touches
and lingering glances. Given the circumstances, it was enough.

Andrew had suffered a stroke upon hearing that M.K. was
safe. Actually two strokes, the last of which had left him unable
to speak and paralyzed on one side of his body. He seemed
aware of his daughter's presence, but he hadn't been told the
details of her rescue. His doctors feared the strain might be too
much on his ravaged body.

M.K. stayed by her father's side, eating and sleeping at the
hospital. Laspada provided a very visible police presence—one
officer stationed outside the ICU at all times, another officer
waiting outside the hospital itself, prepared to escort M.K. to
any location she requested.

So far, she'd refused to leave the fourth floor.

Charteen prepared hot meals and packed a change of clothing every morning for her. But the food went mostly uneaten.
And fashion was the last thing on M.K.'s mind.

She and I sat together in the waiting room when Andrew was too sedated to know anyone was there. Sometimes we sat quietly, other times we talked. But always about Andrew and Amanda, M.K's childhood growing up in Palm Beach, never about what had happened that day by the swamp. Broward Gaines was never mentioned. Laspada had been right—she seemed terrified of Salgo, unwilling to even discuss what had to be done next. I brought the subject up again and again, tried to convince her that we should tell our story to the press. Try Salgo in the court of public opinion if we couldn't get him into a court of law. But she claimed she wasn't ready.

Who could blame her? I understood her fears, but I had the nagging feeling she was hiding something. Something important. And the effort was costing her.

On the third afternoon, it came to a head.

"We have to talk about this," I told her. "It's killing me—every time I turn on the television I see Salgo's face. If we don't do something, he's going to get himself elected governor."

She stood up and crossed the room, pulling open the curtains. "We've been over this. I told you I can't do anything about him now. I won't put my father through any more stress. It's up to the police. They'll deal with Mr. Salgo. Let them do their job."

I shook my head. "They can't do a thing. Not without proof, and I'm not so sure they're ever going to get any."

She turned on me. "And that's supposed to be my fault?"

"No," I said gently. "Of course not. But the election is in less than three weeks. If we don't go to the press now, tell them what really happened, he could win. What would that do to your father?"

"I don't have time to discuss this now," she said, glancing at her watch and beginning to pace. "He should wake up soon. I better go in. I want to be there when he opens his eyes."

"M.K., you can't keep avoiding this. Your father wanted to stop Salgo. We can help him do that. We owe it to him to follow through."

She started toward the door, then stopped and glared at me. "Who are you to tell me what I owe him? It's my father lying back there. He's all I've got. And he's dying. Do you hear me? He's dying. What am I supposed to do? Tell him how I almost got killed? Put more pressure on him? Drag his name through the mud in order to seek some kind of vengeance on Roberto Salgo? I want my father protected—I want him to have time to heal. He's too fragile now. We can worry about revenge later."

I stood and stepped to her side and tried to put my arm around her. But she pulled away. "Don't you patronize me. I don't need that."

"I'm sorry. I don't want to see your father hurt any more than he already is. But you have to—"

She cut me off. "I don't have to do anything! What's wrong with you? My father's got a tiny chance to pull through this. One chance in a million. Can't you understand that? I don't give a damn about Salgo. Not right now. All I want is my father back. He's lost enough already. A wife and a son—it's enough for now!"

I intended to try and soothe her, but my own anger boiled up inside me and spilled over.

I shouted, louder than I meant to, "The man is an animal! He has to be stopped. Can't you see, we owe it to your father. Salgo's responsible for your mother's death. He'd have killed you too! Aren't you angry? Don't you give a damn?"

She tried to turn away, but I didn't let her. "No! A son isn't enough. It's not a big enough price to pay. Guillermo Salgo deserved to die—but it doesn't begin to pay for his father's sins. Roberto Salgo needs to pay his own debts."

She looked up at me, her face ashen. "You don't understand," she whispered.

"The hell I don't!"

She backed up a couple of steps. Tears filled her eyes. "You're wrong. I'm not talking about Guillermo Salgo."

"Then what are you talking about?" I snapped.

"I'm talking about Broward. Broward Gaines." Her voice was so low I wasn't sure I heard her right.

"What are you saying?"

Crossing her arms in front of her chest, she met my eyes.

"Broward Gaines was my half-brother. My father doesn't know he's dead—doesn't know that his own son betrayed him. I'm not going to tell him now. And I'm not going to let you or anyone else—including your goddamn court of public opinion—tell him either. It would kill him."

My mouth hung open. I stared at her, trying to figure out what to say.

Shaking her head, she stepped around me. "If you're finished telling me what I should and shouldn't do, I'm going to go and check on my father."

She left me standing there, staring after her.

50

I DROVE BACK TO THE HOUSE and sat alone on the Stevensons' seawall, thinking about what M.K. had told me, trying to mold it into a shape I could wrap my mind around. Gaines was Andrew's son . . . On one level it was easy enough to grasp. But the ramifications were too complicated to simply accept it at face value. Did Broward Senior know Broward Junior wasn't really a little Ward? Had Broward known the truth? Or was he too busy trying to climb out from under his father's shadow? Which father? Did Amanda suspect? It made my head spin.

As I sat there, I realized how little I knew about these people, how far removed from their world I truly was. What was holding me here? Not the appraisal—that was over. Amanda's body had been cremated; a private memorial service was to be scheduled at a later date. I didn't know what was being planned for Gaines, and I didn't care. I suppose it didn't really matter which shadow he had tried so hard to step out of. He must have believed that whatever promises Guillermo Salgo had made would turn him into a big man. Just like Daddy. I'd always envied rich kids—their cars and girls and easy access to everything that looked worth having. But I'd never thought about the private hell they had to endure to earn it all. It was so predictably pitiful, at least in hindsight, that I laughed out loud, startling a pair of hunting gulls. This was the only mourning Broward Gaines would ever get from me.

What now? I had the pieces of a career to sort through, responsibilities back in New York. I forced myself to think about the things that had to be done. The bank, creditors . . .

The art world beckoned and I tried to convince myself to go through the motions, but I had no stomach for auction deadlines and condition reports, didn't feel like waxing enthusiastic over a few colorful daubs of paint on canvas. The season was about to kick into gear, but I found myself dreading the whole goddamn charade. Who cared what the Germans were buying this year? So what if figurative painting had been declared alive and well after decades of decline? Cézanne had been canonized as the century's greatest visual prophet—ask me if I rejoiced.

For an hour, I sat at the refectory table, staring at the shiny bleached oak of the closed drawers, trying to decide what to do next. The dehumidifier clicked off.

I had my eyes closed when M.K. walked in and cleared her throat.

"Are you working on the appraisal?" she asked.

I shook my head. "No. I didn't think it was a priority anymore."

She hesitated. "No. I guess it's not. Did Broward ever pay you?"

"No. We'll talk about it when your father is better."

She pressed her lips into a frown. "It would be wrong to let money come between us . . ."

I nodded. But how could money not come between us?

Stepping to the table, she stood across from me and searched my face with her eyes. "I came to tell you that I'm sorry about the way I spoke to you at the hospital. This isn't your fault. I know that—I know what you've done for us. I apologize."

I took a deep breath. "I still don't understand—about Broward."

She was quiet for a moment, and the awkward silence built.

"It's not something we talked about," she said finally. "It was just there. Jessica Gaines and my father were lovers before my mother came into the picture. Broward was an accident. They kept it a secret from everyone—including him. But my mother knew—and she made sure he was always welcome, always part of our lives. She told me a long time ago, when Broward got it into his head that I should be his girlfriend. I understand how you feel about Salgo—why you want to go to the press. If there were some way to do it without bringing my father and Broward into it . . ." She fell silent. We both knew that was impossible.

"Your father should be here," I said, changing the subject. "It might do him some good to be surrounded by his collection again."

She looked around the vault. "I don't think he cares anymore. But I could bring a few things to the hospital, see if he responds to them."

I nodded. "That's a good idea."

Her eyes found mine, and held them.

Then, without another word, she stepped around the table, leaned over, and kissed me on the lips.

"There. . . . I've wanted to do that since the night at the museum," she said. "It seems like a long time ago."

I stood up and drew her into my arms.

I closed my eyes and put my face in her hair, breathing her in. "Great timing, huh?"

"Yeah," she whispered into my neck. "Great timing."

We stood in the vault, holding on to each other.

Then she pulled away. "You're not going to let it go, are you?"

"I can't, M.K."

We stared at each other. The moment stretched out.

Then she nodded. "I guess I knew that . . ."

"I won't hurt your father. You have my word."

She turned and looked around the vault. "I hope all of your appraisals don't turn out this way."

I looked around the vault too. Then it dawned on me that I hadn't told anyone about the sketchbook. "This may seem like an odd time to bring this up—but I'd like to show you something special."

I stepped to the miscellaneous drawer and pulled out the Velázquez sketchbook. Carrying it to the table, I said, "I found this in your father's mystery collection. He hadn't gotten around to researching it. It may be the most important thing he owns."

"It doesn't look like much," M.K. said, thumbing through the pages.

"Take my word for it. It's amazing."

I explained how rare and important such a sketchbook was— what it might be worth if I could prove it to be authentic.

She looked dubious. "*If* it's authentic."

I shrugged.

"Take it to the hospital," I suggested. "Tell Andrew what I think he discovered. It might catch his attention."

She picked it up and looked at her watch. "I want to get back before the shift changes. You'll be here later?"

"I'll be here," I promised.

She smiled. Then she kissed me once more and stepped out of the vault.

51

LATER THAT AFTERNOON, I sat at Andrew's desk in the library, nursing a shot of whiskey. I still had the silver lighter and the news clipping I'd saved from his file. I'd considered turning them over to Laspada. But for reasons I hadn't fully thought out, I'd decided to keep them. At least for the time being.

The article shed no new light on the matter, but I brooded over it anyway, sipped whiskey and tried to find secrets hidden between the lines. I sat in Andrew's chair and studied the clipping as though some master plan would jump out at me if only I looked hard enough. It didn't. I picked it up and turned it this way and that in the late afternoon light. I reread it for the hundredth time, trying to see why Andrew had bothered to keep it. The *Miami Herald* reporter, Raoul Hernandez, had written a scathing article about the death of the man named Jonathan Korn. Hernandez had fallen just short of out-and-out accusing big sugar of having engineered the mysterious plane crash that took Korn's life. But there was no mention of Salgo—no speculation of who might actually have tampered with Korn's plane. It was easy enough to imagine Kiki, or someone like him, fiddling a fuel line, or cutting a control cable, but how did that help me now? I set the article down on the desk, picked up the lighter, and turned it over in my hand as I finished the last of the whiskey.

If only it could talk.

There had to be a way to bring Salgo down without involving Andrew. It was there. I could feel it. I just couldn't see it.

I stood up and looked around the library, started to pour another drink, then changed my mind. I thought about going outside for a walk on the beach. Instead, I picked up the telephone. As much as I didn't want to face the responsibilities I'd left unresolved in New York, I couldn't pretend they didn't exist.

I called my answering service. A couple of friends had called to say they'd seen my name in the paper and wanted to know if I was okay. But aside from Ev Lenoir at the bank, and three calls from the Peraltas, the rest of my messages were from bill collectors.

I returned the Peraltas' call first, hoping they'd received a check for the sale of "Sasha." Then I'd deal with Ev Lenoir.

Isaac answered on the second ring. "My God, Wil, Lara and I read about you. Are you in one piece? What happened down there?"

It was dark by the time I finished telling him my story. I hadn't intended to dump it on him, but he'd been so inquisitive and persistent—gently pressing and prying until the words poured out, the details, my feelings for M.K., the promise I'd made to do nothing that might hasten Andrew's decline. Maybe it was the concern in his voice that had set me off. I wasn't sure, but after I finished, I found that I felt strangely relieved.

He was silent for a moment. Only the sound of his measured breathing audible.

Then he said, "Walnut juice. It was walnut juice."

I looked at the telephone. "What?"

Isaac cleared his throat. "The boy who killed this Amanda Stevenson—he'd painted himself with walnut juice. That's what rubbed off on you when you tried to fight him. It was a message. This Salgo was sending a message to Andrew Stevenson."

"I don't understand," I said.

"How much do you know about what happened in Spain during the civil war?"

"Not much," I admitted.

"It was a terrible time," he said. "The Spanish fascists weren't so different from the Nazis. Not that such things can be measured—"

"What about the walnut juice?" I asked before he strayed too far from the topic.

"Of course," Isaac said. "When Franco first came back to Spain from Morocco to put down the October revolution in 1934, he had a large number of black Moors under his command. This was shocking to the general population. It had been several centuries since the Christians had driven the Moors out of Spain, but when these black troops swarmed out of Africa—marching inland through the very heart of the country to put down the miners, killing and looting and raping along the way—they spread before them a wave of terror. Their fearsome reputation made the job of quelling the actual uprising easier than it might have been had Franco used Spanish soldiers. He never forgot this lesson.

"Later, during the civil war, the worst of his officers instructed their men to boil the shells of walnuts to create a dye that would turn their skin brown. They painted themselves with this mixture and from a distance appeared to be Moorish, terrifying all who had the misfortune to cross their paths. It was a very successful strategy. A strategy this Salgo must have assumed Andrew Stevenson would remember. Painting that boy with walnut juice was meant to scare Stevenson into handing over the file, remind him of who he was dealing with."

"You're serious?" I asked.

"I could be wrong," Isaac admitted. "But this Salgo is a man in love with his own history. Why else use the Blue Arrows' name—the graffiti?"

"Did you know him?" I asked.

Isaac hesitated. "Roberto Salgo? No. But I knew enough like him."

I looked down at the article, thinking about what Isaac had pointed out. *Salgo was a man in love with his own history . . .* The thought rolled around in my head. How does a man like that bury his glorious past in a vault of lies? It had to lay, festering, just under the surface. Why else would he have used the old symbol, the walnut juice? His own son had called his actions vain. If the right situation presented itself . . .

"Isaac, would you be willing to come down here—confront Salgo in person, help me draw him out? Even if it means misleading him?"

"Of course," he blurted out without hesitation. "When do you want me? Such men must be exposed. The world must never be allowed to forget."

In the background, I heard Lara's voice. "What are you saying, Isaac?"

He held his hand over the phone, muffling his reply, but I could still hear it. "Wil wants me to come to Florida. He needs my help to bring this animal to justice."

Lara said, "Don't be foolish, Isaac. A hero you're not."

He chuckled softly. "That's because I have you to protect me, no? One hero is enough in any family."

I cleared my throat before they could get started. "If I can set it up so that Salgo trips over his own beloved history, maybe I can get him to reveal himself without drawing the Stevensons into it at all."

"How, Wil? What are you thinking?" Isaac asked.

I picked up the article, the excitement rising in me. Then I explained what I wanted him to do.

"This is possible, I think," Isaac said slowly. "How soon do you want me down there?"

"You're not going without me," Lara said, loudly enough to be heard quite clearly.

52

I⊤ ⊤OOK ⊤HREE MORE PHONE calls to set it up.

The first call was to Raoul Hernandez at the *Miami Herald*. Laspada had used me as a tool. I planned to use Hernandez and his newspaper the same way.

It was late, but I caught him at his office. He picked up on the first ring, sounding harried and less than thrilled when I told him I'd called about Roberto Salgo.

"Mr. Sumner, I appreciate the phone call, but I'm on deadline," Hernandez said. "I cover business, not politics. My only interest in Salgo had to do with his involvement with sugar money. I'll give you the name of—"

"Wait! That's why I called you," I lied. "I thought you might be interested in knowing that Salgo is dirty."

"And your point is . . ."

"Somebody should expose him for what he truly is . . ."

"He's a politician, last I heard."

"He's a dirty politician, Mr. Hernandez. As dirty as they come."

"Yeah—yeah. So tell me something I haven't heard," he grumbled. In the background I could hear the tapping of keys on a computer keyboard. "Listen, I'm kind of busy here; if you have something I can use, fine, I'm all ears. But I've got a copy editor breathing down my throat, so spit it out."

This wasn't going the way I had imagined it would. "My information is good, Mr. Hernandez. Very good."

"I don't pay sources, if that's what you're getting at . . ."

"I don't want money. How far are you from Palm Beach?"

"An hour, hour and a half. Why?"

"If you'll give me that much of your time later in the week, I'll give you a story that'll win you the next Pulitzer."

He went quiet. I could still hear him typing. Then he coughed.

"That's a very nice offer, but I'm not going to win the Pulitzer and you're not gonna get ten more minutes, much less half a day of my time without something a helluva lot more solid than 'Salgo's dirty.' They're all dirty—filthy—how else do you think they get elected? But I'm working on a deadline—so if you have something to say, say it. Otherwise, drop me a line and if it's good, I'll get back to you."

"There isn't time to drop you a line," I said, trying to decide how far to go. If I didn't give Hernandez something, he was going to blow me off—just another crank caller looking to air his own agenda. There were other reporters, but Hernandez sounded tough, nobody's fool, and for whatever reason, Andrew had added several of *this* reporter's past articles to his file. I glanced down at the one clipping I'd managed to save, and decided to lie through my teeth. If everything went as planned, Hernandez would thank me later.

"Mr. Hernandez, I have verifiable proof that Roberto Salgo and his son, Guillermo, were involved with the plane crash that killed Jonathan Korn. They used a group called the Blue Arrows. I can prove it to you, but not over the phone."

He didn't say anything at first. But the tapping on the keyboard stopped.

Then he asked, "What kind of proof?"

And I knew I had him.

Next, I called Galen Tessereau.

He wasn't in the shop, but his home number was listed. I laid out my plan and asked if he would help by setting out the bait.

"Let me make sure I understand you," he said, sounding intrigued, but not convinced. "I'm to call Roberto Salgo's office on the telephone, somehow get him on the line and offer him a Velázquez sketchbook?"

"Exactly! Then—"

"Just a minute, Wil. Why on earth would he take my call? He's in the middle of an election, not to mention the fact that he just buried his only son."

"It may sound crazy, but he'll take your call because he's a collector. A serious collector of Spanish old masters."

"I understand what that means . . . I've been dealing with collectors for longer than you've been alive. But timing is everything—and now doesn't seem like a very good time to try and sell him any art."

"We're talking about a Velázquez sketchbook. Not just some painting he could buy next week or next month. It's a Velázquez! No one's ever offered him anything like it. There are none! They don't exist! It's not a question of timing. He'd get up off his own deathbed to have a look."

"I see . . . But that presents another problem," Tessereau said. "I'm a book dealer—I traffic in the occasional rare object, but my forte is the printed page, not things like Velázquez sketchbooks. Why would Salgo take my call seriously? It all sounds a bit far-fetched."

I held the phone away from my ear and looked at it, wanting to scream. Of course it sounded far-fetched. The whole goddamn situation was far-fetched. Why couldn't Tessereau just go along with the program? I had a lot to do and spending precious time convincing him to help was a roadblock I hadn't expected. But I told myself to calm down—his questions were good, and if I couldn't answer them adequately, then my plan was too flawed to work anyway.

"He won't take your call seriously, Mr. Tessereau. Not at first. But if you persist, ultimately he'll respond because the sketchbook is unlike anything he's ever seen. I'll give you Polaroids— get them in front of Salgo. Do whatever you have to do to make sure he sees them. Once he does, he won't be able to resist."

Tessereau pondered this for a moment. "Suppose you're right? Suppose I get to Salgo . . . ? Then what?"

"I'll provide the sketchbook and all of the background expertise. What we don't have, we'll make up. He won't have time to double-check. I want you to tell him an elderly couple own the book and have decided to sell it rather than try and divide it between their children. Tell him both the Getty and the Prado are interested, but the owners are infirm, that they don't want to wait for acquisition committees to meet. If he acts quickly, he has a shot to buy it out from under both museums. That ought to motivate him. All collectors get greedy when the pot is sweet enough. He'll understand how rare the chance you're offering him is."

"And you truly believe the Peraltas can pull this off? We're not leading the lambs to the lion?"

"You make sure the lion scents the bait, I'll deal with the Peraltas. When you meet Isaac and Lara, you'll understand."

"I see . . . They sound most interesting." I could almost hear Tessereau come around. The tone of his voice changed, his speech quickened. "You know, it just might work. If I were to present myself in person at Salgo's offices in Miami—instead of calling him on the telephone. Nika could drive me. . . . I'm not an easy fellow to turn away. I can be quite convincing when the occasion demands."

"That's why I called you, Mr. Tessereau."

"Wil, it's a bold stroke. A cunning plan. I believe Andrew would approve." He hesitated. "However, one other potential problem comes to mind. . . . Do you think Salgo could possibly connect the two of us? His men picked you up on Worth Avenue, didn't they?"

"Yes. But they got me standing by my car, not outside your shop. They never saw me enter or leave your place."

"You're quite sure they couldn't have followed you up the Via Parigi?"

"Absolutely!" I lied. It was getting easier by the minute.

"In that case, I'm in."

"Thank you, Mr. Tessereau. I know Andrew would be grateful." I hung up, praying I was right about Salgo not being able to connect Tessereau and me.

I thought it through . . . The book had never left Guillermo's car—and Kiki and Lito *had* picked me up on the avenue, not the Via Parigi where Tessereau kept shop . . . I told myself not to worry, that there were a million other things that could go wrong. Salgo wouldn't suspect Tessereau . . . No one would . . .

Who was I selling now?

I saved M.K. for last.

I called the hospital, but they wouldn't allow my call to be transferred into Andrew's room. So I left a message at the ICU nurses' station asking that she call me back as soon as possible.

Five minutes later the phone rang.

"Are you all right, Wil?" She sounded tired.

"I'm fine," I said, closing my eyes and picturing her face. "I know you've got a lot on your mind, but I have a strange request. Can I borrow the sketchbook I showed you in the vault?"

"This is about Salgo, isn't it?" she asked.

"I'm not going to involve you. My promise stands—your father's name will never be mentioned. For that matter, neither will Broward's."

"Wil . . ."

"I have to do this, M.K. I don't have a choice."

I heard someone say something in the background.

"Hold on . . ."

She came back on the line a minute later. "Listen, the doctors are making their evening rounds. Of course you can borrow the sketchbook—come pick it up. You can take anything else you need. But, Wil . . ." She hesitated. "Be careful, okay?"

I held the phone to my ear for a minute or two after she hung up, then I lowered the receiver to its cradle.

Now came the hard part, waiting to see if Salgo nibbled at the bait.

53

SEVENTY-TWO HOURS LATER, Tessereau had the Polaroids in Salgo's hands. It had taken him less than three days to track down the busy politician and make the approach. Once the Polaroids were delivered, Salgo had reacted exactly the way I had predicted he would—greed overcoming common sense.

The meeting was set for the next day, Friday. Less than two weeks before the election.

Salgo was planning to address a Republican fund-raiser at the Breakers Hotel in Palm Beach that afternoon. He had a gap of about an hour in his schedule, and had practically demanded that Tessereau clear his own schedule so that he could stop in at the shop to view the sketchbook at precisely four o'clock.

It didn't leave much time to make the necessary arrangements.

Isaac and Lara flew out of New York early that morning.

Tessereau and I met them at the airport. Once I'd made the introductions, he and the Peraltas lapsed into a rapid-fire conversation in Spanish, the three of them gesturing with their hands, the Peraltas looking around nervously, as though they had entered enemy territory. I suppose they had. I watched them interact, wondering how many languages Tessereau spoke. My stomach was churning.

The ride to Worth Avenue was short, but by the time we reached the shop, the Peraltas and Tessereau seemed like old friends. I drove Tessereau's Bentley, listening to them jabber away. I was sweating, my stomach in knots. I had set all of this in motion and it seemed a little late to be having second thoughts, but now that the Peraltas had arrived in Palm Beach, my brilliant plan suddenly seemed ridiculous.

Isaac and Lara oohed and aahed as Tessereau proudly showed them around his shop, then introduced them to Nika. The place looked as good as I remembered it. Salgo would be suitably impressed.

While Tessereau showed Isaac his rarest books, Lara pulled me to the side. "Is this going to be dangerous?" she asked.

"No," I said, praying I was telling her the truth. "Salgo's coming to look at the sketchbook, but when he gets here, he's in for a surprise. We're going to give him enough rope to hang himself. And he's going to do it in front of a reporter."

She looked doubtful.

I took her hand. "Lara, I've given Isaac something that will shake Salgo to the core. A tangible piece of evidence he can't deny. It's going to be all right. I promise."

Looking nervous, she nodded. "I am hoping you are right, Wil. We are counting on it."

I checked my watch—eleven-thirty in the morning. That left four and a half hours. I had the feeling it was going to be the longest four and a half hours of my life. But there were still things to do.

Hernandez had agreed to meet me at two-thirty; we'd settled on a café a few blocks from Worth Avenue. He was under the impression he was coming to see proof of Salgo's involvement in the death of Jonathan Korn. That was the only way I'd been able to convince him to drop what he was doing and come to Palm Beach on such short notice. Soon, I'd have to tell him the truth, then convince him that it was worth his while to stick around for a few more hours. I wasn't exactly sure how I was going to accomplish that feat, but I decided to worry about it later.

M.K. knew today was the day, but she continued to spend most of her time at the hospital, and I'd been careful to keep her out of the plan. She was expecting a call when it was over.

Hopefully, it would go the way I had planned it.

If Salgo showed . . .

54

O~N~ A HUNCH, I TOOK ISAAC~ with me to meet Raoul Hernandez. We drove Tessereau's Bentley the two blocks to Café L'Europe and arrived just as the lunch crowd was finishing up. A good-looking hostess showed us to a corner table where we ordered coffee and waited for the reporter to show.

He didn't keep us waiting long.

At exactly two-thirty, a stocky, bearded man wearing a rumpled blazer and khakis was shown to our table by the same hostess.

I stood and introduced myself. Then I introduced Isaac.

Hernandez nodded, then sat heavily, as though the world was an exhausting place and the luxury of a comfortable chair was not to be wasted.

He fished in his shirt pocket for a pack of Camels, dropped them onto the table, ordered coffee, then sat back and looked Isaac and me over.

"Sumner . . . Wil Sumner." He repeated my name a second time. "Have we ever met before?"

"No," I said. "But I'm glad you came. We have a lot to talk about."

"I didn't expect two of you," he said, still looking at me, his brow knitted, as though trying to place either my name or my

275

face. Then, reaching into his blazer pocket, he produced a microcassette recorder and asked, "Either of you mind if I tape this conversation?"

"First, let's talk," I said.

He looked at me suspiciously. "That's precisely what I had in mind."

I glanced at Isaac. "I meant before you start recording. You see, Mr. Hernandez, I haven't been—"

But Isaac interrupted me before I could tell Hernandez the real reason I'd asked him to come here today.

Unfortunately, Isaac spoke in Spanish and I had no idea what he said.

Hernandez narrowed his eyes, shook his head, and answered back in Spanish.

Isaac spoke again at length, still in Spanish.

This time Hernandez looked at me, and he didn't look happy. "So this has nothing to do with Jonathan Korn. I should have known. You sounded too good to be true, but I bit anyway, didn't I?"

"Wait a minute," I said.

But Isaac put a hand on my arm. "Mr. Hernandez, I've come a far greater distance than you to be here today. I did so because Wil asked me to—and because it is the right thing to do. I understand that you are a busy man, and I apologize if my young friend misled you, but I assure you he did so with the very best of intentions."

"Good intentions don't change the fact that I stopped what I was doing and drove sixty miles for nothing," Hernandez growled. He knocked a Camel out of the pack and stuck it into his mouth but made no move to light it.

Isaac nodded. "It may seem that way to you, but if you'll give us a little more of your time, I think we can convince you otherwise."

Hernandez glared at me, but he couldn't quite manage to glare at Isaac. I don't imagine many people could. He looked at his watch, then picked up his coffee and somehow managed to swallow some without taking the Camel out of his mouth.

"Okay, gentlemen. I'm all ears. You have fifteen minutes to convince me that I'm not as big a schmuck as I think I am," he said.

Isaac glanced at me. I nodded, deciding that it was best to let him do the talking.

He turned to Hernandez and fixed him with that same warm and knowing look he'd shined on me the first time we'd met. "In that case, I had better come directly to the point, no?"

Speaking softly, he told Hernandez the story Andrew had told me about burning the church, the Capilla del Rosario, but somehow, coming from Isaac, the words gained the gravity of moral outrage. He'd been in Spain, dealt with the fascists, and throughout his telling of Andrew's story, he managed to weave in bits and pieces of his own experiences. He told Hernandez about Salgo's involvement with Franco's *Brigada Diablo*; he brought their violent sadism to life in a deathly quiet voice that raised the hairs on the back of my arms. Without ever saying so, he gave the impression that he'd been there, personally witnessed Salgo order the atrocities in Providencia and Najera. He told Hernandez that although Salgo had managed to sanitize his history for the record, as long as there were victims willing to speak out, he couldn't erase it. Everything Isaac told the reporter was true—but at the same time it was all a fabrication. He wasn't speaking, as it seemed, for himself, he was speaking for Andrew Stevenson, a man who once chose silence, and now had lost the ability speak at all.

When he finished, I looked at Isaac in awe.

Hernandez was staring at him, spellbound.

"Now do you understand why Wil has asked you to be here today?" Isaac said.

"Jesus Christ," Hernandez muttered, shaking his head. He picked up his coffee cup, then set it down without drinking any. "Let me make sure I understand this . . . You're going to confront Ernesto Caldero—or should I say, Roberto Salgo—today? *The* Roberto Salgo? In front of me?"

I nodded. "I apologize for lying to you—I thought you would understand, once you heard the reason."

"And you want to use the newspaper as a weapon—you expect me to write about this?" He still looked dubious.

"Only if you think what you witness is significant," I said.

Isaac reached across the table and put a hand on Hernandez's arm. "It is our hope that you will bear witness and tell the truth—that is all we ask. An animal like Salgo should not be allowed to bury his past and rise to such heights of power—not here, not in America. Wil has planned this carefully; we meet Salgo in what seems to be a safe environment, then I will provoke him. He will not be able to deflect my provocation—and I will prod him hard enough that he will be forced to respond. When he does, his mask will slip away. Ultimately, he will reveal himself—not because he will recognize my face, but because he will recognize what I am. The truth can be more devastating than a bullet to such a man."

Hernandez looked at me. "Is this on the level?"

I nodded. "All of it. Salgo is going to arrive at Galen Tessereau's shop at four o'clock. He thinks he's coming to buy a rare work of art—but he's in for a surprise. If you're there to make a record of it, we can expose him for what he is."

Hernandez thought for a moment, the cigarette dangling forgotten in the corner of his mouth. "It's a goddamn crazy idea—but if what you say is true . . . Given the right push, anyone will explode. Problem is, if I hear something I want to use in print, I'm going to have to identify myself as a reporter." He looked over at Isaac. "If he knows I'm there, he won't let you get to him. He'll simply walk out on you. There must be a way around that . . ."

Isaac and I waited for him to work it out for himself.

Then he nodded. "There's no ethical reason for me to identify myself as soon as he walks in . . ."

"Then you'll come with us?" I asked.

Hernandez grinned at me. "Are you kidding? Wasn't it you that talked about a Pulitzer? If this turns out the way you two seem to think it will, we're talking front page above the fold all over the world."

55

Salgo was late. Four-thirty had come and gone without a sign of him. Not even a phone call saying he was running behind schedule.

Isaac and Lara sat on Tessereau's sofa, nervously plucking at their clothes, jumping at any unexpected sound. Tessereau sat behind his desk, having placed the sketchbook in a well-lit locked cabinet next to the emerald-encrusted gold crucifix. The two objects looked good together.

Every five minutes or so, he stood, walked to the case to look again at the arrangement he'd created, moved the sketchbook a quarter of an inch in one direction or another, only to get up and reverse the move five minutes later.

Nika, Hernandez, and I waited in the back room. I was sweating again, glancing involuntarily at my watch every time Tessereau stood and walked to the case.

Earlier, I'd persuaded Hernandez to don a white smock so that he would look like a gallery assistant. I had Tessereau give him an extra key to the case holding the sketchbook, and instructed him to enter the front room and make a show of unlocking the case when Salgo arrived. Hopefully, this would render his presence in the room plausible. He'd have a front seat and would miss nothing.

Nika was going to leave with a stack of correspondence as soon as Salgo entered the shop, presumably headed for the post office. Her job was to scout the exterior of the building and make sure no one was lurking about. If she spotted anything suspicious, she was to call from Tessereau's car phone and warn us.

I planned to stay in the back room, out of sight. I doubted Salgo would know me if I walked up and shook his hand, but I didn't want to prove it. So I kept the door leading from the front of the shop to the back room cracked open, hoping I'd be able to see and hear everything that happened.

Assuming Salgo showed.

Which I was beginning to doubt.

As five o'clock drew closer, I was ready to give up.

"All right, enough," I told Nika. "Let's can it . . ."

"Wait!" she whispered, peeking through the door. "Someone's coming."

Hernandez and I crowded around her, trying to look through the crack too.

Salgo stood half in and half out of the shop's front door, his back turned to us. He was talking to someone outside. "Wait in the car with Juan. This will take no more than half an hour, that will leave us plenty of time to get to the airport."

He waved, then turned and entered the shop.

My breath caught in my throat.

He walked into the shop like he owned it. He had a military carriage, erect and balanced on his feet—there was power in the set of his shoulders, strength that belied his age in his thick arms. His presence was electrifying.

Tessereau calmly stood and greeted him. They shook hands.

Isaac and Lara stayed seated as Tessereau gave Salgo a brief tour of the shop, pausing in front of the case that held the sketchbook.

Salgo had to see it. But Tessereau didn't point it out.

Not yet.

Then he walked Salgo over to the desk and introduced him to the Peraltas.

Isaac nodded, but didn't offer his hand.

Lara looked like she was going to faint.

"The Peraltas are the owners of the sketchbook," Tessereau was saying. "They must approve its ultimate sale. I know you have a time problem—I'll have my assistant unlock the case."

This was Hernandez's cue. Nodding at me, he clicked on his tape recorder and stuffed it into the pocket of his smock. He looked deadly serious, his eyes far too predatory for a gallery assistant. I hoped Salgo would be too focused on the sketchbook to notice.

Hernandez and Nika entered the main room together, a couple of employees winding down another busy afternoon in the art business. I stood there, my eyes glued to the crack in the door, a trickle of sweat sliding down my back.

"I'm off to the post office, do you need anything?" Nika asked her grandfather.

"Just a moment, Nika," he said. "Let me introduce you to Señor Roberto Salgo. I think you know who he is."

"I know *exactly* who he is," she said ironically.

But the irony went right over Salgo's head.

IIc bowcd graciously, and took Nika's hand in both of his. "It's a pleasure to meet you, Nika." His voice was deep and authoritative. His own hands enveloped hers—they were large and square, heavy hands, hands that could do a lot of damage.

Isaac and Lara hadn't said a word yet.

Nika walked out of the shop.

As she was leaving, Hernandez unlocked the case and removed the sketchbook. He carried it over to the desk and handed it to Tessereau, then he drifted casually over to the bookshelves and began moving the volumes around as though he were actually accomplishing something.

Nobody paid him the slightest attention.

Salgo took the sketchbook from Tessereau and began thumbing through the pages, his face a study in concentration.

He licked his lips, his face coloring as he examined the sketches.

Fighting the urge to step out there and snatch the fragile book out of his meaty hands, I looked over at the Peraltas. Lara was clutching Isaac's arm, barely breathing, while Isaac studied Salgo.

After a moment, Isaac cleared his throat. "Put the book down," he said firmly.

Salgo tore his eyes from the sketchbook. "Eh?"

"I said, put the sketchbook down, Caldero. I wouldn't sell it to you if I were starving."

Salgo looked from Isaac to Tessereau, the color draining from his cheeks. "Is this some kind of game?"

"I'm afraid not, old boy," Tessereau said, deftly plucking the sketchbook out of Salgo's hands and retreating around the far side of his desk.

Hernandez drifted a little closer.

Salgo turned on Isaac Peralta. "What's this about? I demand an explanation."

Isaac let go of Lara's hand and stood. "*You* demand an explanation?" he said softly. "An explanation . . . You have no right to demand anything of me. I know you." He pointed a finger at Salgo's face and his voice broke like thunder. "I know you, Ernesto Caldero. I was there—at the Capilla del Rosario, at Providencia and Najera. You can't hide from me—not anymore."

Salgo's face twisted, then he regained his composure. "You must be mistaken. I don't know what you're talking about." He looked at Tessereau. "I don't know what kind of game you people are playing, but I have neither the time, nor the interest, to join in."

Tessereau said nothing. Hernandez watched carefully.

Isaac shook his head. "This is no game, Caldero. You may have found a way to hide all these years, but I know about the *Brigada Diablo*. Sadistic butchers. Animals masquerading as men."

Salgo's face reddened. "I think you are mistaken."

He turned and started toward the door, but Isaac grabbed the sleeve of his suit and spun him around, a move that I would have thought impossible.

"Why do you scurry away, *Capitán* Caldero? Do you only face your enemies when you outnumber them—when you are surrounded by thugs? Go and get your bodyguard if it will make you feel braver, but he can't help you—no man can shelter you from the truth. How many innocents have you killed, *Capitán* Caldero? How many women and children died at your hands? Did you really think you had gotten away with it?"

Face tight, Salgo tried to walk around Isaac.

But Isaac refused to let him, moving into the larger man's path.

"You are a coward, like all of your type," Isaac said so softly that I could barely hear the words.

Then, he smiled and spat in Salgo's face.

Even then, Salgo kept his composure. Reaching into his pocket for a handkerchief, he tried to walk around Isaac.

It was all going wrong in a hurry.

Hernandez glanced in my direction, frowning. Tessereau looked like he was about to jump out of his skin.

Lara wasn't breathing. Neither was I.

But Isaac wasn't finished.

Calmly pulling the silver lighter I'd given him out of his pocket, Isaac dangled it in front of Salgo. We'd put the lighter in a small plastic bag for this purpose.

It was now or never.

"Perhaps this will jog your memory, Ernesto," Isaac said.

Salgo reacted instinctively, reaching for the lighter.

But Isaac pulled it back out of his reach.

Salgo's hand closed on empty air. "What kind of game is this?" he said.

"No game," Isaac stated. "The lighter has your fingerprints all over it. How will you explain that, *Capitán*? How will you explain the story behind this lighter?"

For the first time, doubt clouded Salgo's face. He looked around the shop, gauging the threat facing him. Seemingly satis fied that he could handle the situation, he turned back to Isaac. "Give it to me!" he demanded again.

Isaac smiled and shook his head, as though he were admonishing a wayward child. "You don't give orders here, *Capitán*. Not to me. I am your jailer. I am the man you have always feared. And because of me, it's beyond your reach. All of it. The lighter, the governor's office, everything you've worked for . . . Because of me, the world will know the truth. With this proof, the world will know you for the coward you are." Isaac dangled the lighter again.

Salgo grabbed for it.

Again, Isaac pulled it back, out of his reach.

And that was the final provocation. Not just the lighter, but Isaac's words—the stark truth that this little old man dared to speak.

Enraged, Salgo took a step forward and backhanded Isaac, knocking him to the ground.

Isaac, still clutching the lighter, looked up at him, and he smiled. "You are afraid now, aren't you? How does it feel? How did those boys in Najera look before you hanged them? Like you do now, I'd imagine. You are through, Ernesto. And you will end up like all cowards—screaming your innocence as they lead you away."

"Innocence?" Salgo shouted. "What would you know of guilt or innocence? Where were you during the war? Counting money, like all the other Jews? Oh, yes, I know a Jew when I see him. I did what had to be done. Nothing more. Nothing to be ashamed of. We stood for something important. We took the country back from *mierda* like you—from the communists and the kikes—and we fought to put it into the hands of men who knew how to lead. Great men like Franco! Now give me the lighter!"

Isaac climbed slowly to his feet and faced Salgo again. "You are worse than a coward, Ernesto Caldero. The men you speak of acted openly—they at least had the courage of their convictions. You no longer have even a name."

Salgo was apoplectic, his face bright red and sweating now. He drew back to hit Isaac again, but before he struck, Lara was on her feet and moving.

She slapped Salgo across the face, a stinging blow that echoed throughout the shop.

Salgo put a hand to his cheek, looking like he was going to explode.

"That was a mistake," he roared. Turning on Lara, he balled his hand into a tight fist . . .

I was halfway through the door before he could cock his arm.

But I wasn't fast enough.

Before I could get to him, he made a ghastly gurgling sound and clutched his chest.

Then he was on the floor at the Peraltas' feet, gasping for breath.

At first, no one moved.

Then Isaac stepped over Salgo and calmly walked to the desk. He picked up the telephone and dialed 911.

Hernandez pulled out a pad and started to scribble furiously.

Tessereau and I hurried to Lara's side.

"Are you all right?" I asked, taking her arm.

Looking down at Salgo, who struggled for each breath, his face gray and greasy, Lara shook her head and whispered, "*This is what killed my Sasha? Animals like this?*"

Then the tears started to stream down her wrinkled cheeks, her expression a mixture of horror and pity.

Tessereau and I led her to the sofa, where she was joined by Isaac.

He took her hand and said, "It's over. It's over. You did well, my hero."

56

SALGO HAD SUFFERED A SERIOUS heart attack, but he'd sur-
vived to face what for him must have been an unbearable
humiliation. Within hours of the first press reports, everyone
from the Cuban American Political Federation to the United
Sugar Refiners moved to distance themselves from the once
popular candidate. He'd been air-lifted from Palm Beach to St.
Mary's Hospital, and judging from the published medical
reports, due to complications, he would remain hospitalized for
a long time.

Forever wouldn't be long enough for me.

Raoul Hernandez had been right. Within a day, the story was
an international sensation. Isaac and I had refused to tell him
what the significance of the lighter had been—it was the only
way to keep Andrew out of the story. But armed with Salgo's
real name, Hernandez had been able to dig up enough information to bury the man without any more help from us.

Almost immediately, Laspada made his move, raiding Salgo's
offices, confiscating documents and computers. Within forty-
eight hours, a statewide sweep produced dozens of arrests of
suspected members of the Blue Arrows.

The Peraltas became Tessereau's house guests. Overnight they became media darlings—international heroes. There wasn't a newspaper in America that didn't run a picture of the two of them holding hands. The tabloids played the story as David and Goliath, Isaac having been given the David role. There was talk of movies, television, and book deals.

My name appeared in a few articles, but quickly faded from sight. No one was talking book and movie deals with me.

But Andrew knew. I sat one afternoon by the side of his bed and read to him from a half dozen different newspapers. The left side of his face was wooden, and his lopsided expression never changed as I read, but his eyes burned bright. When I stood to leave, I pulled his father's silver lighter out of my pocket and placed it in his good hand. Tears streamed down the old man's cheeks as I walked out of his room.

He and M.K. made it clear that I was welcome to stay in Palm Beach as long as I wanted, but I had problems of my own to sort through, a career I didn't want to face—a future that looked uncertain if not bleak.

But Tessereau had ideas of his own about that problem.

He asked me to meet him at the shop two days after the story broke.

"I have a proposition for you, Wil," he said without preamble. "As you know, I plan to retire, and Nika is going to attend medical school. I'd like you to take over the shop—run things while she's in school. If it works out, I think we might find a suitable arrangement for you to buy me out."

I smiled at him. "That's a kind offer. But my interest is in art, not books."

He held up his hands. "I'm aware of that. And I'm willing to commit a certain amount of capital for you to begin trading in fine art—here, out of the shop. I'll continue to provide the expertise for the books, you'll be the art expert."

I told him I needed to think about it.

In any case, I needed to get back to New York. There were too many loose ends that needed attention before I could seriously consider Tessereau's offer, an offer that sounded better than I was prepared to admit.

That night, I found out that M.K. knew all about it. I'd brought her one of Charteen's meals, and a bottle of burgundy. As we sat in the hospital waiting room eating and drinking, she said, "I've decided to move back into the main house. I know you and Mr. Tessereau have been talking, and if it makes your decision easier, you could have my apartment while you sort things out."

I started laughing. "Are the two of you ganging up on me?"

She smiled. "The three of us. My father is in on it too."

I promised I would give it serious thought, then told her I was leaving early in the morning.

At this, she grew pensive. "I want your word that you'll come back and finish the appraisal. I'm not sure what my father wants to do with the collection, but I want your promise that you'll come back, no matter what you decide to do about Tessereau's offer."

I looked at her and frowned. "So I should come back down here—*just* to finish the appraisal?"

She laughed. "I might find some other odd jobs for you."

"Like what?" I asked, reaching for her.

I pulled her to me and kissed her.

When I pulled back, she smiled.

"Well?" I asked. "What other kinds of work do you think I'm qualified to do?"

She pretended to consider this. "If I remember correctly, you were a lousy cabana boy—so I think it will have to be something in the house."

My mouth must have dropped open.

"Did you think I didn't recognize you right away?" she asked, amused by my reaction.

"I wasn't sure," I admitted.

She kissed me again. "You're not very forgettable, Wil. Not then, not now."

The rest of the evening passed in a pleasant blur.

We kept our good-byes short and sweet.

"You never told me what happened in London," I complained as she walked me to the elevators.

She laughed. "Always leave them guessing. Now you have another reason to come back, don't you?"

The next morning, Maj drove me to the airport in his truck.

"Damn fine t'ing you do, mon. But why you not be letting your old friend Maj help?" he asked.

I started laughing. "Next time, I promise to call."

"Ain't gone be no next time," he grumbled.

As he pulled up to the departure concourse, he asked, "Wil, all dis mess—it turn out the way you planned?"

"The meeting at Tessereau's shop?"

He nodded. "All of it—how you be feelin' 'bout thc way it turned out?"

He was the first person to ask me that question and I wasn't sure how to answer it.

I looked at him and thought about it for a moment. "I don't know, Maj. I came down here to do an appraisal, ended up killing a man. Then, M.K. . . . It turned out . . ." I shrugged. "It didn't turn out the way I expected."

He flashed those white teeth. "Nothin' ever does, you know. Miz M.K. give me dis," he said producing a small package from under his seat. "Said to tell you not to open it 'fore you get on the plane."

I took the package and smiled. "What's in it?"

He shook his head. "Don't know. Good-bye, mon. I'm gone miss you."

"I'm gonna miss you too, Maj." I shook his hand.

Then he gave his truck a little gas and eased away from the curb, whistling a Bob Marley tune and shaking his head to the beat.

I opened the package over Georgia. Inside was another smaller parcel wrapped in plain brown paper, along with a note from M.K.

Dear Wil,
    By now you're on the plane. My father and I have talked it over, and we're both sure that we want you to have this. It's a gift— from us to you. We didn't know

how else to say thank you. You've done more for us
than you could possibly know, so accept this gesture
and use it wisely. Think about Tessereau's offer . . .

                              M.K.

I put down the note and tore open the parcel.
Inside was the Velázquez sketchbook.

57

New York was cold and gray. Usually I loved the fall, the way the women dressed, the crisp energy in the air, the change of color on the trees in the park. But not this year. I waited impatiently to hear back from the Velázquez experts, sure in my own mind of the sketchbook's authenticity, but unable to market it without the blessings of the Prado.

A few days bled into a week. I met with Ev Lenoir, promised that I would settle my debt in full if he would grant me a short extension. He refused. Hernandez sent me copies of his articles, begging me to tell him more about the origins of the lighter. *I* refused. Laspada called to tell me that he was close to bringing charges against Salgo—but he doubted the man would live long enough to see the inside of a courtroom. It was cold comfort. I tried to put together a plan, some brilliant move I could make that would bail out my business. But the only real hope I had was the sketchbook.

Then October turned into November and I couldn't get the smell of M.K.'s hair out of my nostrils.

Tessereau's offer was never far from my mind, but I wasn't ready to go to work for someone else. I'd been my own boss for too long.

I tried to pass the time constructively. Another picker out pounding the pavement, searching for that overlooked master-piece, the one in the back of the bin that everyone else had overlooked. But I was faking it, because no matter how hard I tried, I couldn't put Palm Beach out of my mind.

M.K. and I spoke every day on the telephone. Andrew was making small strides, but he was a long way from well. She sounded as lonely as I felt.

After two weeks, I was ready to get on a plane and fly to Madrid myself. I hated waiting for the experts to render a ver-dict, but without their opinion, the sketchbook was just so much old paper. No matter what I thought.

So I told myself to be patient, and then went to work. I spent the day pawing through a collection of nineteenth-century fur-nishings in a friend's shop on Tenth Street. A good find would buy me time, get the bank off my back. The afternoon was winding down by the time I finished digging through the junk in his basement. It had been a waste of energy. I was dirty and tense, in no mood for polite chitchat when I found a stranger waiting for me outside my apartment.

Before I could run him off, he introduced himself, produced a card and acted very pleased to meet me. The card identified him as Juan Carlos Ortiz, a senior curator of paintings from the Prado museum.

He seemed so happy to find me, I invited him in.

"Let me come directly to the point, Mr. Sumner," he began, without taking the time to remove his overcoat. "I've just flown in from Madrid. I wanted to meet you in person. You see, I was on vacation until two days ago when I returned to find the photographs you sent us on my desk. It was some-thing of a shock. I mean to say, I was absolutely overwhelmed. I've spent the last forty-eight hours studying our archives, and if the sketchbook looks as good in person, we at the Prado would like the chance to bid on it before you offer it else-where."

I just stared at him.

"Are you all right, Mr. Sumner?" he asked, suddenly looking worried.

"I'm fine, Mr. Ortiz. I was just thinking I might need a drink. Would you like a drink?"

"No, thank you," he said, even though he looked as thirsty as I felt. "I don't want to impose on you. I'm staying at the Plaza. I'd like to set up an appointment to examine the book—before you show it elsewhere."

I nodded. "I'll show it to you, Mr. Ortiz. But I'm not prepared to make any other commitments. Not yet."

He looked vaguely disappointed. Then he smiled. "I'll tell you straight up that if it's what I think it is, I'm authorized to offer eight figures if we can conclude a quick and private sale."

"Eight figures—that's conservative, don't you think?" I said, putting on my best poker face.

He frowned. "We're open to discussion, of course. But there are limits . . ."

I saw him to the door, promising I would get back to him to set up an appointment.

When he left, I floated over to my desk and fell into my chair.

Eight figures . . .

I wondered what the Getty would pay.

I imagined a number. Then I imagined a bigger number. I whispered it out loud a couple of times. Attempted to grasp it. But my head was spinning and it was too much to hold on to.

I tried to picture a new gallery, my name in gold leaf . . .

Madison Avenue . . .

Maybe Park Avenue . . .

Big. Spacious. High-tech lighting. Elaborate security. Fancy openings. A statement.

But as hard as I tried, I couldn't draw the picture in my head. It was Palm Beach I kept thinking about.

Not Palm Beach—M.K.

She was standing on the seawall, sipping beer and talking about trouble coming when you least expected it.

Trouble . . .

I sat there, picturing her face, until I was sure I could control my voice. Then I picked up the telephone.

"Mr. Tessereau," I said when he answered, "I want to discuss your offer . . ."